DEAD INNOCENT

TIM LAURIE

Dead Innocent
First published 2014 by
Clock Hill Publishing

A CIP catalogue record for this book is available from the British Library.

Visit www.timlaurie.com
to read more about the author and his work.

ISBN 978-1-908387-67-7 (Paperback)
ISBN 978-1-908387-68-4 (iBook)
ISBN 978-1-908387-69-1 (Kindle)

Book design and typesetting by
Oxford eBooks Ltd.
www.oxford-ebooks.com

Author's Note

The forensic processes detailed here, like the public buildings, are all real. The legend of Ankh Hor does exist, as do the chalk works and flint mines under the city of Norwich.

PART I

I am more and more convinced that man is a dangerous creature, and that power... is ever grasping, and like the grave, cries 'Give, give.'

Abigail Adams, *quoted* 1775

1

'How much further?' demanded Harry Scarfe. The edge in his voice betrayed the strain of the last twenty-four hours.

Howard Kingsley, breathing heavily, eyes stinging with sweat, was trying hard not to think about what lay ahead. 'We're close,' was all he said.

They struggled on through the tunnel, forced by their awkward load to shuffle in tandem, until at last they reached a heavy-set door. Grunting with relief, they lowered what they were carrying carefully to the ground.

'No noise.' Kingsley's throat was dry. 'The guards.'

Producing a large key, he guided it into the lock. The primitive mechanism refused to turn.

Scarfe struck the door with the side of his fist.

'No noise!'

'*Open it,* then.'

'I am.' Kingsley worked the key in frustration.

With a sudden click the lock gave way and the door swung aside. Half expecting to be seized immediately, Kingsley was unable to move. But no hands reached out to grab him, and so nervously he leaned over the threshold. The light was muted, giving little away. He listened. The chamber appeared empty.

Standing back, the roll of blue tarpaulin they had carried here lay at his feet, dark slicks running across it. Trussed untidily with short lengths of twine, a nauseating bulge had formed in the middle.

This was madness.

They would never get away with it, thought Kingsley. If only he hadn't been so greedy, never gone to Petrova in the first place. Faced with the reality of the tarpaulin and what lay inside, he realised what a mistake he had made. He looked longingly past Scarfe to the tunnel, sloping away behind them, the torchlight fixed to his head quickly losing its strength in the blackness.

'We're not going back,' said Scarfe, the menace in his tone clear – too much was at stake. 'Not until this is done.'

Knowing he had left it too late to argue, Kingsley concentrated instead on his efforts to block out why they had come. They. Now he was part of it.

'Ready?'

Staggering through the doorway and into the low-ceilinged room, their final destination, the two men managed a last few steps before bending to lay down the tarpaulin once more. It had a distinct odour now, sharp and acrid.

'This place couldn't be better.' Scarfe looked around him. 'Perfect.'

To one side of the room, a steep staircase led above ground, while embedded halfway up the opposite wall, which curved noticeably, was a metal grille. Beyond this dropped a well, from which rose a penetrating coldness, even more so than in the tunnel. Scarfe walked over to it, pressing his face against the grille. The top of the well was about fifteen feet above him, ground level, affording the chamber what little light it had. He couldn't see the bottom.

'Have you got your keys to upstairs?' Scarfe asked unexpectedly.

'My keys?' Kingsley patted the set he always carried. 'Why?'

'I want you to go and get me something.'

'What, now? Get what?'

Scarfe told him. At a loss to understand at first, the truth hit Kingsley like a punch.

'She's still alive, isn't she?' He took a step away. This was too much.

'Of course she's not still alive.'

Far from being comforted, Kingsley instead began to fear for his own life. Did Harry intend returning through the tunnel alone? He hung back. 'What do you want it for then?'

'Reasons. Just go and get it.'

Kingsley could see nothing but danger for himself. 'What if I get caught? Why don't we just do what we came here for and go?'

'Don't get caught. That wouldn't be good for either of us. Five minutes, and you can have it back.'

Kingsley chewed his lip. The dagger of Ankh Hor. Harry didn't intend using it on him then. So what did he want it for? Some kind of unholy ritual? Atonement? There seemed no other explanation. Whatever the answer, time was ticking away.

'What are you waiting for?'

Reluctantly, Kingsley obeyed. Climbing the stone steps, he paused to switch off his torch before carrying on into the darkness.

Eventually he came out into a cavernous hall, as high as it was wide. It felt eerie and unfamiliar in the moonlight. No sign of Barry or Clive, but then he had no idea of their routine. They could appear from anywhere. Moving to the next room, he did his best to ignore the hundred lifeless eyes following him as he passed, entering the tall atrium at the other end. Taking the middle set of stairs, he raced up them two at a time, wincing at the sound of his heels on the bare wood, keenly aware he was visible from any number of directions.

Safely reaching the top, he rounded a banister and stopped outside a large plate glass window that formed one side of a room. Displayed inside was a valuable collection of Egyptian antiquities, including the mummified remains of Ankh Hor, who when alive had been a priest at the Temple of Amun. The middle of the room was dominated by a huge sandstone plinth, its top bare of any ornamentation. Finding the right key, Kingsley opened a glass door cut into one end of the window and entered, pausing briefly to look at the priest's elaborate sarcophagus. Superstition got the better of him.

'I'll bring it straight back,' he promised.

'You will.'

Kingsley yelled out, jumping as if touched by a red-hot poker.

'Quiet, it's me.'

Kingsley collapsed against the wall.

'I didn't want you getting lost and not coming back.'

The sound of footsteps came from nearby stairs.

Kingsley motioned manically for Scarfe to hide behind the sandstone plinth. Crouching, he then swung the glass door back into place before joining him. Too late, he realised he had left the door unlocked, the latch clearly visible.

'I'm telling you, it came from up here. Someone called out.'

Kingsley recognised Clive's voice, listening as both guards moved towards them, stopping outside the Egyptian display.

'All seems okay. What do you reckon?'

Barry, sounding as if he had already lost interest.

'I dunno. None of the alarms have gone off. Could've sworn I heard someone, though.'

Barry gave a drawn out exhalation. 'Tell you what, we'll do another walkabout, just to cover ourselves, then we'll get a good brew on the go.'

Without warning, strong torchlight strobed through the glass, lighting up the sarcophagus and casting a shadow barely an inch from Kingsley's right foot. Kingsley tensed, trying to shrink.

'So long as he's not on walkabout with us. Gives me the creeps. Come on then, let's get started downstairs.'

After waiting as long as they could bear, Scarfe and Kingsley crept out from their hiding place.

'That's it. We need to get out of here, fast.' Kingsley was in no doubt.

Scarfe plucked from its stand the golden dagger he had sent Kingsley to fetch. Even in the subdued light, it glowed like cold fire. 'I still need this.'

'Harry –'

'Let's move.'

Scarfe pushed him roughly out into the corridor. Kingsley secured the display before setting off with Scarfe in the opposite direction to the guards.

A short time later they were back in the underground chamber next to the well, their torches switched on again.

'Will they search down here?' Scarfe asked.

'I don't know. Whatever you're doing with that, be quick.'

Scarfe bent down to untie the tarpaulin, placing the dagger beside him on the brickwork floor. Disturbed though he was, Kingsley looked on in horrified fascination. Suddenly the bundle was flapped open, and the naked corpse inside revealed. Kingsley could barely recognise her. The skin was a ghostly pale, except for one shoulder, blackened by ugly stretches of bruising. A dark crust of lumpy gore blocked the nose and mouth, the same mass forming dark lines around the neck. Worst of all were the eyes. They stared out at Kingsley, distorted by shock. His gullet shrank, quickening his breath.

'Oh my God, Harry. Oh my God.'

'What did you expect?' snapped Scarfe.

Lower down the body and tied to the waist with orange netting were two large ornamental stones, of the sort normally used to decorate ponds. The reason she had felt so heavy thought Kingsley, his head thick and dull. The toes were still neatly varnished.

Scarfe leaned over the dead woman and twisted her face

down. The exposed back was disfigured on the upper part by a deep gash, a scarlet slit ripped out between the delicate shoulders. Using thumb and forefinger Scarfe split open the wound and held it there, taking up the dagger and resting its weight in the gap. Kingsley saw him hesitate, and then, very slowly, begin to force in the blade. The sound of metal against bone grated through the air, stopping only when mashed clots of blood started to press over the hilt.

Kingsley stifled his retching with a handkerchief. Scarfe stood up, for the first time looking shaken. 'Here.' He held out the dagger, dull now, a tiny thread of sinew stuck to its point.

Trembling, Kingsley removed the square of cloth covering his mouth and closed it round the knife.

'Make sure you clean it properly. Your fingerprints are on there too.'

Kingsley nodded dumbly before finding his voice. 'Why did you do that?'

'Doesn't matter.'

Kingsley had other questions, questions he didn't want answers to. He looked again at the girl. Dead, her nakedness seemed more indecent than if she were alive.

'Aren't you going to wrap her up again?'

Scarfe shook his head. 'Plastic might make her float. Get the grille open.'

Doing as Scarfe said, Kingsley leaned warily through the waist-high gap the grille left in the shaft of the well. The coin bucket was above him; good. No one had moved it. Below, a hundred feet or more, a solid black disc of water waited silently. Would Barry or Clive hear?

'Hurry up. Come and get the other end.'

Kingsley suddenly froze. 'I can't. I can't touch her. You'll have to cover her up.'

'We're doing it like this, so come and get the other end.'

After a short silence, Kingsley started nodding to himself.

'Okay... okay.'

Swallowing hard, he took hold of the ankles, the skin cold and loose. Scarfe gripped under her arms.

'One, two, *three*.'

Lifting with great difficulty, they wrestled the dead woman up onto the open ledge of the well, manoeuvring her until the top half of her torso was suspended above the abyss. There was no dignity left her. Catching his breath, Kingsley delayed the point of no return a little longer, hardly able to bear to send her finally over the edge. At last he could avoid Scarfe's eye no more. The time had come.

'Now,' said Scarfe.

With a single movement they both pushed. She was gone.

2

HARRY SCARFE EXHALED noisily. 'That was good.'

Still out of breath, he turned his head to look across the pillows at Anneka, stretched out on top of the duvet. Sex was his antidote – to the stress of business, to the stress of life in general. She looked incredible. Less than half his age, and naked except for a pair of red high-heeled shoes. It was a great feeling. Very different from the effort it took coaxing a performance out of Caroline these days. Maybe every marriage reached that point.

His lust satisfied, the same question as always hung on Scarfe's lips, but he chose not to ask it. Levering himself awkwardly to the edge of the hotel bed, he stood up, glad of the subdued light. The jaw of a prize-fighter, he had powerful shoulders to match, his heavy frame exaggerated by a lack of height, black hair slicked straight back. Founder of Scarfe Industries, despite the size the company had grown to he still held control of its board, which he governed as would a medieval warlord – without mercy or regret.

Anneka yawned, propping herself up on the pillows and emptying the last of the champagne into a glass. She gave Scarfe an ambiguous smile before taking a sip. Scarfe slid on his boxer shorts and grinned toothily back, snapping his waistband in a self-congratulatory manner. His dark eyes glinted.

Politics could be so rewarding.

Not that he could have imagined his campaign for Parliament leading to nights like this one, any more than he could have foreseen the seat for Norfolk South becoming vacant in the first place – a once-in-a-lifetime opportunity to elevate himself from Norwich Councillor to Conservative MP. The local party's decision as to who should stand in the by-election, a decision still to be made, meant more to him now than even his Norwich Eye project.

The man who had held the safe seat for the previous twenty years, one Douglas Bassett, had caused uproar when his body had been found. Never included as part of Bassett's circle, Scarfe had read the newspaper reports with a mixture of satisfaction and contempt. Sex being thicker than politics, journalists of all persuasions had been quick to print the story.

At around two thirty one Wednesday afternoon, Bassett had suffered a fatal heart attack, that much the press were agreed on. Whether this could be entirely attributed to natural causes was more hotly debated, as at the time of his demise he had been wearing only a mask and collar. The appointed Coroner had also observed that the red stripe marks he'd found on the decedent's chest and back were "consistent with having been whipped or beaten". Consistent also, both tabloids and broadsheets had been fast to point out, with Bassett having been found dead on the third floor of a Mayfair brothel.

Scarfe fumbled with his cufflinks, wondering at the necessity for Bassett's deviance. Why couldn't the upper classes get their end away like everyone else, instead of dressing up like perverts and having the crap beaten out of them?

'You've gone very quiet,' said Anneka uncomfortably.

Scarfe looked down at her but said nothing, pulling on his trousers.

In the hope that press coverage would improve, the committee responsible for appointing Bassett's successor had been ordered by Central Office to prolong the process for as long as possible. That had given Scarfe time to ensure his was one of three names agreed on for consideration. Time also for him to charm what members of the committee he could into giving him their support, employing every means at his disposal. Within a matter of weeks, all that stood between himself and guaranteed victory was a single vote.

He was made for politics.

And for that crucial vote, he knew he could rely on Howard Kingsley. A fellow Councillor, Kingsley was also married to his wife Caroline's older sister, Judith. That made them practically related. Kingsley's loyalty therefore wasn't in doubt, which was why he sounded him out last, one morning in the main debating chamber at City Hall, waiting for a meeting to begin. He seated himself beside Kingsley with a friendly nod. When, however, he broached the subject, the conversation didn't go quite as he had expected.

'I can't discuss it,' Kingsley told him irritably, 'you know that.'

Scarfe frowned.

'What is there to discuss?'

'Can we just leave it? I haven't decided, if you want to know the truth.'

'You're not telling me you're thinking of voting for one of the others?'

'Why not?'

'Because they're no different from Bassett, that's why not.'

Arrogant silver-spooned arseholes who assumed power as their birthright, Scarfe nearly added.

'And you are, I suppose? Well, like I say, I haven't decided yet.'

At that moment the meeting was called to order, and Scarfe was left to fume in silence while he listened to a breakdown of the Council's latest proposed budget cuts.

Anneka brought Scarfe back to the present, staring past his shoulder to whatever was behind him.

'... going to break your legs,' said a man's voice.

'What the –' Scarfe swung round.

It was the TV. A black and white film showed three men standing over another, slumped in a chair. 'No!' the lone man pleaded. 'Please. I'll do it.'

'Wanted to see what was on,' Anneka pouted.

Scarfe sighed. Maybe threatening to break Kingsley's legs would have worked too. In the end, money had provided the answer. It usually did.

Not a briefcase full of banknotes – in his estimation, Kingsley would have reacted badly to that, despite the financial problems he periodically whinged about. Not a risk he was prepared to take. No, the briefcase needed a disguise, something more palatable to Kingsley's tastes. Everyone had a taste for something.

But what that was had proved elusive. He had spent many wasted hours in Kingsley's company, even allowing himself one afternoon to be shown around the museum Kingsley worked in, all to no avail. Then, on one of the Council's junkets to their twinned city of Petrova, an outpost of Eastern Europe, his luck had changed, and a deal was struck. He got his vote, and Kingsley an arrangement he'd been more than willing to accept.

Fully dressed in a dark blue tailored suit, Bond Street, Scarfe checked his reflection, shifting his glance to stare unobserved at Anneka's nude profile. No need for collars and masks to get turned on by that. Surreptitiously pocketing her tiny lace knickers, he adjusted his tie.

'I've got to go.'

Eyes hazy, Anneka looked up at Scarfe. Now he was dressed, his remarkably hairy body was more imposing. Naked in bed, she'd told him he could pass for an ape, only she was sure apes didn't have such dirty habits. They had laughed as if sharing a joke, though inside Scarfe had been pissed off as hell.

‘When will I see you?’ she asked him blandly.

‘I’ll call.’ Scarfe watched the curve of Anneka’s hips change as she moved her legs. She was still wearing the red shoes.

Not for the first time, he was struck by her resemblance to the young woman in the blue tarpaulin – same blonde hair, same foreign accent, same age even. It was three months ago now, late spring, though it seemed far longer.

It had been her own fault, thought Scarfe. Threatening his candidacy. What made her think she had the right? Stupid girl. No one stopped him from getting what he wanted, least of all a nobody like her. There were winners in life, and she wasn’t one of them. Anyway, all that mattered now was that she was gone.

He was in the clear.

Anneka seemed faintly displeased by Scarfe’s reticence.

‘I need the bathroom,’ she said, kicking the red shoes from her feet and swaying off unsteadily in the direction of the en-suite.

Scarfe switched the TV to standby.

When she returned, Anneka climbed groggily back onto the bed, slumping diagonally across the sheets. After a minute she raised her head, before realising she was alone.

3

THE NEXT DAY, Monday morning, Howard Kingsley gripped his steering wheel, long face grimly intent on the traffic signal across the junction. His weak chin and round glasses gave him a faintly colonial look. A pith helmet would have completed the picture. The lights changed, and he shot off with uncharacteristic speed towards the next set, which turned red in anticipation.

'Bloody hell!'

His day hadn't started well, and now he was late. The car park at Norwich Castle Museum, where as Curator he had a space reserved, was difficult to get to at the best of times, without all the extra traffic he'd hit.

He was late because at breakfast, he and Judith had had one of their regular battles over what he called her 'conspicuous consumption'. On this occasion, she had commissioned a pair of electric gates, without his knowing.

'We agreed we should discuss these things first,' he had reproached her over his bowl of cereal. He took a handkerchief from his jacket and dabbed unnecessarily at his nose, a habit of his whenever troubled. Monogrammed in blue, it was one of a set Judith had bought him last birthday.

'So you can say no?'

'Well, do we need them? The neighbours are going to think we've gone mad.'

'I've had a design made up now.'

'Judith...'

'It's got lilies in it. You never buy me flowers any more,

and you know they're my favourite.' She fixed him with an unblinking stare, the one that told him the gates were non-negotiable. Her curly shoulder-length hair framed a strong, though not unattractive face. Smartly dressed in a fashionable skirt and white cotton blouse, she had an air of efficiency about her.

Howard sighed inwardly.

'You've had a design made, have you...?'

Judith leaned over and kissed him on the forehead. His soggy cornflakes half-eaten, Howard managed a weak smile.

As newly-weds, he could remember the two of them making trips to the launderette, renting a TV. Far-away days. True, he was glad not to have to carry bin-bags of damp clothes through the streets anymore, but of the woman he had married – at times like this, there seemed very little left. Competing with Caroline Scarfe, her rich younger sister, had changed her. He had lost count of similar arguments they'd had, he insisting that with only one income, and a young daughter, they couldn't afford a new kitchen, an extension, another holiday. All in vain. Little wonder then he'd proved such an easy target for Harry, angling for his vote on the electoral selection committee. Not that he wouldn't have taken his debts back, if he could have done. Anything not to have seen inside that tarpaulin.

'I must ring Belinda about the weekend.' Judith was ready to move on, now the issue of the gates had been resolved. 'Did you get a new shirt like I said?'

'A new shirt?'

'For Saturday, we're going over to Belinda's for lunch, remember? She's all on her own now. You can't wear any of the shirts you've got.'

'There's nothing wrong with the shirts I've got.'

'They're scruffy,' Judith admonished her husband, stretching out an arm and pulling at his collar. 'Look at this one, it's all frayed down one side.' Howard rolled his eyes, used to his being regarded as a work in progress. 'I'll go to House of Fraser and get you a nice set of new ones,' Judith decided firmly. 'You need smartening up.'

*

Moving slowly around the one-way system that strangled Norwich Castle, Kingsley turned off the car radio. He wasn't in the mood. The fate of the girl in the blue tarpaulin, though months ago now, was never far from his mind's eye. Images he couldn't erase. He often tried to bottle up his conscience by telling himself that she really had died in an accident, as Scarfe had said, the secrecy necessary only to protect Scarfe's precious campaign from slanderous accusations.

So why the dagger?

In Kingsley's darker moments, when the nights closed in on him most tightly, he would often imagine he was about to be found out, a thought that frightened him more than anything else. He would have to fight the urge to confess what had happened – to Judith, to anyone. To let it all out and plead for their forgiveness, for their understanding. The guilt seemed not to recede, and it scared him that it never would. Easy money had drawn him into a world of which he knew nothing, and which seemed intent on slowly consuming him from the inside.

The car's tyres rumbled as Kingsley slowed to navigate a cobbled avenue. He swung right and crossed over the bridge that led to the truncated mound on which the castle sat, overlooking the centre of Norwich. Two huge stone pillars guarded the bridge's entrance, crowned by black ironwork from which prisoners had once been hanged in front of vast crowds, though not for some one-hundred and fifty years. More's the pity, Kingsley sometimes thought.

He parked in the space reserved for him, close to the main entrance. The castle had been built by the Normans as a royal palace in the eleventh and twelfth centuries, then used as a jail until the late nineteenth century before being converted into the museum it remained today. It was packed with treasures, from Egyptian antiquities and famous paintings to prehistoric skeletons and a mock-up of a First World War trench system. A massive stone fortress formed the dominant centrepiece of the buildings. Technically known as a Keep, it was Romanesque in style, with arcading and fine decorative sculptures carved into its square faces. Together with its lofty battlements it made an impressive landmark, visible for miles. Kingsley delayed entering, late as he was, instead walking over to the railings that ran the circumference of the mound, to a vantage point from which he could look out over the city.

It was a view he never tired of. The rest of the world appeared a safe distance from here. Passing over the bridge was like entering a sanctuary, his worries and fears left behind, at least until evening, when he would have to cross back. He gazed down at the lawns and flowerbeds that curved along the base of the mound, often thick at lunchtime with sprawling office workers.

It started to rain.

Summer this year seemed to have had only two settings, much like the year before – either hot and humid, or windy and wet, with nothing inbetween. Hurrying to avoid getting soaked, his tweed jacket already damp, Kingsley made his way to a small arched door at the rear of the castle, tapped in the security code and stepped through, unaware as yet that today his greatest fear had crossed the bridge with him.

He was immediately met by the cool dimness of the interior. Even on days when outside the sun baked the air, the castle's twelve-foot-thick walls maintained a constant twilit atmosphere. He rounded a small buttress and entered the Great Hall, a large square filled with exhibits, the ceiling soaring some forty feet or more above him. Balconies ran at different heights around each of the walls, galleries on which bowmen had once stood, ready to defend the castle when it had been a royal household. In each corner a stone staircase spiralled tightly upwards towards the battlements, while from a wide central beam hung Snap, a massive and ancient model dragon, swinging gently on its cable ladder.

Normally Kingsley would have made straight for his office, threading past the various displays of armour and instruments of torture and on to the first emails of the day – a more up-to-date method of torment. But in the middle of the Great Hall a small number of staff had gathered, at intervals peering down at the floor and chattering noisily.

Brian Finch, Kingsley's deputy, was the first to notice him as he approached. What could be seen of Finch above his neatly trimmed beard shone with excitement. Together with his grey hair, parted in the middle, he had the appearance of a man much older than he actually was. Rumour had it he thought this gave him an air of gravitas, a quality suited to his position as Forensic Archaeologist and second-in-command.

'Howard, you're here; come and see this.'

Muttering 'Morning,' to everyone in general as they stepped aside to let him through, Kingsley stopped at the edge of a large metal grate that sat flush with the floor of the Hall, sealing in the castle's well. The elaborate ironwork allowed visitors the peculiar sensation of standing right over the borehole, looking straight down a full one hundred and thirty feet to the water far below. Except the water was no longer that far away – it had risen considerably, like the liquid in some huge thermometer. Alarm seized Kingsley, rooting him to the spot.

'Oh my God!'

'Quite a sight, isn't it?' said Finch enthusiastically. 'Must be all the rain we've had. I've sent Ian to check on the dungeons.' Ian Chapman, Finch's assistant.

Kingsley felt faint. He dabbed at his nose with his handkerchief. The rain had been no worse than last year, and the well hadn't flooded then. He bent over, trying to see more clearly down the shaft. Anyone who had read the castle's guidebook would know that the well tapped into a fast-moving waterway, deep in the ground. Scarfe had insisted that that was a good thing, but what if the waterway's route became obstructed? Bile burned at Kingsley's throat. What might be causing any obstruction seemed all too obvious.

'And I've called Tom Lomax,' added Finch, clearly pleased at his presence of mind, 'see if he'll take a look. We won't get another opportunity like this. Big insurance job I told him, if it floods the Mall. Or us, come to that.'

The Castle Mall Shopping Centre was close to the castle itself, half-submerged on the site of what had once been the cattle market. Not that Kingsley was concerned right now with flooded shops.

'Who's Tom Lomax?' he asked sharply.

'Don't think you've met. He leads the Police Search and Rescue unit – worked with him a few times.' This was a reference to the occasions when the local CID, on their colder cases, had made use of Finch and his anthropological expertise, when the more usual forensic evidence was hard to come by. 'He couldn't promise he'd make it over, but said he'd try. This afternoon, or tomorrow at a push. Might swing it with his boss as a training exercise. That's if they're not called out on a job.'

Kingsley gaped at his deputy.

'You called the police?'

Finch had expected a more positive response.

'Well, Tom's unit, yes. Any blockage, he'll find it. Doesn't matter even if he doesn't – wasn't really why I called him.'

'What's that supposed to mean?' demanded Kingsley, more angrily than he'd meant to, drawing curious glances from those around them.

Finch affected not to notice. 'Don't you see?' He pointed at the metal grate. 'For the last nine hundred years, the well has been a tip longer than it's been a water supply – think what Tom might find down there!'

The sense of shock that had struck Kingsley the moment he'd seen the flooded shaft now thickened into a numbing panic. What a team of highly trained divers might find at the bottom of the well, and police divers at that, he didn't dare contemplate. With a flicker of hope he remembered something.

'The well was dredged, Brian, back in the nineteen-twenties. They took everything, there'll be nothing left to find.'

'It was dredged, I know, but what did they miss? No one's ever actually been down there, have they? The technology wasn't the same as now.'

'No one's been down there because it's too dangerous, whatever the technology. You'll have to call this dive team off.'

'Call them off?' Finch was incredulous. 'I've asked Tom as a favour. What's he going to say if I –'

Kingsley decided he needed to assert his authority, before it was too late. Before his life came crashing down around him.

'It doesn't matter what he says, Brian. I'm in charge here.'

'Yes, but you're missing the point.' Finch appeared confused. 'At least let Tom take a look, he might say it's an easy job. And we have to report what's going on to someone – what if we do flood the Mall? We'll have insurance claims coming out of our ears.'

It was a fair point, Kingsley conceded to himself, trying to think of a response. At that moment Finch's assistant Ian Chapman arrived, out of breath. Kingsley noticed the number of staff that circled himself and Finch had grown considerably.

'Two of the dungeons you can't get to,' panted Chapman, 'and there's water in some of the tunnels, all over the place.'

At this, the staff's interest in watching the squabble between their curator and his deputy rapidly evaporated, the mood switching to one of concern. Some ventured their support in allowing the police divers to do whatever they could to unblock the well.

Kingsley realised he was losing the argument. Over-ruling the common consensus for no apparent reason could prove difficult. And if there were insurance claims, or the flood threatened the castle itself, the Joint Museums' Committee would want to know why nothing had been done. He would be held to account. Was that worse than taking a risk on whatever the dive team might find, if they showed up? And even if they did find anything, why should they link it to him?

He couldn't decide what to do. Maybe the water would go back down of its own accord, as quickly as it had risen. Then there would be no need for any police dive teams. Now he thought about it, he did vaguely recollect reading something about the castle having flooded before. Whether it had been caused by the well or not, he wasn't sure. How long had the flood lasted that time? The castle archives would hold the answer. They often did for historians like himself.

'Okay.' Kingsley stared gloomily through the grate. 'I want to be informed the minute this Search and Rescue team gets here.'

'Thanks Howard,' said Finch, a picture of relief. 'I think that's the right decision.'

The rest of the staff added their approval, nodding to each other and exhaling through puffed cheeks, as if catastrophe had been narrowly averted.

'When did you say they were coming?' Kingsley asked Finch.

'This afternoon, I'm hoping. Like I said though, Tom didn't make any promises.'

Kingsley remained silent, squinting as he searched the well shaft again, but the rope that held the coin bucket remained all that was visible. He made his exit, the group closing back behind him as he passed.

Head down, Kingsley found the nearest stairs and began to climb, taking each step like a man ascending the gallows.

4

LATER THAT SAME morning, Harry Scarfe sat alone. In spite of his many business interests and the millions they generated, it was when in this particular chair that he felt most gratified.

It wasn't an opulent environment. The desk was standard issue. On it, a phone, computer, stacked wire trays, unread paperwork, two pens in a grey plastic pot. A few badly chosen prints hung on the walls, and a small coffee table with an unconvincing veneer glared under the strip lighting. The carpet, interspersed with patches of some un-named grime, was an unfashionable shade of pink, while the chair itself groaned and ached as he spun round to either answer the phone or click on his mouse. It was a far cry from the state-of-the-art suite he used to conduct his business affairs.

But none of that mattered. What made this room so special was what was written on the other side of the door – COUNCILLOR SCARFE. In its own small way, this unremarkable office inside City Hall held power. Provincial, often inconsequential, but power none the less.

Putting this influence to use on behalf of his various businesses was the only reason Scarfe had entered local politics. What he hadn't anticipated, however, was how his position would awaken in him a latent desire to pursue higher office. Something about the way important people discovered they needed you; doors were opened where before they had been closed, invitations were extended, everyone suddenly a friend. It was intoxicating, a kind of fame. When Douglas

Bassett had been found dead, he had taken it as a sign.

A buzzer sounded on the phone. Scarfe leaned forward and pressed a button.

'Yes?'

Scarfe knew his secretary well enough, but preferred not to be familiar. Different, with better legs.

'Mr Kingsley to see you,' Tracy answered, in her sing-song voice.

'Send him right in.'

Kingsley entered in a hurry and hovered next to the low visitor's seat. He was a picture of worry, hair lank over his face. Never much of a poker player, thought Scarfe. When would he learn to take Council business in his stride?

'Howard, good to see you.' Scarfe pressed the button again. 'Tracy, two cups of tea please.' He tilted back in his tatty leather chair, every bit the indulgent host.

In the next room, Kingsley could hear the secretary's heels clacking on the lino as she bustled out to the machine, somewhere down the corridor.

'So, to what do I owe the pleasure?' Unexpected visits usually made Scarfe wary, but where Kingsley was concerned, there was no need. Minutes later, he'd changed his mind.

'How did you let this happen, for Christ's sake?' The well had seemed like a bottomless pit, but nothing was bottomless.

'I didn't let it happen. I did everything I could, but Brian –'

'Never mind him. You've got to stop these divers.'

'I will – there's a good chance they won't even turn up.'

'What makes you think that?'

'Brian said –'

'Brian again. Aren't you supposed to be in charge?'

'You don't understand, it's not that simple.'

Scarfe sat back in his chair, eyes on Kingsley, gesturing for him to do the same. This needed sorting out, and arguing over Kingsley's inability to control his workers wasn't going to help. He needed to know the worst case scenario, build from there.

'Let's think this through... what happens if these divers do turn up?' Scarfe spoke matter-of-factly, as if he had every confidence in the man sat the other side of his desk.

To his surprise, Kingsley had a ready answer. He spoke in a rush, as if eager for agreement.

'That's what I asked myself. Then I remembered reading somewhere about the castle flooding before, so I dug out our records. I was right. The well flooded the dungeons back in the nineteen-twenties, when it was dredged. The important thing is, it cleared up after a few days.'

'That sounds in our favour.'

'It is, I'd say. So if Lomax does –'

'Who?'

Kingsley explained Tom Lomax's role as lead diver of the Police Search and Rescue Team. 'So if he does show up, I think I can make him see there's no point going down there, not for the sake of a day or two.'

Scarfe twisted the lobe of his ear. Promising, but no guarantees.

'What if he disagrees?'

'If he won't listen to that, I can scare him with our survey maps.'

'You have been busy. How do they help us, then?'

'They show several big cavities under the water, close to the wellhead. One of the notes says that with the type of rock, there are probably a lot more, a network. And strong currents, which is what carved them out in the first place.'

'Dangerous, is that what you're saying?'

'Very. Not only that, it means there's probably no blockage for Lomax to find, it's just the weather we've been having this summer.'

'So why take the risk?'

'Exactly. Our insurance covers us, I've checked with

accounts.'

Over his initial shock, Scarfe saw reason for hope. Whether Lomax could be dissuaded from diving or not, his finding anything in those cavities seemed highly unlikely. The body, or what was left of it, had probably been dragged by the currents somewhere far underground. Not forgetting Lomax might not turn up at all. Of greater concern was Kingsley himself. He looked under obvious strain, barely coping with the situation. A dangerous state of mind for someone who knew what he did.

'And in a few days, you say this flood will have gone by itself?' Scarfe asked, wanting confirmation.

'That's what happened last time.'

'So by the weekend, there'll be no more problem. Next week, it'll all be forgotten about.'

This seemed to reassure Kingsley, relieved anyway now he had unburdened himself. Scarfe told him to go back to work, to act normally and call the minute Lomax arrived – if he arrived.

On his way out, Kingsley passed Tracy as she entered with their tea. Scarfe dismissed her too, waiting until she had closed the connecting door before swivelling around in his chair to face the window.

On the opposite side of the market square overlooked by his office ran a terrace of mainly Victorian and Georgian buildings. They were split in the middle by a wide walkway, Davey Place, at the far end of which a set of steps led up to Castle Meadow, a wide road used exclusively by buses and taxis. From there rose the mound on which sat the castle, neatly perched, facing back towards City Hall. Kingsley's castle. It had doubtless hidden many crimes over the centuries, thought Scarfe; one more wouldn't hurt it.

The odds were that though Lomax and his team were outside of his control, they posed little threat – it was Kingsley who was his main concern. His conscience was never far from the surface, though he tried to hide it. Something like this might push him over the edge, make him lose his bottle and talk. Scarfe wished he could turn the clock back, not have used Kingsley to help hide the body. He'd known it was a risk at the time, but mistakes were easy to make with a corpse in the boot of the car.

It was time to take certain precautions.

He flicked through the name list on his mobile, stopping at Doyle and touching the call icon. The Private Investigator answered on the second ring.

'Mr Scarfe. What can I do you for?' The tone was hopeful.

'I've got a job needs taking care of.'

'Who is it?'

'I'll email everything you need to know. Start straight away – whatever else you've got on, drop it.'

'Sounds like my rate needs to go up.'

'Don't fuck me about. The name I give you – I want him watched, his phones tapped, the works. And you don't sleep unless I say so, clear?'

'Crystal, as they say in Chinatown.'

Scarfe ended the call. Chinatown? Whatever else the army had done to him, they'd blown away what sanity the PI might once have had. No matter; Doyle was the best he'd ever used. If Kingsley gave cause for alarm, he'd know about it first. Then it would be time to call in some insurance of his own. Not a piece of paper, covered in illegible text, but a dagger, covered in blood. Property of a long since dead Egyptian priest. Intended as protection against possible blackmail, the dagger would work just as well as a means of making sure Kingsley didn't talk.

With any luck, he wouldn't need to use it.

5

LATE MONDAY AFTERNOON, still at his City Hall office, Harry Scarfe received a call. It was Howard Kingsley, sounding relieved. The dive team hadn't materialised, and the floodwater had begun to drop. Not only that, his deputy Brian Finch, cause of all the trouble, was apparently pessimistic that the dive team would make it tomorrow either, as his calls to their office hadn't been returned.

Scarfe calmly replaced the receiver. They were in the clear, or as good as. He toyed with the idea of calling off Doyle, but decided against. Better to wait until Kingsley was settled again, his conscience too.

Distracted, he looked across to the castle. This time next year he would be MP for Norfolk South, and Kingsley, the dead girl; neither would matter. He remembered how different it had been, months earlier, when his Parliamentary campaign had still hung very much in the balance.

Petrova had changed all that.

*

He had flown to Petrova from Stansted in the early spring, along with several of his fellow Council members, as part of an exchange visit. The Eastern European city, a fascinating and lively place, had been twinned with Norwich since the aftermath of the Second World War. The original intention had been to spread a greater understanding of different cultures, in the hope that this would make conflict less likely in the future. Now the primary purpose of these regular visits was to form new trading links, though in Scarfe's view, more often than not, an exchange of emails would have been as productive. He, on the other hand, had put to better use the network of local government officials he'd met over the years, and with their backing had formed a lucrative property company, based in the city.

Caroline had questioned why he should want to take on such a venture – it couldn't be for the money. She was right of course, he knew that, but he shied away from telling her the true reason. Although the company did provide a healthy return on investment, with its mixed portfolio of residential and commercial units, its real value lay in something less tangible. The risk and the thrill of building up once more something from nothing. Making deals, just as he'd done as a young man, an eternity ago, so it seemed to him. Petrova made him feel alive. He had that feeling now, as he approached the city aboard the airport shuttle.

The view from his seat made Petrova appear at first a poor choice of destination. It had suffered badly under Communist rule, the surrounding countryside denuded of hedgerow and woodland, ripped out to make way for farming machinery and five-year plans. The suburbs consisted almost entirely of great concrete monoliths, towering concentrations of people with few facilities for pleasure.

As Scarfe alighted from the train in the heart of the city, however, the impression was altogether different. It was as if the Brothers Grimm had built a stage set. The architecture enjoyed a Gothic fantasy, spiralling and pirouetting in a fairytale of colour and texture. Shops crooked with age sold wooden toys and fresh cakes, while narrow cobbled streets completed the sense of fantasy, ensuring a steady trickle of the more adventurous type of tourist.

Carrying only hand luggage, Scarfe opted not to queue for

a taxi with his colleagues, choosing instead to walk from the train station to his apartment, hidden in one of the many tall winding streets only five minutes away. Something he would never have done at home. It was a pleasant stroll, taking in the early morning sights and smells, though the problem of Kingsley's undecided vote on the selection committee was never far from his mind. He put that to one side to mull over the days forthcoming meeting with his foreign counterparts. First some housekeeping, then onto the main agenda item; educational links of some sort, according to his notes. Scarfe could think of nothing duller, but then these meetings often were. Nothing much ever got actually *done.*

It was the same when the idea of building a Norwich Eye had been proposed, to match the Ferris Wheel in Petrova's main square. A feasibility study had been set up, only to be put on hold indefinitely once the hundred thousand pounds set aside for the study was used up with various consultancy fees. Luckily for Norwich, Scarfe thought, the concept had appealed to him. He had taken on the idea as his own, recruiting a team to see the project through and investing heavily with his own money. Planning permission was fast-tracked under the latest green legislation, which allowed the usual due processes to be steam-rolled over. In a short space of time, the Eye moved from drawing board to preliminary excavations. The publicity machine he put in place managed to label objectors as lacking in civic pride, anti-progress and anti-jobs, while at the same time successfully portraying himself as a no-nonsense man of the people who made things *happen.*

Scarfe entered the ornate building where his apartment occupied the top floor. He pressed the button that would summon the elderly lift. Waiting for it to appear, he imagined the Eye complete, the Norwich skyline reshaped. As the man responsible for building it he would be immortalised, a part of the history of the city he'd moved to as a child. The thought energised him, as the lift arrived to carry him up.

Scarfe's apartment was impressive. Early nineteenth century and furnished in lavish style – oriental rugs, antique furniture, and with walls covered in original oils, each painting lit individually. A distinguished suite of rooms in which to entertain business associates, or, for that matter, company of a more intimate nature. Stopping long enough only to shower and change into a fresh suit, Scarfe was soon in the lift again, ready for the brief walk to Petrova's City Hall and Administrative Centre, where the meeting for which he'd come was to take place.

The meeting passed very much as Scarfe had expected. The main order of business, the proposal to set up educational links between the two cities, descended into fruitless bickering and point scoring. This was due in no small part to the inability of Kingsley and another colleague Donald Rayburn to agree on anything, even a definition of terms. After lunch, any decisions that needed to be made were put off until another meeting could be arranged. With time on their hands, most delegates spent the rest of the afternoon shopping for their families, or seeking refreshment in one of the many bars and cafés.

That evening, in a well-heeled corner of Petrova's historic quarter, the Norwich Councillors and their opposite numbers found themselves in a private room on the first floor of The Toy Soldier, a restaurant favoured by any who could afford it. Everyone looked very satisfied as the last of their plates were taken away. Having poured himself a decent measure of port, Scarfe slid the bottle along the dining table to his neighbour.

'I believe that should be passed the other way, old chap.'

The casual rebuke hit Scarfe like a hard slap. The man who offered the advice, Donald Rayburn of course, red face heavily lined, continued to puff extravagantly on his cigar, at ease in his surroundings.

'Of course. Must have had more than I realised,' Scarfe

replied, his teeth bared in an attempt at a smile.

Rayburn had been a highly vocal critic of the Norwich Eye. The wheel would tower over St Peter Mancroft Church, where he was a member of the congregation and its board. He had been silenced only when a large compensation payment had been agreed.

'So what did you make of today's business?' Rayburn asked him. 'You didn't say much.'

'Not my area of expertise, education,' Scarfe responded cautiously. Rayburn was no friend.

As the evening grew late and noisy, Scarfe noticed Kingsley looking detached from the group, despite the warm hospitality of their hosts. After listening dutifully to a rather long-winded joke – 'And he said, they enjoyed it so much, I'm taking them to the beach!' – there were guffaws of laughter – he went over and sat down quietly next to him. With his vote on the selection committee still an unknown quantity, any opportunity to change that had to be taken.

'I thought you made some good points at the meeting today, Howard.' In fact, Scarfe knew very little about what Kingsley had actually said, having spent much of the time on his BlackBerry.

'Really?'

The crude flattery seemed to bring Kingsley back to life. Dismissing Rayburn as a self-serving bureaucrat, he recounted his argument for the introduction of History Scholarships. Funded by Norwich City Council, they would enable selected students from Petrova to be enrolled at the University of Norwich, where they would be taught in part by himself, who already gave lectures to undergraduates twice weekly at the castle. The scheme would satisfy all the criteria listed on that days agenda. Scarfe listened patiently, and then with increasing interest. Glimpsed as if through muddy waters, the vague outline of an idea materialised. The outline of a vote.

'History Scholarships,' Scarfe repeated thoughtfully. 'I didn't know you lectured. Shouldn't you be working?'

Kingsley looked at him sternly. 'It *is* work, Harry. It's taken years to build up the partnership we have with the university. Helps with our funding.' He lowered his voice, glancing across the room at Rayburn. 'So would a sponsorship deal. Never used to have to worry, but these days, well. You know how it is.'

Scarfe nodded sympathetically. 'I can imagine. You know, now you've explained these scholarships again – I like the idea. Problem you've got is Rayburn. You'll be lucky if you ever get the thing off the ground. I think you'd be better off with a private sponsor, cut out the red tape.'

'Not much chance of that,' said Kingsley defeatedly. 'We're talking a lot of money.'

Scarfe smiled. The muddy waters cleared.

'Your glass is empty. Let's top you up, shall we?'

*

Scarfe awoke alone in his apartment in central Petrova. Throwing back the bedclothes, he walked into the kitchen where he fixed some coffee, taking it out onto the small balcony that led from the main room. He sat in the early morning sunshine, slanting down through the narrow street, still elated by his success the previous night at The Toy Soldier.

Kingsley had taken him up on his offer to fund the History Scholarships he wanted, and accepted a very generous "consultancy" fee. In return, the Curator would vote for him on the selection committee. All of which meant he was now guaranteed to be the Tory candidate for the Norfolk South by-election. Beautiful, thought Scarfe, squinting in the light. Money – was there anyone immune to its power? Nothing seemed to motivate people so much as their greed. He sipped his coffee, and enjoyed the warmth on his face.

Within weeks, with the scholarships hurriedly organised and five successful applicants enrolled mid-term at the university, each a young Petrovan woman, Harry Scarfe made sure the press were fully briefed on his philanthropic venture. The political capital to be made for himself and his campaign couldn't have come at a better time, he thought. Soundbites like 'promoting closer cultural ties with our twin city,' and 'opening doors for those less fortunate,' gave him, so he believed, a statesman-like air.

Less statesman-like were the affairs he began with two of the students.

Harry saw Anneka and Odette as nothing more than an unexpected bonus to his arrangement with Kingsley. Conquests he could be proud of. He found Anneka the most fun, adventurous and feisty. Odette began that way too, but soon became more intense and demanding, believing it seemed that there was more to their affair than there actually was. He bought her gifts, believing that would be enough to satisfy her.

Then one afternoon, lying exhausted in a familiar hotel room, Odette caught him completely by surprise – she wanted them to live together. He tried laughing off the suggestion, though it was clear she was serious. The next few times they met the tension grew, until, at a quiet pub beside a river, she threatened to make their relationship public. That, Harry knew, would leave his political campaign in ruins. He stared at a hire boat as it chugged by, thinking darkly how an accident on the water would stop her from talking. He bought himself time with vague promises for the future, and they parted without a visit to the hotel room.

But time was shorter than either of them knew.

Working from home one morning the following week, Harry received a text. Odette wanted to see him. He still had no more idea how to deal with her than he had at the pub by the river – apart from that accident. Maybe if she saw him at home, he thought, she'd feel guilt of some sort, feel Caroline's presence. Caroline herself was at a lunch meeting with a business associate, and his next phone conference wasn't until two.

Time enough.

They never made it to the bedroom, succumbing to each other instead on the kitchen floor. Pinning Harry down, Odette mounted him, moaning softly. Then came a different sound. Harry lifted his head and peered over Odette's shoulder. Standing by the sink was Caroline, her face burning red. Her lunch appointment had obviously cancelled. Sensing suddenly that something was wrong, Odette twisted round, following Harry's fixed gaze. Sweat ran down her cleavage, a small silver 'O' dangling from its thin chain. A pause crackled the air, before Odette shrieked. But it was a shriek of laughter. She flopped onto Harry's rigid torso in a fit of helpless mirth, offering Caroline a view of her husband's penetration of her – no embarrassment, no remorse.

Harry knew Caroline had suspected his infidelity many times before. Now she had the proof. Even as his wife's tears formed, his mind leapt to what the political fallout would be if Caroline left him – no different than if his affair became public knowledge.

His options were running out fast. He had to take back control.

Forty minutes later he started the engine of his car, pushing the button on the central console. In the boot lay Odette's body, wrapped in a sheet of blue tarpaulin he'd retrieved from the garage. The mess had been unbelievable, making him gag even to think of it. Despite having showered and wearing a fresh suit, the smell of death still clung to him, metallic and raw.

He looked back at the house. Caroline stood at a window

in the hallway, her face whitened by shock. He nodded, and she nodded in return. What had taken place in the kitchen was to remain their secret, neither wanting to test the consequences of betrayal. With unusual meekness, he eased the car forwards in an arc, waiting for the driveway gates to open before pulling out slowly onto the road.

That afternoon he drove for hours, looking for a place to hide the body. But however far he roamed from the main roads, a rambler or cyclist would appear, as if out of nowhere, eyeing his distinctive coupé with distaste. If the body was discovered, Scarfe thought, any one of them might remember him. And discovered it could easily be, if the news was anything to go by. Increasingly anxious, he headed back to his office at City Hall, needing to think, the body of Odette still in his boot. He told Tracy he was not to be disturbed.

Standing at his office window, he watched as life around him carried on as if nothing had happened. The market bustled, Gentlemans Walk packed with shoppers, while sat serenely on its high mound was the castle, flag fluttering contentedly in the light breeze. Out of habit, he bent his head right to catch a glimpse of his Norwich Eye project. From this height, he could see past one edge of the hoarding to the building site the other side of it. The building site, he suddenly thought – was that the answer?

He hurried over to the scale model of the Eye he kept in his office, taking out the blueprint stored beneath it along with a map from the City Planning Office. Back when building work had first begun, his foreman had commented that while digging out the foundations, they had shaved through two tunnels that ran close by – two of the many flint and chalk works that criss-crossed under central Norwich. They would have to be blocked up again, before the foundations were filled in with hundreds of tons of concrete.

Would he be safe, dumping a body in one of those tunnels? Might a workman find it? Possible. How far in would he have to go? He traced each of the two tunnels with a finger, using the map from City Planning where the blueprint ended. One of the two led to another tunnel that then ran directly into the castle, terminating in a symbol he didn't recognise. Checking the legend, Scarfe became animated. He traced the route again to be sure, and ended once more at the symbol.

No one would find her there.

The only problem, he realised, was that he would need Kingsley's help. How else could he gain access? But dare he take such a huge risk?

Scarfe pulled on his ear. For the life of him, right at that very moment, he could think of no other way. He was mentally exhausted, just wanting to be rid of the problem. Every moment the body lay in his car, there was a chance he could be caught – the end of everything he'd worked for. Kingsley had already taken his money once, he reasoned. That meant he could be persuaded to do so again, the only unknown being the price. Money had never let him down yet.

Ten minutes later, Scarfe arrived at the castle, bursting in to Kingsley's office.

'I want you to do something for me.'

'Afternoon to you too,' said Kingsley, taken aback.

'There's been an accident.'

Glossing over the details haphazardly, Scarfe gave the story he'd decided upon. Kingsley would be less happy to co-operate if he knew the truth. Listening, Kingsley became pale, his jaw slackening in disbelief.

'I can't believe it. I was teaching her this week.' Kingsley stared at the floor, shaking his head. He looked up. 'This accident – why was she with you in the first place? Where is she now? Have you called an ambulance, or someone to take her?'

'If I do that, the papers will make out I was having an affair.'

Behind his glasses, Kingsley blinked. 'Were you?'

'Think very carefully before you speak,' said Scarfe, dark eyes flaring.

'So why *were* you both out on a boat together, then?'

'See how it would look? I can't take that risk.'

Both knew Scarfe meant the damage such a revelation would do to his campaign for Parliament. He would be deselected.

'So what are you going to do? You'll have to tell the authorities what's happened sooner or later.'

'There's a way round it.'

Scarfe unrolled the map and blueprint he'd brought with him, using several books from a shelf to weigh down their ends onto Kingsley's desk. He explained his plan to avoid scandal, and prying eyes, by carrying the body underground from the Eye to the castle's well.

'There must be a door here,' Scarfe finished, his finger at the point where the tunnel met the castle's boundary. 'I need you to get us in.'

Kingsley was incredulous.

'Us?' he said. 'Tell me you're joking.' It didn't take much to see that Scarfe wasn't in a joking mood. Kingsley's voice rose indignantly. 'What makes you think I'd help you do that? Here, where I work? Harry, think about it. You've got to tell the authorities what's happened.'

'I have thought about it. I don't expect you to help for nothing. You'll get paid.'

'Paid? Are you trying to say – you think because of Petrova –'

'I'm talking a lot of money.' Scarfe let the thought percolate the air.

Kingsley took out his handkerchief, picking at a plucked thread. The same look entered his eyes as it had at The Toy Soldier in Petrova. The clock on the desk ticked indifferently.

'How much?' he asked, with as much dignity as he could

muster.

'Say a price.'

Kingsley took off his glasses and pinched his nose between forefinger and thumb. 'I think fifty's reasonable. For what you're asking me to do.'

Fifty thousand pounds. He really was a greedy bastard, thought Scarfe. Would he come back for more when the money ran out? Blackmail? Before they dumped the body, he'd have to find a way to connect him to the murder – insurance against future claims.

'That's quite a sum, Howard.'

'I don't think you realise what you're –'

'All right, all right. Fifty it is.' Scarfe pondered the logistics. 'You'll have to take it in instalments. That kind of money gets noticed. The scholarship fund will hide it.' It was time to get down to details. 'So where exactly does this tunnel come out? Do you know?'

Kingsley nodded. 'I do.'

*

The next night, Scarfe and Kingsley drove to the site where the Norwich Eye was being built. It wasn't a particularly busy evening in the city, and no one paid them much attention as Scarfe swung open the entrance gate before driving through. Inside, and with the gate secured once more, they were able to hide their movements behind the builders' hoarding, disconnecting three security lights to make sure of themselves. With the boot lid open, the two men reached down and lifted out the blue plastic tarpaulin that was wrapped around Odette's lifeless body. They carried it to where a ladder poked up from a wide gulley in the ground.

'We can't carry her down that,' said Kingsley.

They had no choice but to drop the body instead, flinching at the sickening crunch it made hitting the concrete floor, some fifteen feet below.

A gentle drizzle began to fall. Scarfe pressed his car key, closing the lid to his boot without a sound. They wouldn't be coming back this way. Kingsley had suggested they returned via the tunnel that led to City Hall, and he'd agreed. Cover their tracks as best they could.

Scarfe climbed gingerly down the ladder and into the darkness, Kingsley following close behind. At the bottom they took one end each of the tarpaulin again and moved cautiously forward, a wall of earth on one side, slabs of metal and huge steel cables the other. Within a dozen feet a break appeared in the earth wall, pitch black.

'Switch your torch on,' whispered Scarfe.

The cycle lamp attached to Kingsley's head blazed into life.

'Point it towards me, you idiot.'

A rough opening, propped up with steel poles and a horizontal section of wood, materialised out of the shadows. A temporary entrance to the tunnel on Scarfe's blueprint. Stumbling over the debris left by the builders, they entered, both wondering nervously just how accurate their maps were. If they got lost, thought Scarfe to himself, then Odette would have company for all eternity.

But they didn't get lost. Instead, after more than an hour's effort, Scarfe and Kingsley found themselves at the door they had come in search for, the other side of which was the well.

Kingsley unlocked it, and they staggered through.

6

Fisher Bayley was seated at the window of a coffee bar, one end of the market square in the centre of Norwich. His coffee tasted good; hot and bitter. He was seldom up early enough to enjoy coming here before work, unless he'd stayed over at Ginny's.

Yesterday's excitement at the castle was fresh in his mind. Being the museum's Marketing and Communications Officer, he'd been disappointed when the dive team Brian Finch knew had failed to appear. Would have made a good story. He took a swig from his cup. Dark hair briefly combed, eyes friendly and with a ready smile, Bayley had an air about him almost of innocence, as if he were unsullied by the world and its iniquitous ways. It was a quality most people he met found attractive.

He gazed out towards the market stalls. The summer sun reflected strongly off the brightly striped canopies, under which fruit, vegetables and flowers spilled out onto the flagstones of Gentlemans Walk. The stallholders were already doing a steady trade. One figure stood out amongst the early shoppers, tall and gangly, shirt too large around the shoulders, fair hair long over his ears.

Gulping down the last of his drink, Bayley left the coffee house and made his way over to where his friend was busy assessing the ripeness of a plump avocado. The stallholder spoke with barely concealed annoyance.

'If you want to squeeze it like that, mate, you'll have to buy it. You can squeeze it as much as you like at home.'

Reddening, Phillip Henderson bought it, and three more.

As far as Fisher was concerned, Phil Henderson, despite his eccentricities, had grown from hippy youth into some semblance of an adult far more convincingly than he himself had. Happily married to Penny, a successful artist, for years now he had worked as Resident Archivist at City Hall, the large brick edifice of which overlooked the market square. Fisher often thought this a curious occupation for someone so naturally untidy, but Phil claimed to enjoy the peace and quiet of his basement domain, no one there to look over his shoulder.

They had been friends since school, and even when at the age of twenty-seven Fisher had moved to London, had still kept in touch. When several years later he returned from the capital, a broken relationship behind him but little else, the two of them had picked up where they'd left off, as if the years had been days.

'Always hard to tell, isn't it?'

Phil turned. 'Fisher!' His eyes were red and swollen, the skin around them crusty. 'You're out of bed. Hard to tell what?' He took his bag of fruit from the stallholder, and his change, dropping a ten pence piece amongst the bananas in his haste.

'Whether they're ripe or not.' Fisher squinted at him. 'You all right?' he asked inquisitively.

'Ah, you've noticed.'

'Difficult not to.'

'I have had a bit of trouble,' Phil began to explain.

Not many new-age fads passed him by, usually health-related. They came and went on a regular basis, forgotten as quickly as they arrived, nothing having changed in their wake. This time had been different. Recently turned thirty-six, Phil admitted he'd developed a dread of the milestone birthday that seemed to be accelerating towards him. Fisher wasn't keen on the idea either, but hadn't realised the full extent of his friend's phobia.

'A sunlamp, with your eyes wide open? No wonder you blinded yourself. A tan *gives* you wrinkles, Phil.'

'I wasn't getting a tan, I was training my eyes to see people's auras. Normally they're invisible.'

'Your brain's what's invisible.'

'You're so small-minded. For your information, negative auras are a main cause of aging. They sap the spirit. That's why you have to train to avoid them.'

'You'll still be turning forty in a few years time, same as me.'

'Don't say that. Anyway, it's not about numbers, it's about being young inside. Healthy.'

'And burnt to a crisp on the outside.'

'I seem to remember you using sunbeds, before they went out of fashion.'

Which was true. Fisher changed tack.

'What did Penny say?'

Phil shifted uncomfortably. 'It's all done with now. Anyway, forget about that. I've been meaning to call. Boys' night out – what do you reckon? It's been a while.'

'All the old gang, eh?' said Fisher absently. Himself, Phil, Chris and Sean. Not as close as they'd once been, but their shared history ran deep. He continued to search his friend's eyes, as if at any moment they might pop out or explode.

'Weekend after next – are you about?'

'I'll check. What's wrong with this weekend?'

'Can't, Penny's got Caroline coming round. Going through another sticky patch at home. I've always thought her other half was a bit too old for her, if I'm honest.'

'Caroline... Do I know her?'

'Not sure. You might have heard of her husband, he's trying to get himself elected MP. Harry Scarfe. Ring any bells?'

7

FISHER BAYLEY WALKED away from the market and along Davey Place. He hadn't told Henderson about his own "sticky patch". He and Ginny Carmen had been together only two months, but already their honeymoon period was over. Climbing the steps that led up to Castle Meadow, he tried to put his finger on what had gone wrong between them, as if by dissecting the past he might be able to change it.

All he did was run out of fingers.

He let himself into the castle by the staff door, the bright morning at once cut off by the medieval dusk of the interior. When he reached his office, on the top floor of one of the buildings linked to the Keep, he was greeted by Jane Meadows, with whom he shared the tiny space.

Jane was pretty rather than striking, and her glasses, though fashionable, gave her a slightly studious look. A geologist, she was usually surrounded by samples of rock and uncut precious stones, shining amongst the papers and various optical devices that otherwise filled her desktop. Whenever Bayley asked her about her work, the explanations that followed often made him think geology was written in a different language. Despite this intellectual gulf, Bayley found Jane good company. They laughed a lot together. She had what Phil Henderson would no doubt call a positive aura.

There was a Post-It note on his desk from Howard Kingsley, asking to see him. 'Best see what he wants, as if I didn't know,' he said, and left again in the direction of the

Curator's office.

Barely out of the door, he bumped into Ian Chapman, Brian Finch's assistant, red hair and the beginnings of a paunch. Too much beer, Ian often commented about himself, usually in the pub after work with a pint in his hand.

'Morning,' they chanted to each other as they passed, neither inclined to stop and chat so early in the day.

'Jane's in,' Fisher called back, knowing Ian's destination. He often wondered if Jane knew how Ian felt about her.

Kingsley was tapping away at his keyboard when Bayley arrived. The computer was the only object in the room it was possible to tie with any certainty to the twenty-first century, including the Curator.

'Morning Fisher, let me just send this... Done.'

As Bayley had expected, all Kingsley wanted was for him to prepare another PowerPoint presentation, for a lecture he was to give. Bayley often got the impression Kingsley thought of him as little more than his personal assistant. The phone on the desk rang, interrupting his instructions. It was the security guard, Barry Cleaver. His message, whatever it was, didn't appear to go down well.

'Are you sure?' Kingsley spoke into the receiver. His mouth was turned downwards, making his chin almost disappear altogether. 'Where are they now?' There was a pause as he listened. 'I see. No, no, I'm coming straight away.'

He replaced the receiver.

'Everything all right?' asked Bayley, intrigued to know what had been said.

Kingsley looked at him as if he'd forgotten he was there.

'It's the dive team Brian called yesterday. They're here.'

8

BRIAN FINCH WAS enjoying his newfound celebrity and Howard Kingsley's moodiness in equal measure. Professional jealousy, Finch thought. He locked his laboratory and descended a small staircase nearby, a bounce in his step.

Another interview, this time for a Sunday magazine. Finch found it difficult to believe it had been only a week since Tom Lomax and his team had spent the day diving the well. What they found in that time had exceeded his wildest expectations.

*

Harry Scarfe stopped toying with his ear. 'Will you get a move on,' he shouted up the stairs. 'I've got other things to do than this charity of yours.' He picked up his BlackBerry from the console table standing in the hallway.

Caroline ignored him, studying herself in the bedroom mirror with a ruthless eye. An amazonian figure, someone had once said to her. Strong features to match, and long, light brown hair, stylishly cut.

Giving up on the trouser suit, which didn't seem to be working like it had in the shop, Caroline instead slipped on a dress and descended the staircase that fluted out onto the tiled hall. Her husband paced the floor, BlackBerry in hand, thumbing the keys.

'I'm ready,' she said.

'At last. Wait while I finish this off.'

Caroline opened the front door and stepped outside onto a large circle of gravel, at its centre a fountain, cherubs gushing into a clear pool of water. She climbed into the passenger seat of the Bentley parked there.

Inside the house, having pressed the send button on his email, Harry pocketed his phone and activated the burglar alarm. Slamming the door shut he joined his wife in the car, pressing the start button and accelerator pedal in quick succession before whipping around the fountain and speeding off towards the gates as they opened. He glared at the driver of a passing car as she prevented him from pulling straight out. His phone rang.

'Shit.'

'Give it to me, I'll put it on speaker,' said Caroline.

'No. It'll have to wait.'

*

Mid-morning, Brian Finch returned to his laboratory, his mood even better than when he had left it. The journalist for the magazine had been gratifyingly enthusiastic. He took off his jacket and donned a lab coat that hung on the back of the door.

The simple white coat felt familiar and comfortable, with its stains and pens, and odd pieces of equipment that always somehow found their way into the deep side pockets. Finch loved equipment. Here, it was all around him, some state of the art, some held together with tape. The radiocarbon dating apparatus had its controls inside the laboratory, though most of the machine was housed separately in a room next door. It could produce results in less than a day, if properly coaxed, though after years of patching up that was rare. Several other expensive looking machines flanked it, their dials and readouts unintelligible to most visitors. Finch preferred to keep it that way. If asked to explain their function, he would do so using technical terms designed to be as baffling as possible.

The door swung open again, nearly braining him.

'How did it go?' Chapman asked, though Finch's expression was enough to give him his answer.

'Very well!' Finch beamed. 'The story's being published in two weeks.' He picked up a box from a shelf next to him and pulled out two pairs of latex gloves, eager for the task that lay ahead. 'We'll talk about it at lunch, shall we?'

They crossed the floor to a wide bench, laden with some of the dozens of objects recovered from the well by Tom Lomax and his team.

The cause of the flooding, Lomax had told Finch at the time, was likely due to the abnormally wet summer, the fast currents disturbing more debris than was usual. Searching the caverns at the base of the well, their own activities had had the same effect, raising the water level again for a few hours, much to Kingsley's fury.

On the bench were an assortment of arrowheads, pieces of armour, and several sections of sword. There was pottery too, some of it still decorated, but mostly fragmented and worn. Everything required documenting and tagging, before being sent off to various departments around the castle, or occasionally further afield. As a Forensic Archaeologist, however, it was the bones that most interested Finch. A find rare enough to make his name.

Many of the bones were small and unremarkable, but amongst these there were more exciting pieces – the end of a shattered femur, a slice of pelvis or shoulder blade, Finch wasn't sure yet, and a partial jawbone. Not all the skeletal remains appeared human. It was a newsworthy haul, though the object that had most captured the public's imagination Finch had isolated inside the laboratory's fume cupboard. A ribcage, nearly intact. He had examined it already on several occasions, his touch delicate, nervous of tainting whatever secrets it might hold. He rationed his time spent with it, putting off the day when there would be nothing more to analyse. The ribcage would then become the star exhibit of a new display, somewhere in the castle.

On first seeing the bones, particularly the ribcage, Chapman had been struck by their surprisingly good condition. They were not the darkened relics he would have expected, centuries after death. Finch had explained.

'Bones that have aged in air can tend to darken. Or when preservative is added. Water's different. Silt in the currents acts like sandpaper, and when the water's acidic, as we know it is in the well, there's bone dissolution too. Makes our job all the harder.'

From the way he spoke, it was clear this was a challenge Finch relished.

He now picked up a small finger bone, fixed to a card, a six digit number inscribed in one corner. The size and features were also recorded, and a sliver had been taken for DNA analysis. The carbon dating machine had calculated the metacarpal to be mid fourteenth-century, the same as it had many of the other bones. Finch passed the specimen to his assistant. 'This one's ready to be put away.'

Chapman took the finger bone to a cabinet, filled with small trays, placing it in one of them.

'We need Fisher here,' Finch thought aloud. 'Have you seen him?'

The Deputy Curator wanted Bayley to capture every moment, every detail of the find. After all, Bayley's job was to publicise the castle and its work. The last week had been a gift for him.

Chapman sent Bayley a text, then asked, 'Are we carrying on with the jawbone?'

Like the finger, it too was fourteenth-century. Chapman was fascinated by its history. The lesions that scarred it had been caused by the Black Death, the Plague that had decimated Britain's population in the thirteen-hundreds. It was a tangible connection to that hellish time, which to Chapman made the disease seem very real. He was never tempted to touch it with his bare hands, wary that somehow the horror might still hide there, ready to mortally infect him.

'We most certainly are. I want another ten scrapings mounted on slides, all from the sockets.' Finch had cursed his luck at there being no teeth. 'Anything you're not sure of, call me over. Ah, Fisher.'

'I got your message. Where do you want me to start?'

Finch directed Bayley to the many arrowheads, yet to be photographed, at the same time giving advice on how he wanted the castle's website updated. He deferred Bayley's questions about his interview until later, as he had Chapman.

The three of them set to work, Finch sifting through computer printouts, making meticulous notes. For half an hour, the only sounds were of pencil on paper, metal on bone. Then the door opened again. It was Kingsley, eyes tired behind his glasses.

'How's it all going?' he asked. He had been a frequent visitor to the laboratory over the past week. Finch had put up with his incessant questions only because he hoped he would change his mind about the funding of further dives. Lomax was unable to repeat the favour. 'Anything unusual?'

Finch sighed, rubbing his beard. Different day, same question. Why wasn't what lay on the bench enough? He gave Kingsley a brief update on the day's work, irritated at being disturbed.

'The Black Death,' Kingsley murmured, touching the jawbone in front of Chapman.

'Not without gloves,' rebuked Finch.

Kingsley drew his hand away. 'Fourteenth century... worst time to be alive.'

'Thirteenth wasn't a bed of roses,' Finch said.

He had dated nearly every bone to either one of these two periods, placing the exceptions as seventeenth-century, eighteenth at a push. The more recent the time frame, the less accurate the process. He'd been made to repeat these facts every visit to the laboratory Kingsley had made. Why those particular centuries, he told him, he wasn't sure. Maybe because the churchyards were struggling to cope with the number of corpses caused by the Plague.

Kingsley gave a satisfied grunt and left. Ruffled, Finch hung up his lab coat and disappeared too, muttering about needing some fresh air. Chapman followed him out of the door to buy a pastry from the cafeteria.

Alone, Bayley stretched his legs, wandering over to where the glass-fronted fume cupboard stood. The human ribcage inside had a clean break through two of the ribs, leaving them joined only by the sternum. Bayley had listened to Finch speculating on how the injury could have been sustained, the favoured theory being the most dramatic – a lethal blow suffered in battle. Bayley thought of Kingsley's comment. Fourteenth century – worst time to be alive. He was with the Curator on that. Though if the broken ribs did signify a brutal death, he thought, at least their assailant was long dead too.

9

GINNY CARMEN GAVE Fisher an appraising look. It was lunchtime, and they were seated together in one corner of the busy cafeteria that served visitors to the castle. Her porcelain face was immaculate, each wave of her blonde hair shimmering under the spotlights. The castle's Art Curator, she often drew as much interest as the Cotmans and Cromes people came to see.

'You're quiet,' Fisher ventured.

He seemed unsure of himself. As he should, Ginny thought, after their last row. He was dressed casually, his approach to life in general, as if he didn't realise the importance of things. So exasperating – the reason she lost her temper with him so easily. She'd considered ending it, but then changed her mind.

Ginny never had a problem meeting men. Instead the problems came later, somewhere down the line. And when they did, she didn't hang around. But that had got her nowhere. Nights in alone, a takeaway curry and too much to drink. She wanted this time to be different, to give things a chance to work out. In the meantime, she had an idea how they could put the arguments behind them. Men were so predictable.

'I've been thinking,' she said.

Fisher nodded non-commitally. Ginny leaned forward, not wanting to be overheard.

'I want to make love,' she whispered.

'Okay,' said Fisher, drawing the word out, as if suspicious

of what Ginny might mean by this statement.

'You don't understand. I want to make love here, inside the castle. Where we work. What do you think?'

The idea of it aroused her, even more now she'd said it.

'Here in the castle?' Fisher glanced around at the assortment of visitors nearby, stirring drinks, biting into sandwiches, slicing through triangles of cake with the edges of forks. He grinned suddenly.

'Sounds kinky. Let's do it!'

Ginny looked directly at him, eyes alight with anticipation. 'I thought the Egyptian room would be good. Tonight, when everyone's gone.'

'Tonight! Don't we need to plan? What if we get caught?'

'We won't. Come over to my office after six – everyone will have left by then. I'll go out and get something nice to wear, if you like.'

Fisher perked up. 'What sort of something?'

Ginny smiled knowingly. So predictable.

'You'll have to wait and see.'

*

That Thursday afternoon Bayley found it difficult to concentrate. He was back in the laboratory, on hand to record the progress of Finch and Chapman.

Finch had decided to once again examine the ribcage, and his excitement was evident. Bayley thought there was something unsettling about such enthusiasm. These were after all the remains of a person. At what point had they lost their humanity?

He watched as Finch unlocked the glass window to the fume cupboard and slid it to one side. Finch then picked up the ribcage by the base it rested on and carried it over to the wooden examination table in the middle of the room. He moved slowly and with great precision, as if worried any sudden movement might see his great prize collapse like some ghoulish soufflé.

With the partial skeleton securely placed on the bench, Finch gently touched the jagged ends of two of the ribs, severed from the spine and held in place only by the sternum, which they curved to join at the front of the chest.

'Whatever happened to you, my dear fellow, we shall do our best to find out.'

Chapman had another theory to add to the mix.

'Could it have been a sacrifice?'

'That's an interesting idea.' Finch rubbed his hands, taken by the suggestion. Even more newsworthy than dying in battle. 'Not unknown, around the time of the Plague. Difficult for us to prove, though.'

Bending closer to the bones, Finch frowned slightly.

'You know, it's difficult to tell, the way the backbone's been twisted, but I'm not entirely convinced this is a man.'

'Female warrior?' offered Bayley. 'Like that one who fought the Romans... Boudica,' he remembered.

Finch momentarily froze. The castle had an entire gallery devoted to the great warrior Queen.

'Pass me my toolkit,' he said urgently.

10

THAT EVENING, ALONE in the office he shared with Jane Meadows, Fisher Bayley logged off his computer. Since the discoveries made in the well he'd been kept very busy, which was fine by him, but updating the website and social media feeds were among his least favourite tasks. Online meant twenty-four seven, which always left him with a sense his work had never really finished for the day. For once, however, banishing such thoughts wasn't a problem. He wondered what purchases Ginny had made at lunchtime.

Ginny Carmen occupied a bright and spacious office attached to the art galleries. Fisher made his way there, relieved to find the castle deserted, except for a solitary cleaner busy washing the floor of the cafeteria. What time the security guards started their patrols, he had no idea – not for another hour he hoped. He passed through the Natural History galleries without stopping. Normally he would pause to stand in front of the fierce-eyed pride of lions, imagining what it would be like if they were alive and about to pounce on him. But not this evening. As he entered the first of the art galleries, which contained a Rembrandt and several rare Cotman oils, he met Ginny coming the other way. They kissed, smiling at each other almost shyly.

'Er – are you ready?' Fisher spoke as if they were about to go for a drive somewhere, or see a film.

Both could sense in the other the nervous thrill of the unknown.

Together, they made their way to the castle's central atrium and climbed the stairs that led towards the Egyptian display. Fisher used the key he'd collected from the staff lounge to open the display's glass door. Ginny stepped inside, sliding on a pair of velvet gloves over her bare arms as Fisher joined her, closing the door behind him.

They kissed in full view through the glass. Fisher found the gloves' texture erotic as Ginny stroked his face. Eventually she pulled herself away, and began to produce magician-like from her handbag tiny items of nylon and lace. She placed them on the huge stone plinth that stood in the centre of the room like a raised bed.

'Classic Egyptian attire?' Fisher queried.

'Are you complaining?'

Fisher replied by unbuttoning his shirt.

Their surroundings were unusual to say the least. Close to the viewing window were mounted the exhibit's rarest items, a plaque to describe the provenance of each. The most dazzling object on display was a golden dagger, radiating brightly on its stand. The same ambient glow gave the sarcophagus near to Fisher a slightly sinister appearance. He swayed backwards and forwards, checking to see if the eyes in the mask followed him. They did.

'What on earth are you doing?'

'Nothing. It's the mummy. It's like he can see us.'

'I thought you might prefer to watch me.'

'I do.' Fisher looked at Ginny's near naked body. 'I really do,' he said, moving towards her meaningfully.

'Wait, I'm not ready! Cold hands, cold hands!' she gasped, pulling away.

Fisher stood back reluctantly, throwing down his shirt and undoing the belt of his trousers. He watched as Ginny unfurled another stocking over her calf, a soft furrow forming as she let it cling to her thigh. Above, a single piece of lacy lingerie cut high into her hips. Cliché, thought Fisher, but who was he to fight tradition? Then suddenly Ginny had grabbed him and was kissing his lips forcefully, pulling him down with her onto the plinth. Fisher had never been so aroused, kicking off his trousers and running a hand down her arched back. The world outside ceased to exist, as he abandoned himself completely to the moment.

Some time later, lying exhausted beneath the stone plinth, Ginny curled up beside him, Fisher found his eye wandering once more to the ornate wooden sarcophagus. He stared at it intently, as if to pre-empt any sudden movement that might catch him off his guard. Its intricate hieroglyphs gave it an alien appearance.

'He's still watching us. You can see where the legend came from.'

Ginny moved her head on Fisher's chest to see. 'Legend?'

'The legend of Ankh Hor – you know?'

Ginny had caught snippets in conversation, but that was all. She seldom left the art galleries, and then only because she needed to visit one of the art archives or restoration room, located in one of the buildings linked to the Keep. Once, she had stopped to take a closer look at the gibbet that hung in the Great Hall, when Ian Chapman had told her that if she examined it closely, the bloodstains from prisoner's bodies, locked in and left to decay, could still be seen.

'I heard there was some sort of tale,' she said vaguely, propping herself up and resting her chin on the palm of her hand, looking at him.

'It's more than that,' said Fisher, a little aggrieved Ginny had clearly never read any of the guide books he'd put together. 'When the sarcophagus was X-rayed in the seventies, they saw something that shouldn't have been there.'

'The new iPhone?'

'Very droll. The mummified body of Ankh Hor and his organ pots were inside, as expected, but there were several metal brackets too, which they dated to the nineteenth century.'

'Meaning the Victorians took a look first.'

'Except they couldn't have done. The seals around the coffin were never broken, still aren't. Impossible to fake.'

'So how do you explain the brackets?'

'Can't. No one can.'

Ginny digested this. 'Bit of a puzzle, I suppose. Not exactly Curse of the Pharaohs though, is it?'

'He was a priest.'

'You know what I mean.'

'Anyway, I haven't told you the most interesting part yet. It's not just the fact that these brackets were there, it's the reason *why* they were there.'

He paused enigmatically.

'Go on then, why were they there.'

'It was obvious from the way they were put in that they were designed to hold the priest down.'

'What – you mean – to stop him getting out?'

Fisher nodded solemnly. 'Legend is, he'd been seen wandering about the castle, trying to get home.'

A short silence ensued. Ginny's eyes flicked to the sarcophagus and then back to Fisher.

'He's creepy, I'll give you that, but come on...'

'It's a mystery, that's all I'm saying.'

'The real mystery is why anyone would believe it.' Ginny rolled on top of him. 'No brackets holding me down,' she said mischievously.

Fisher nuzzled her neck, her perfume mixing with the scent of her hair. She gripped his midriff between her knees.

'What are you waiting for,' she breathed in his ear.

*

They left the castle without being seen, the novelty of their illicit lovemaking giving them both a heady sense of exhilaration. Walking hand in hand through the city towards

Ginny's flat, she reeled off a list of other locations around the castle she would like to "christen". Fisher was enthusiastic, except for one suggestion, which was unfortunate, as it was the very one Ginny seemed most keen on.

Ginny's flat was a sleek affair, off-white furnishing and clean modern lines, interrupted only by the blazes of colour that swept across several frameless canvases. While Ginny showered, Fisher gazed down at Chapelfield Park, which the flat overlooked. Dusk wasn't far off. The park's perimeter was marked out by leafy horse chestnut trees, while at its centre a wooden bandstand cast a long shadow over the grass and flowerbeds. A jogger passed by the bandstand, crossing the giant chessboard next to it, the pieces locked away this late. The siren of a squad car sounded from the city police station, one block away.

Mulling over Ginny's list, sequels to the Egyptian room, Fisher could see no problem with the battlements or dungeons. It was her insistence that their next venture should be the dragon that concerned him.

Named Snap, the popular medieval effigy was made up of a timber carcass, cloaked in a skin of stiff faded cloth. Centuries earlier it had been the mainstay of countless parades, when two or three actors inside would entertain the crowds. Enough room then for Ginny and himself, he thought, but that wasn't what worried him. Rather, it was the fact that Snap the Dragon was suspended some forty feet or more above the floor of the Great Hall. The huge beam it hung from, with its thin metal rail to one side, could be navigated, but only by those with a good head for heights. He didn't count himself among that happy number. And then there was the awkward descent into the dragon itself.

One mistake, and he, Ginny, and Snap would all plummet to the floor below, the beast's inanimate wings unable to save them.

11

Friday dawned clear and bright, the early morning sunshine promising much. Traffic in the city built quickly to a background hum, those yet to head out of their doors bustling about at home, preparing for the day ahead.

Ginny Carmen and Fisher Bayley left her city flat for the short walk to the castle. People were moving in a steady stream along the pavements, take-out coffee clutched in one hand, peeling off to disappear into shops and businesses. Most wore an expression of contentment – the weekend was nearly here. So too, thought Fisher, was the night out Phil Henderson had organised, straight after work that evening. Inside the castle he kissed Ginny before each went off to face their day's business.

The morning shuffled slowly towards midday. Outside the window to Fisher and Jane's office, the sun burnt off any remaining haze. A rippling, drowsy heat descended on the city, the Indian Summer showing no signs of flagging. At lunchtime the bars and cafés filled quickly, sending out aromas of beer and grilled meat. By afternoon the heat had intensified, and at five o'clock the bars were heaving again, restaurant tables buzzing with chatter and laughter.

Fisher left work later than intended, making his way through Chapelfield Park and towards the Hendersons' house accompanied by Ian Chapman, having invited him along too. The evening light gave them both a tanned glow as they passed by a roundabout, snarled up with traffic, then continued along Unthank Road, a busy route that led away from the city. Dodging cars and cyclists, they crossed over and into a quieter street, to where Phil and Penny Henderson lived.

Arriving at number forty-two, Fisher and Ian were greeted by the sight of a warm redbrick terraced house, its windows high and elegant. A small house, but, as Phil never tired of saying to his friends, perfectly formed. Lifting the front door's heavy brass knocker, Fisher felt its pleasingly tactile weight before rapping out a short jingle.

Light female steps approached from the other side and the door swung open.

'Fisher!' Penny Henderson hugged Bayley enthusiastically. Her small frame felt delicate to him under the bob of dark hair. Her skin looked more olive than ever, her mischievous eyes bright and clear. 'And you must be...?'

'This is Ian.'

Ian gave a lopsided smile. 'Hi.'

Penny pecked him on the cheek, causing him to blush the colour of his hair.

'Come on, follow me. Phil's out the back. He's made a cocktail for you all, to kick things off.'

Fisher gave Ian a look, which said avoid anything made by Phil's hand.

Together the three of them passed through the house to step outside again onto a small patio, at the top of a long narrow garden. There was a heady perfume coming from the flowerbeds, which gave the warm air a sultry feel. Phil Henderson was sat at a garden table, a long blue drink in one hand, reading a paper. His eyes, Fisher could see, had resumed their normal appearance.

'Fisher, you're first here for a change!'

Fisher introduced Ian before accepting a glass of Phil's cocktail. It tasted strong, though a little sweet for his taste. Ian made himself an instant hit with Phil and Penny, enthralled to hear first-hand about the discoveries made in the well.

Hearing the doorbell, Fisher offered to answer it.

Sean Cooper and Chris Stokefield had been friends of Fisher's since they had all been in their early twenties. As the years had passed, however, Fisher had begun to find their company less of an attraction – like a couple, who, if they'd met years later, would never have got together in the first place.

Sean looked surprised to see Fisher answering the door, but with his protuberant eyes and thick, expressive eyebrows, he looked that way most of the time. Hair cut in an old-fashioned short-back-and-sides, from a distance he could have passed for a sixth form prefect, rather than the middle-ranking civil servant he was. He worked on the outskirts of Norwich, at County Hall, though what he did exactly he could never seem to explain, at least not in a way that could be understood.

'Moved in, have you?' he said, wiggling his eyebrows suggestively.

Chris laughed, already a few drinks ahead it seemed. 'Always fancied Penny, didn't you Fisher?'

Fisher was pleased to see Chris in a good mood. All too often his quick temper caused trouble. A sales rep for one of the big pharmaceuticals, he was sharp faced, like a bird of prey, an impression accentuated by his dark, gelled-back hair.

'Leaves Phil free for you then, doesn't it?' he said drily.

Chris scowled. 'Out of the way Fishy, I need a drink.'

He pushed past Fisher, short and wiry, smelling of cigarettes as he always did. The smoking laws had been brought in to screw him over, like everything else in life. Sean followed him in.

*

Within half an hour the party of five were making their way

on foot into the city. They walked past the clock tower at one end of City Hall and descended a steep square, edged on one side by the market place that sprawled across the heart of Norwich. Dominating the square was the medieval Guildhall. Its chequered stonework had once housed the city's courts, and a tunnel still led from its cells under Bayley's feet to the castle where he worked, perched a few hundred yards away, used when the castle had been a prison rather than a museum. According to popular myth, many more such passageways groped their way under Norwich, snaking between the chalk works and other excavations long since lost or forgotten.

Reaching the bottom of the square, a change of plan diverted the group from Tombland, a wide boulevard next to the Cathedral, lined with bars and restaurants, to the Lamb Inn, closer to the market.

The tables outside were packed. The five entered the coolness of the main bar, taking their drinks back outside to stand in the last of the sun before it dipped down behind the roofline overhead. Fisher took a long draught, eyes closed. After the sweetness of Phil's cocktail, the beer tasted good. Local.

The next hour or so was devoted to alcohol and talk; news, opinions, jokes, gossip. Chris smoked three cigarettes to a pint, still managing to drink faster than anyone else. He didn't add much to the conversation, constantly looking over shoulders to survey the ebb and flow of women around them.

Sean, eyes bulging earnestly, was eloquent on the subject of himself and his girlfriend, Eleanor Rayburn. Their love had apparently reached a new level. He looked at the others with something akin to pity.

'Not being Christians, you can't really appreciate what I'm talking about.'

'Not being Christians,' said Chris, 'listening to you it's difficult not to be sick. What's she like in bed?'

Sean did his best to ignore this remark but failed, giving Chris a look of contempt. 'My point exactly,' he said, as dismissively as possible.

Fisher, a little embarrassed with Ian there, swung the conversation round to Phil's episode with the sunlamp. Phil was still adamant that being able to avoid negative auras was the key to a long and healthy life, though he was curiously reluctant to share what method had succeeded the sunlamp. Whatever it was, Chris gave it no more than a week before he blinded himself a second time. Keen to disagree, Sean said at least it showed some spiritual awareness. Ironically, thought Fisher, Phil had begun to look worse for wear, and not just from the drink. Chris had picked up on it too.

'Phil,' Chris said, looking upwards at him, 'is it just me, or are you turning orange?'

The four of them studied Phil's face.

'I think he's right!' exclaimed Sean.

'Bit under the weather, that's all.' Phil emptied his glass. 'Why don't we go eat? I need some food.'

*

They chose a lively bar on Tombland, a short walk away. A modern hybrid mixing diners and drinkers together, it too was packed, the noise level high. Chris pounced on the one free table. Perched on the stools circled around it, the five of them ordered food.

At a table nearby, a group of four young women were each silently focused on their mobile phones, fingers darting nimbly, ignoring each other and Chris' rapt attention.

'What do you reckon?' Chris asked Ian, giving Sean a reason to tut and shake his head, the look of pity returning.

Ian frowned in the women's direction, as if assessing the possibilities. Fisher also cast his eye over the four girls, glad not to be called upon as wingman. Before Ginny he'd been single himself, for longer than he would have liked. It was a brief fling with one of Kingsley's students that seemed to have brought him to Ginny's attention, even though she'd never responded before to his flirting. Like buses, Chris had said at the time; nothing, then they all come at once.

Sounding ill at ease, Ian said, 'Which one do you fancy?'

'Whichever one will have him,' remarked Sean archly.

Chris gave a menacing scowl. Before he could reply, however, Fisher saw that Phil was rubbing at his temples, something very wrong.

'Phil... your head – it looks like it's swollen or something.'

He had also turned a definite shade of orange. The others peered closely at him now.

'You're turning into a space-hopper,' pronounced Chris.

Phil got up suddenly. 'Call of nature,' he said hurriedly, making off in the direction of the toilets.

Fisher watched him as he reached the stairs. 'Do you think I should go with him?'

'He'll be fine,' said Chris. 'What about those girls, Ian?'

The waiter approached with their food.

'Let's eat first, shall we?'

The note of relief in Ian's voice put Fisher in mind of a soldier in a First World War trench, told he wasn't going over the top just yet.

The drink made them eat greedily. Phil had not yet returned from the toilets, his plate left untouched, bar a few fries.

'Ah, shit,' exclaimed Chris, a moment later. To general giggling, two young men had approached the four girls, dressed in designer suits, accents from places they'd never been. 'Absolutely bloody typical.'

One of the suits let the cork from a bottle of house fizz fly off into the crowd. They'd come prepared.

'Still leaves two,' said Chris, but no one was paying him any attention. Phil had returned. He balanced himself on his stool, giving assurances he was better. Fisher wasn't convinced.

'You look worse, if anything. Are you sure –'

Phil interrupted with the release of a spectacular bout of flatulence. The four girls and their admirers looked over in disbelief, before laughing hysterically. Chris rounded on the perpetrator.

'Thanks a bunch, Phil. Very attractive. Just the image I was trying for. What the fuck is wrong with you?'

'Do you have to swear like that?' Sean reprimanded.

'Sorry Chris,' mumbled Phil. 'I've been sick...'

'Sounds like food poisoning,' said Fisher. 'We should get you a taxi. What did you eat before you came out?'

'I think it's the pills…'

Chris rolled his eyes in exasperation. 'What pills?'

Phil's bowels gave another loud fanfare.

'For the love of God!' Chris gave up. Any chance he may have had with the four girls had gone. One of the suits raised his glass to them, to which he gestured back by way of a single finger. Fisher laid a restraining arm on him.

'No handbags Chris. We need to sort Phil out.'

Chris sat back and drank deeply straight from a bottle, looking mutinous.

'What pills did you take?' Fisher felt anxious now.

'Vitamin A, that's all. For the eyes. Vegetables are too bulky.' Phil leaned heavily on his forearms, his expression glazed.

'How many did you take?'

'A bottle. Two bottles.'

Chris spread his arms in disbelief. 'That's like eating your own fucking weight in carrots, you idiot.'

'It's the only way to see the auras.'

'Here he goes with the auras again. What do you think you are, a fucking Jedi? Bloody new-age hippy bullshit.'

Phil chose that moment to convulse, retching onto the

plate of food in front of him. Everyone sprang up.

'Phil!' yelled Fisher, pulling him upright. 'Phil! Look at me!'

But Phil's eyelids were closed, fluttering lightly. It was a frightening sight. A taxi was no good, decided Fisher – an ambulance was required.

A crowd had formed, the designer suits and four girls laughing uncontrollably.

'You think this is funny?' shouted Chris, striding over to their table.

One of the men pushed him backwards.

Fisher draped Phil's right arm over his shoulder, Sean taking the other. Ian hovered around them, unsure how to help.

'Dial 999,' Fisher told him, as they tried to push through the crowd that had thickened to watch Chris and one of the suits fighting. Two bouncers flew past. As nights out with the boys went, thought Fisher, he'd had better.

*

The following afternoon Fisher drove to the Norfolk and Norwich Hospital, located outside the city since the original site had been demolished to make way for housing. At this time of day, it seemed an entirely different place from the night before. When he and Phil had arrived at the Accident and Emergency wing, the hospital had resembled the first circle of hell. The drunks and junkies who flooded the waiting area, loud and abusive, reminded him of his time in London, Trafalgar Square in the early hours, waiting for a night bus home.

Phil had received little sympathy from the hard-pressed doctor, his condition falling into the category of self-inflicted injuries. After her examination of him, he was admitted to a ward for intestinal problems, which was where Fisher headed now.

The ward had a distinctly unpleasant odour, like an open drain in the sun, made almost worse by the strong tang of disinfectant. Each of the twelve beds were occupied, men in varying states of distress. They watched as Fisher passed. Phil looked apologetic as he saw him approach.

'Sorry about last night,' he said dejectedly. 'I'm an idiot.'

Fisher sat on the low chair next to Phil's bed.

'Don't worry about that. What did the doctors say?'

'I'll be fine. Bit of liver damage probably' – Fisher looked alarmed – 'but nothing much, not really. They said I'd been lucky.' Phil rotated his head around the room to indicate his fellow patients, lowering his voice. Fisher leaned in to hear. 'Someone else wasn't though. Didn't make it through the night. I heard them talking. Not sure who – the beds are all full again.'

Fisher shuddered. 'Where's Penny?'

'You just missed her, she's gone to get me the papers.'

'How did she take it?'

'Not too well.' Phil looked remorseful.

'You've got to sort out this fixation of yours.'

'I know. I'm going to.'

The two friends chatted a while, but with every passing minute, Fisher found the ward's putrid smells evermore overpowering. And then there were the noises. A nurse, attending to a pale man in the next bed but one, drew the curtains to provide what level of privacy she could. Fisher tried not to imagine what horror might be going on behind the inadequate screen. He needed to get out of here, and Phil looked tired. Rising from his chair, he promised to visit the next day and left the room at a fair trot.

Taking the stairs to the ground floor, Fisher found the foyer that led to the main exit. He was halfway across when something caught his eye. His stomach flipped. He flung himself against a pillar, breathing heavily. Was he mistaken?

Cautiously he peered out, darting back in again. No. Using the pillar as cover, he made his way towards a side corridor, attracting a few curious glances.

He found another route to the outside of the building, and bewildered and relieved, walked quickly to where his car was parked. Penny was devoted to her husband, the two of them one of the strongest couples he knew. So why, with Phil on his sick bed close by, was she standing at the Hospital entrance with Sean Cooper, the two of them locked in a passionate embrace?

12

The following week, Fisher Bayley stayed over one night with his parents, a response to his mother's accusation that they never saw him. The next day, after having consumed a full fried breakfast, he left for work. The country lanes that led from his parent's village to the nearest main road didn't seem as familiar to him as they once had – perhaps his mother had a point.

The journey into Norwich from this direction always struck Bayley as like driving through the age rings of an imaginary tree. Outermost were the sharp lines of the latest suburbs, flimsy and unappealing. Planners had tried adding character, alternating the features of each house or terrace, only to achieve the effect of a Lego landscape that repeated itself like a lazy cartoon. Past this, more traditional homes sprouted vigorously, dotted with the council housing hurriedly built to fill the spaces the Luftwaffe had left behind. Eventually, larger and more established properties loomed, before Bayley reached the grand Victorian piles that lay just outside the city walls. Standing in impressive plots of mature grounds, they formed a convenient vantage point from which the people who had designed the suburbs could contemplate their efforts.

Arriving at work, Bayley was stopped in the reception hall by one of the security guards, Barry Cleaver.

'Sorry, Mr Bayley sir,' said Cleaver. 'Could you make your way straight to the canteen area? Everyone else is in there. Only there's been an incident.'

This was announced by Cleaver in a tone that suggested whatever had happened was nothing short of a catastrophe. Bayley wondered if the well had flooded again, this time reaching the top. Cleaver admitted he didn't know as yet the exact nature of the emergency.

'But Mr Kingsley is in a right state about it,' he added, not wanting to seem uninformed.

Bayley continued through the entrance lobby and straight ahead up a long ramp. Normally a few people would be wandering about, but not this morning. The place was strangely deserted, causing Bayley to feel apprehensive. What could have happened that demanded the attention of the entire building?

He entered the large open area that contained within it the cafeteria, overlooked by a mezzanine floor. As Cleaver had said, it looked as if all the staff were here. Some were milling about, others sat, waiting patiently. Two colleagues he vaguely knew were attempting to coerce a hot drink from Margaret, the cafeteria's manageress. She was having none of it.

'I've told you,' she said, tying a clean white apron around her bulky frame, 'I'm not open yet. Use the vending machine like everyone else.'

The two men gave up, looking despondent.

Spotting Jane, Ginny, and Ian sharing a table, Fisher went over to join them. At the same moment Howard Kingsley and Brian Finch both appeared, with them a dark-haired man who Fisher didn't recognise, the stranger's face at once open and inquisitive. Around forty-something, his skin was a darker olive than Penny's, the cheeks lightly pockmarked. Silence fell as Kingsley spoke.

'Morning everyone, thank you for waiting.' He sounded tense, thought Fisher. 'I believe we're all here now – is that right, Brian?'

Finch held up the clipboard given to him by the security

guard. 'All here, except two off sick and Kate on maternity. I told Barry to put the closed for training sign out until we're done.'

'Good idea. Yes. Well.' Kingsley turned to the stranger on his right. 'No doubt you will all have noticed we have a visitor here today. This is Detective Inspector Morello.' Kingsley looked as if he could hardly believe his own words.

The Inspector smiled. 'Morning.'

'Perhaps you'd like to explain why you're here, Inspector,' Kingsley offered, then promptly sat down, sagging slightly in his chair.

'Thank you.' The Inspector's audience faced him expectantly. 'I'll come straight to the point. As you all know, Mr Finch here, your Deputy Curator, has been working on a collection of bones recovered some weeks ago by our Search and Rescue team.'

Finch tried to look modest, not quite managing it.

'A collection of great archaeological interest, so I'm told. All except one item – a ribcage.'

Fisher exchanged a puzzled glance with Ian. The ribcage was the most significant find of all; Finch certainly thought so.

'The reason I say that it is of no archaeological interest, is because that particular item dates back to no earlier than the nineteen-fifties, which is why it was brought to my attention.'

Some of the staff looked confused by this statement, others frowning, not sure they had understood correctly. Then everyone began to talk at once. The noise eventually distilled into one question, asked by a woman Fisher could see was Catherine, sat at the next table.

'Are you sure?' she asked.

Morello decided there was no harm in allowing the facts to be known. There would be a press release anyway. He turned to Finch. 'Would you like to explain?'

Finch happily took up the baton.

‘I’ll keep it simple. It comes down to bombs.’

Fisher was mystified. Finch hadn’t confided any of this. The Deputy Curator continued.

‘Let me go back a bit. As most of you are aware, I’ve been using carbon-dating to estimate the age of the bones from the well. The process works better the older a piece of organic material is, so when the results for the ribcage came up inconclusive, I took a closer look at its graph profile.’

‘Skip the lecture Brian,’ muttered Ginny, rolling her eyes at Fisher.

He ignored her, listening intently.

‘When I did, I noticed several peaks in the radiocarbon levels, which could indicate only one thing.’

Finch paused before pronouncing his conclusion. His previous experience on police investigations had made it easy for him to recognise the anomaly.

‘The effect on living bone of nuclear weapons testing,’ he said finally. ‘Since the nineteen-fifties, testing has caused the amount of radiocarbon in all our skeletons to increase, to levels higher than at any other time in history. So in answer to your question, Catherine, yes, I am sure.’

Once again the meeting broke up into a myriad of chatter. Finch looked on, satisfied with the stir he had caused. Morello waited for calm. Eventually, all eyes faced him once more.

‘Thank you, Mr Finch,’ he said, only a hint of sarcasm at the Deputy Curator’s melodramatic style. ‘So now you all know the situation, it will save time when it comes to interviewing each of you.’

There were a few grumbles at this.

‘Routine on this sort of inquiry, I’m afraid. When a body is found, or body part, certain procedures have to be followed. That’s all I can say. I’ll make it as painless as I can.’ Morello’s keen gaze swept the room. ‘Unless there are any more questions...? No? Then thank you all for your time.’

The Inspector looked to Kingsley, who jumped up as if

suddenly aware of his surroundings.

'Right. Thank you, Inspector Morello. Thank you everyone. Let's get back to work, shall we?'

*

The cafeteria was largely empty by the time Sean Cooper arrived. A certain weariness about his features, he seemed at a loss to as to why Fisher had wanted to meet. They sat down together. One of Kingsley's students greeted Fisher as she passed and he waved in return, before beginning his interrogation.

'How long have we known each other? Long time, isn't it?'

Sean ignored this prompt. 'Why did you want to see me?' he asked, uncharacteristically direct.

For some reason, this blunt reply made Fisher unsure of himself. Was he making a big mistake? This was going to be more difficult than he had thought.

'Last Saturday I went to see Phil in hospital, after those pills he took. Remember?'

'Not a night any of us are likely to forget, is it?'

'Yeah, I know what you mean. Anyway, that's not what I wanted to talk about. It's what happened at the hospital.'

'What did happen at the hospital?'

Sean didn't seem concerned in the slightest.

'I saw you. With Penny.'

Having finally explained himself, Fisher looked away, embarrassed. To his astonishment, Sean laughed.

'That's it? I see. Hmm.' He rubbed his chin, looking at Fisher as if deciding whether or not to let him into his confidence.

Fisher stared back, angry now. This was not the reaction he had expected, not from someone caught with a friend's wife.

'I don't see anything funny in what I just said.'

Not speaking, his expression impossible to read, Sean remained calm. Seeming to come to a decision, he finally spoke.

'All I can say is, I would never do anything to upset Phil.'

'What's that supposed to mean? What do you think will happen when he finds out? I want you to promise to stop seeing Penny right now.'

Sean looked pained.

'I can't promise you that.' He stood up. Fisher was stunned. 'All I can do is repeat what I just said – I would never do anything to upset Phil.'

And with that, Sean weaved his way back across the cafeteria and left.

'You two-faced bastard!' Fisher shouted after him.

An elderly woman sat two tables away looked round, startled.

'Sorry,' Fisher offered, before scraping his chair back and leaving himself.

13

In Howard Kingsley's office, Brian Finch and Detective Inspector Felix Morello each took a seat. Kingsley made coffee for the three of them before sitting down himself. The clock on the desk ticked away, five minutes slow.

'So what happens now?' Kingsley asked the Inspector.

'As I said to your staff, I'll need to interview everyone who works here.'

'I understand. And after that?'

'It depends. I have to determine as best I can who this person was and how they died. And when.'

Not that Morello expected much in the way of answers. Without a body or any other clues, he had to agree with Kingsley's assessment earlier that morning that tracing the person, or establishing an ID, would be virtually impossible. His first instinct, to treat the death as suspicious, had waned when Kingsley had also shown him several photographs from the castle's archives. They revealed that prior to the metal grilles now in place, the well had been protected only by a safety rail. Easy enough to fall over if you were determined to take a closer look. An accident then, decades old in all probability.

'I thought we'd discussed all that?' Kingsley said.

'We did, sir, but there are procedures to follow, as I've mentioned.'

'I see.' Kingsley took a sip from his mug

Morello turned to Finch.

'They tell me at the station you're something of an expert

when it comes to bones.'

Finch looked pleased at this recognition, confirmation that his specialist forensic skills were held in high regard.

'Very kind, whoever said so.'

'Yes. Well, with that in mind, I would prefer it if the remains stayed in your care for the time being – if they can be kept secure.'

'Of course. I was hoping you might ask.'

'Good. We can make other arrangements once I've completed my report. Speaking of which, I believe you mentioned earlier there were more tests that can be done? Aside from showing us the ribcage glows in the dark?'

Kingsley sat up. This was news to him.

'More tests, yes, most definitely. Let me see...' Finch organised his thoughts. 'I can confirm gender, of course, with a straightforward PCR test. And the İşcan method should make it possible for me to give you their age at death.'

'I'm impressed already. And PCR, Iss-can, they are...?'

'The PCR test is just an extension of DNA analysis.'

'Ah.' Earlier, examining the ribcage in Finch's laboratory before talking to the staff, Morello had suggested the number of ribs would tell them if they were looking at a man or a woman. Finch had explained this to be a biblical myth – Adam giving a rib to make Eve. Men and women had the same number of ribs. 'And Iss-can?'

'Method,' said Finch pedantically. 'Gives an approximate age using the pit shape at the fourth costochondral junction.'

Didn't miss a beat, thought Morello.

'And in English?'

'The shape of the rib where it joins the sternum. That's all I need to tell their age.'

Morello nodded. He liked this room. The old-fashioned radiator chugging cheerfully away, the archaic hat stand, naked except for a single broken umbrella. He ploughed on.

'What about cause of death? Drowning being the clear

favourite.'

Finch nodded. 'We'll never know for sure.'

'Where the ribs are broken at the back. An injury from the fall?'

'I would say so. Either that or a submerged rock. I'll check the break for fragments, in case there's anything interesting.'

'Very thorough,' Morello approved. 'And time of death? Can that be narrowed down?'

'Much more difficult, as I said when you arrived this morning. What I can tell you is, two months or less after immersion, I would have expected to see soft tissue still present, which of course there isn't. Encrustation would develop after that, but only if the bones had been exposed above the surface, and then only for about a year...'

Morello waited expectantly, but Finch made it clear anything further would be speculation on his part.

'Are you saying that time of death could have been anywhere between the nineteen-fifties and a year ago?' Morello asked him.

'Technically, the fifties and about two months ago – there's no way of knowing if the body was ever exposed to the surface. But as Howard said, this sort of accident couldn't happen now, not with the safety grilles in place, so the two months parameter isn't really relevant.' Finch became earnest. 'That's what makes this find so important, Inspector. It's a rare chance to add to our knowledge base. That's why I think Tom should be given another chance to search the base of the well.' He looked meaningfully at Morello.

'I can't sanction doing that, Mr Finch, not unless the skull can be located, which Sergeant Lomax tells me would be unlikely. His team would need dumb luck, was how he put it.'

Finch looked set to debate this as Morello jotted down another note, but then seemed to think better of it. Sunlight glinted through a small stained glass window set high above the radiator, lending the room an ecclesiastical air. Morello finished his note and drummed his pencil on the notepad balanced on his lap. Something else occurred to him.

'Are the safety grilles ever removed for maintenance?'

'I'm not sure,' said Finch. 'Do you know, Howard?'

'Never,' said Kingsley emphatically. 'We open the small grille downstairs to empty the bucket, but there are always two people, and they're tethered to the wall. Health and Safety.' He put down his mug. 'Inspector, I hope you don't mind me saying, but isn't this all a lot of effort for nothing? Speaking as a taxpayer?'

'I understand what you're saying, Mr Kingsley, but what you have to remember is that someone has died. When that happens, as I've mentioned before, there are procedures.'

Procedures, thought Morello to himself, and a boss who would like nothing more than a chance to mark him down for not following them. Punishment for leaving the Met and taking up a promotion promised to one of his own lads.

'But you said yourself,' Kingsley insisted. 'Without an ID, it's a waste of time.'

Finch intervened on the Inspector's behalf.

'I can't give you an ID, but I will be able to tell you *something* about who they were.'

Kingsley looked taken aback, while Morello found himself newly interested in what Finch had to say.

'How can you do that?' he asked, wondering why Finch hadn't mentioned this before now.

'Two ways. Firstly, DNA again – we can use it to establish ethnicity.'

Morello knew plenty about DNA evidence, but had never seen it put to this use before.

'That could be useful,' he agreed, adding as an afterthought, 'run the profile through our database as well, we might get lucky. Ring the station and they'll sort you out a login.'

Finch nodded. 'I've done it before.'

'We may not get a match,' said Morello, 'but at least we'll

have it on the system. And what was the second thing?'

'The bone composition itself,' said Finch, like a conjurer who had saved his best trick until last.

Morello stared keenly at the Deputy Curator.'What will that tell us?' he prompted.

'Where they came from,' Finch replied.

'Really? You mean, which city, or...?'

Finch gave an indulgent smile, as if to an eager student.

'Not quite. More geographical region. There are different isotopes of oxygen embedded in all our bones, unique to where we grew up. It's possible I can narrow down where this person lived to within a few hundred square miles – if they're from Europe or America, that is. They're the only places we've got data for.'

Morello made another note, pleased to have made more progress than he'd expected to.

'If the victim originated from south-east England it won't be much help,' Finch cautioned, 'but... well, we'll see.'

Morello snapped shut his notebook. 'I appreciate the effort, Mr Finch. Whatever the outcome, we'll have given it our best shot. Thank you for the coffee, Mr Kingsley.'

Morello stood up and shook hands with the two men, giving Finch his business card.

'My details are on there. Email me.'

14

HARRY SCARFE PACED the thickly carpeted floor. He was at his business headquarters, a large modern office block situated on an elevated ridge to the east of Norwich. Howard Kingsley sat bolt upright at one end of a huge leather sofa, facing the floor to ceiling plate glass window that gave a panoramic view over the lengthening shadows of Whitlingham Country Park.

Scarfe spoke with a vicious intensity.

'You've left nothing out?'

'I've told you everything.'

'Like last time. Now look where we are.'

Scarfe's first thought had been to steal the ribcage and destroy it. But even if they didn't get caught, it would attract attention. Too many unknowns.

'He told me he'd dated it, like everything else. He must have assumed –'

'So what's he not told you this time?'

'I was there, I heard.'

Scarfe stopped at the wall of glass overlooking the park. 'And they think it was an accident, years ago? A tourist or something? Maybe it was. Maybe these ribs do belong to someone else.'

He saw Kingsley's expression, and had to agree.

'All right, unlikely. But you say there's no chance of an ID?'

Kingsley nodded. 'That's what it comes down to.'

'Which means this Inspector is going through the motions. Ticking boxes so he can file it all away.' Scarfe turned to face Kingsley. 'Right. I want you to keep me up to date. Whatever your deputy finds, I want to know. You can manage that, can't you?'

'I'll make sure he reports to me.'

'Good. This might be a wild goose chase, but I don't want any more surprises. Understood?'

Nodding dejectedly, Kingsley had to lean away as Scarfe joined him on the sofa, uncomfortably close.

'I'm beginning to worry,' said Scarfe, almost in a whisper.

Kingsley said nothing, not making eye contact. Scarfe continued.

'And what worries me is, what if you go soft on me? Decide you'd be better off telling the nice Inspector everything you know – cut a deal. After all, it wasn't you who killed her, was it?'

Kingsley made an attempt to meet Scarfe's stare.

'I wouldn't do that, you know I wouldn't.'

Scarfe gave a mirthless laugh. 'It's written all over you, Howard. Not got what you'd call a poker face, have you?'

'I mean it, I –'

'Thing is, you see, I took out some insurance. In case anything went wrong.'

'Insurance?'

Through the plate glass, in the office itself, everywhere was shadows.

'Insurance. Which means if they do find out who she is, it'll be you they lock away.'

Kingsley was confused. 'What do you mean? Why would they do that?'

'Think about it. You knew the girl, taught her. Tried it on, but she was having none of it. Humiliated you, made you angry. So you killed her. Who else but you would use a dagger kept locked up inside the castle? And dumping the body in the well – very handy for someone who works there. Always the quiet ones, isn't it?'

'The dagger,' said Kingsley. 'That's why you...' The realisation drained from his face what little colour it had. 'You bastard!'

'Language, Howard. That's not a word I really care for.'

'You're insane. Why are you saying all this?' Kingsley's voice had a manic note to it, until he remembered something Finch had been clear on. 'Wait a minute – only the ribcage is left. They can't tell how she died now, Brian said so himself.'

Kingsley's look of triumph angered Scarfe. He hadn't expected to be challenged.

'I think with a bit of encouragement the Inspector would have enough to go on. And that's before he finds out you're a thief, defrauding my scholarship fund. It would be the end for you, Howard, guilty or not. Mud sticks.'

'It's not fraud...' Kingsley faltered.

'That's what you like to tell yourself, is it?'

'I didn't kill her. No one can prove I did.'

'Want to put that to the test? Want me to ask Superintendent Drake what his view would be, next time I'm up at the lodge?'

At the mention of Drake's name, some of the fight seemed to leave Kingsley. He didn't know the Superintendent well, just his reputation, which was none too clean.

'Why are you doing this to me?'

'I haven't done anything yet. Like I said, it's my insurance. Now you know the small print if you don't keep your mouth firmly shut. Am I making myself understood?'

Kingsley's reflection in the plate glass window looked back at him, helpless. You should never have taken the money, his reflection told him.

*

After Kingsley had left, Scarfe poured himself a whisky, the eighteen-year-old malt. Switching off the light, he stood by the window with it, able to see out into the near-darkness.

With the stakes so high, he felt as if the pressure on himself was becoming more intense by the day.

He could see now how weak was the link between the dagger and Kingsley. And with only the ribcage left, it wouldn't be possible to match the dagger to the fatal wound anyway, if indeed it ever had been. Another mistake, risks taken for nothing, any leverage over the unexpectedly defiant Kingsley only temporary. A few strands of hair plucked from the girls head and left in Kingsley's car, or his home perhaps, would have had a much greater impact.

Instead, thought Scarfe, how long before Kingsley overcame whatever fears he may have and recognised his "insurance" for what it was, no more than a bluff? That if necessary he could counter-accuse, with the consequences for himself being far worse. First, the termination of his candidacy for Norfolk South, swiftly followed by a long prison sentence were the police to search his house. His complete destruction. How his enemies would enjoy that.

He had to do more to protect himself. Certainly something other than simply have Doyle continue with his surveillance of Kingsley. That had provided peace of mind, but not any longer. Not with this Inspector hanging about, asking questions. If he found more evidence, something that brought him closer to the truth, what then? Would Kingsley keep his nerve and remain silent?

The likely answer filled Scarfe with fear.

The more he thought about it, the more he realised he had to be ready to take the only action that would guarantee Kingsley's silence. He could decide whether to follow it through when the time came – if it came.

Preparation was the key, just as in business. If he decided to act, he would need to do so quickly. Or at least Doyle would.

He refilled his whisky tumbler, an inch and a half, drank it in one go and poured a third, then went to sit behind his desk. He switched on a table lamp.

He judged that Doyle would follow his instructions whatever they were, as long as the price was right. A Falklands war veteran, Doyle was well into his fifties, fit and strong, but bitter, not a friend in the world. Just a society that didn't care. That much Scarfe had gleaned over the years he'd used him, though nothing more. Doyle had also shown himself to be discreet, no awkward questions or reasons why.

Which was perfect.

Flicking on the computer, Scarfe opened up a new Word document. After deliberating for a few moments, he began to type. Kingsley would want to explain himself, as anyone would, before taking his own life.

15

'YOU'RE WHAT!' DONALD Rayburn exploded.

His already ruddy complexion deepened to a rich crimson. Eleanor had known this was going to be a difficult conversation. She looked at her mother, searching for some shred of understanding, but there was none.

'It's not true, I won't have it!' ranted her father. 'What will they say at St Peter's? At the lodge? Good God, I'll be made a laughing stock!'

'Don't blaspheme dear.'

'Oh, shut up woman.'

Eleanor was on the verge of tears, her long brown hair hiding half her plumpish face. Naturally shy, this confrontation with her parents was torture. 'This isn't about you,' she said defiantly.

But Donald wasn't listening.

'When I think of how he's been running around my church, helping with this, helping with that, and all the time he was – you were...'

The image defied words.

'Please try to understand, father. I love him. He loves me. It just sort of – happened.'

'It "just sort of happened"? Are you listening to this?' Donald turned to Mary.

'I –'

'And he chooses now to give up his job? How does he expect to support you and... and... because if he thinks I'm going to stump up the cash, while he floats around "finding himself" as you put it, he can think again.'

Eleanor had been unable to face telling her father the truth about why Sean had suddenly left the civil service, and hadn't yet asked the question she so desperately wanted an answer to. She looked at her father. Clearly there wouldn't be a best time.

'We want to get married, at St Peter's. Will you let us?'

'That's it!' Donald looked suddenly relieved. 'A quick ceremony and no one need be any the wiser.'

'Will you stop thinking about yourself and start acting like a father!'

Eleanor held her hand up to her mouth, barring any more words from spilling out.

Mary stared at her husband, horrified. Donald didn't speak. Walking to the window, he stared out, hands held behind his back. An eternity later, he half-turned his head, and nodded.

Eleanor let the tears fall as she recalled a night not very long ago.

*

Sean had made a real effort. Not gifted in the kitchen, dinner was nonetheless all homemade, except for desert, a chocolate torte defrosting on a plain white dish. But from the moment she had arrived at his flat that evening, she could sense his mind was elsewhere. Biding her time, she tried to act as if all was well, sitting down opposite him to eat, while he chatted distractedly. Eventually, however, his demeanour sombre, he acknowledged the look on her face and admitted there was something he had to tell her. She prepared herself as best she could, which was nowhere near enough.

Eleanor had had her doubts about the Church before, finding it difficult at times to keep her faith when she felt there was so much wrong in the world. What answers the

Church did offer seemed flawed, as if created to fit the facts. Her belief in God, so it seemed, had to be constantly tested. But Sean's revelation was a test too far, and in that instant, her faith was broken.

Dinner forgotten, they stood together in each other's arms, for a while saying nothing as Eleanor took in the news. When she had recovered enough to speak, she asked Sean why he hadn't told her as soon as he'd known.

'I was afraid.' Sean looked at her. 'Afraid I might lose you. No future.'

'How could you think that?' Eleanor wiped away her tears. 'You should have told me you were going for tests. Before Penny.'

'She happened to be there when I came out, that's all. When I saw her, a friendly face... She's a good friend.'

'So am I. Your best friend.'

Sean smiled, stroking her face. 'I haven't said anything to the others, I can't face it. Fisher saw me and Penny, but he doesn't know.' There was no need to explain the conclusion that Fisher had come to. 'Penny promised she wouldn't tell anyone, not even Phil.' He wiped away fresh tears from Eleanor's cheek and tried to lighten the mood. There would be plenty of time for tears in the months ahead. 'I've still got my hair,' he said, pulling a short tuft towards his forehead before allowing it to spring back.

Eleanor gave a dutiful smile.

'Not for long, maybe.' Sean contemplated this. 'How do you fancy me in a wig? I've always wanted to be curly.'

It wasn't funny, but they both laughed, laughed until they ached, released from care by the enormity of it all. For a few short moments, they lived purely in the present. Then suddenly Sean was angry.

'I'm not a bad person. I don't deserve this. Where's the justice? Where's the justice in anything?'

Eleanor's laughter died.

Where *was* the justice? She had presented Sean to her family with some trepidation. The only other boyfriend she had ever introduced to her parents had worked out badly, and so it had come as a huge relief when this time it was different. Her father had been particularly taken, using his influence to find Sean a role on the committee of St Peter Mancroft Church, comfortable it seemed with the idea of having him as a son-in-law. Had all that been for nothing? Eleanor decided she must be strong, for both their sakes.

'I want to get married,' she said

This brought Sean to tears, something he had promised himself he wouldn't do.

'We can't,' he told her. 'We don't know if –'

'I do know. And I know I want you. And I know I want our baby.'

'Our baby...?'

Eleanor stood up. Without a word, she led Sean to the stairs.

Behind them, the chocolate torte oozed seductively on its plate.

16

ADRENALIN PUMPED THROUGH Fisher Bayley as it had in the Egyptian room, though this time for a different reason. He looked down at the floor of the Great Hall, a good forty feet below, and groaned. Then the floor disappeared, and the wide balcony came back into view. Too far to jump if anything went wrong. Ginny groaned too, her eyes closed.

Both were positioned as if riding tandem, Fisher leaning forward over Ginny so that his head poked from Snap's mouth like a giant fur-ball. The dragon effigy swung on its beam, keeping rhythm with the half-hearted performance going on inside it, a use for which it had never been intended.

Created as the centrepiece for medieval feasts, in previous centuries Snap had led cheering revellers dancing through the streets of Norwich, the procession becoming ever larger as the crowds watching joined in. Three actors inside the colourful woven skin would ignite tiny bags of gunpowder to produce a fire-breathing monster, the sulphurous smell and violent explosions adding to the carnival's already chaotic atmosphere.

As often as not, a badly placed detonation would set fire to the clothing of one of the actors, and the dragon's scaly skin would be ripped apart as the unfortunate artiste escaped, yelling for water. The spectators would enjoy this every bit as much as seeing the flames erupting from Snap's mouth and nostrils. Later, the skin would be patched up and the wooden skeleton repaired where it was charred or broken. These battle scars only increased the peoples' affection for the dragon.

On one memorable occasion, a drunken carpenter set fire to Snap deliberately, just to watch the occupants flee, screaming. This went against the popular sentiment of sportsmanship, and the miscreant was publicly flogged and put in stocks for a week. Fisher would have swapped places with him in an instant.

'I'm going to be sick.'

'Keep going!'

'Wait until it stops swinging again. I'll be all right if I can stay still for a minute.'

'That'll be the third time,' Ginny complained.

'I know, but I really –'

Fisher let out a blood-curdling yell. A splinter from the wide pole they were sitting on had driven itself deep into his scrotum.

'Oh my God, stop, stop!'

Ginny twisted round, trying to look.

'Don't move!' Fisher closed his eyes. 'Stay perfectly still.'

'What's happened?'

Before he could explain Fisher threw up, the rocking motion of the dragon allowing equal amounts to cover the back of Ginny's head and fall with a loud splat to the floor below.

Ginny screamed.

'I can't believe you just did that! I'm covered!'

But Fisher already had a new worry.

'*Quiet*.'

'What?'

'*I said quiet.*'

There was only one thing he feared more than having sex inside Snap – getting caught doing it. Even the pain searing through his groin would have to wait.

'I can hear voices. Someone's coming.'

Snap continued to swing in the murky light, more gently

now as two silhouettes appeared at a doorway below.

'I'm sure I heard something,' said one of the figures.

Fisher recognised straight away Kingsley's slightly nasal tone. Why the buggery was he working so late? And who was that with him? He prayed they wouldn't look up, only to see him peering from the jaws of one of the castle's most famous exhibits.

'There's no one here. You need to get a grip.'

A man's voice, one Fisher couldn't immediately place. Whoever he was, he and Kingsley seemed to have been arguing.

'Let me guess – or it's insurance time?' Kingsley's tone was belligerent, as if he'd had a drink or two. 'Maybe I should organise some insurance of my own, what do you think, Harry? Ankh Hor will do – they can blame him instead.'

'Don't try my patience.'

Now Fisher remembered. The second man was Harry Scarfe. Not so long back, he had been a frequent visitor to the castle. Strange argument they were both having, he thought, before another sudden stabbing pain in his groin nearly made him cry out. It was as if the splinter was injecting itself into him. He opened his eyes again to see Kingsley walking towards the centre of the Hall, the man called Scarfe following.

'There's a funny smell coming from somewhere.' Kingsley stopped directly below Snap, kneeling down. 'Someone's been sick.'

'Nice class of visitor you've got.'

Kingsley tutted his agreement, standing back up. 'I'll have to have a word with the cleaners in the morning.'

'You do that. I've got to go. Lodge night.'

Kingsley and Scarfe made for the door they had entered by, the rest of their conversation lost as the two of them disappeared from sight.

Once Fisher felt sure they weren't coming back, he

breathed out heavily. ‘Phew, that was close. Are you all right?’

The pain in his groin had subsided a little, though he wasn’t looking forward to having to detach himself from the pole.

‘Get me home,’ Ginny demanded, her hair hanging in wet ringlets over her face.

17

Leaving the castle on foot, Harry Scarfe had another appointment to keep before he was due at the Lodge. He made a detour past The Bell Hotel, walked a short distance up Timber Hill and entered a pub on the left, called, appropriately enough, The Murderers.

It was fairly busy, music Scarfe didn't recognise playing on an old-fashioned jukebox. Whisky in hand, he found Doyle sitting in a raised recess, a half pint of lager in front of him. There was just enough space for a small table and three barrels, converted into stools. Scarfe took a seat, his back to the bare beams on one side.

'You wanted to see me,' Doyle said, by way of greeting.

Scarfe took a measure of whisky before replying.

'How would you like more money?'

He didn't feel subtlety would make any difference.

'You're the boss. What do you want?'

Scarfe passed him an envelope containing one piece of typed A4. 'Take a look at that.'

As he read, Doyle's expression stiffened. 'Last I saw, Kingsley was fit and well,' he said guardedly.

'He still is,' said Scarfe, giving Doyle cause to look marginally less tense. 'But there may come a time when his – how can I put it – current problems become too much for him... Force him to decide there's only one solution.'

Doyle nodded his understanding.

'You must really have it in for this guy. What's he done?'

Having read the contents of the envelope, the Private

Investigator was for the first time showing curiosity, not something Scarfe wanted to encourage.

'Question is, will you do it? If I need you to?'

It took a moment for Doyle to reply, his half pint of lager going down steadily.

'I don't know. Killing a man in combat, that's one thing. This though...'

'When I said more money, I didn't say how much.'

Scarfe told him. Doyle gave a long whistle.

'You really have got it in for this guy,' he said, but more interested now, eyes fixed on Scarfe.

'Think about it. Enough to set you up for life. How much is that worth?'

Doyle did think about it. It was worth a lot. His dream of retiring abroad made reality.

'I've always fancied Spain,' he said slowly. 'A boat, maybe. Come and go as you like, nobody knows where.'

'Sounds very nice.' Scarfe breathed more easily. He hadn't liked to consider the possibilities if Doyle had refused. 'I want it to be poison. Something quick and painless.'

'You're all heart. Why not a gun? Quick and simple.'

'But not painless.'

'He won't –'

'No, I want poison. And I want you ready by the end of tomorrow.'

Doyle began to argue this wasn't enough time, but Scarfe insisted. Until the risk Kingsley posed was sorted out, he felt vulnerable. Doyle drained his glass, staring at Scarfe as he did so. He put it down silently.

'I'll need something up front.'

'You'll get ten percent when you tell me you're ready. The rest if I decide to go ahead.'

'So I keep the ten percent whatever?'

Scarfe smiled. He was going to be all right.

18

Harry Scarfe joined several other members clustered around a low-lying table, nestling back into a well-worn leather chair. The entire room resonated to the bass notes of many other of his kin, sat in similar groups – contacts being made, allegiances reaffirmed, the occasional innocent after dinner conversation.

This inner sanctum of the Lodge had an opulent, almost decadent feel. The lighting was mellow, and a satisfying aroma of game and cigars hung in the air. The smoking ban didn't penetrate this far inside the building. Scarfe added his own contribution from an ostentatiously large Havana, ordered specially from London to ensure its pedigree. Waiters in bowties glided unobtrusively between the tables, smiling obsequiously at the practised familiarity of the patrons, careful not to trip over any of the many identical briefcases that littered the floor.

It was no coincidence that Scarfe had chosen to sit at this particular table, but he bided his time, enjoying his cigar, to any observer seemingly at peace with the world. His eye flicked over the dark wooden panels that covered most of the walls, punctuated by alcoves filled with books and ornaments. The panelling itself was adorned with symbols of many kinds, archaic, mystic, exotic, all competing for space alongside oil paintings that depicted past Masters of the Lodge, in full regalia.

'No room for anyone else.' It was Donald Rayburn, sat unfortunately close, his cold eyes faintly mocking. He had noticed the attention Scarfe was giving the portraits. 'Not even The Architect who re-invented the wheel.'

'Re-invented the wheel?' repeated a sharply dressed man, sat next to Rayburn. 'Oh, I see what you mean. Yes. Very good. How is your project coming along, Harry? The Norwich Eye. Had to be called that, I suppose?'

'It's going very well, thank you Alistair,' replied Scarfe, ignoring Rayburn's thinly veiled hostility and the unwelcome attention it brought from the others seated around the table. 'Ready in time for next Easter.'

He said no more about it, much as he would have liked to. Many of his Brothers considered his Ferris Wheel to be unsightly, wedged as it was between the Forum and St Peter Mancroft Church, right in the heart of the city. And his methods for securing planning permission hadn't gone unnoticed.

Rayburn looked set to continue in the same vein, but before he could do so, Superintendent Frank Drake began a lengthy complaint about a new recruit who had been foisted upon him. An outsider from the Met, given a promotion Drake had earmarked for one of his yes-men.

'Fast track smart-arse, all books and no trousers.' The lines on the Superintendent's heavyset face concentrated in resentment.

Scarfe nodded understandingly. Maybe the task he'd set himself tonight wouldn't be so difficult after all. Drake was made from the same mould as himself – worked his way up from nothing, and didn't see why some moisturised college boy shouldn't have to do the same.

An elderly attendant arrived to replace the decanter of cognac, before making his slow way back to the bar.

'Refill anyone?' Rayburn offered, after helping himself first.

Scarfe took the bottle from him, over-filling his own glass before passing it on.

'Don't mind if I do,' said Drake, pouring liberally.

Only Alistair abstained.

'Need a clear head for the morning,' he offered by way of explanation, attracting a Mexican wave of disapproving eyebrows. His first mistake as a new member.

The evening wore on. Scarfe said little, while the conversation ebbed and flowed around him. There was only one person he was interested in talking to, and he wanted to do that in private. An hour or so later, he got his chance. Superintendent Drake left the room to relieve himself, and Scarfe followed him as far as the bar, where he lay in wait. He called Drake over when he returned.

'Fancy a quick round with the sticks, Frank?'

'Why not?' The Superintendent studied the optics, his grey hair thin under the bar's spotlights. 'You in the chair?'

*

The snooker room was as heavily panelled as the room they had just left, only without the symbols or paintings to act as a distraction. Scarfe and Drake placed their drinks on a side-stand before facing the vast table that stood at the centre. The balls were sat neatly in place, brightly illuminated by three green glass lamps that hung low over them. The two men each selected a cue, the Superintendent rolling his backwards and forwards along the baize, making sure it was straight. Scarfe watched while onto the end of his own cue he meticulously worked a cube of blue chalk, licking his finger and dabbing the tip before trying to rub in more powder.

'I'll break, shall I?' said Drake.

The question was rhetorical. The Superintendent lowered himself, and without taking aim struck the cue ball hard. It rocketed down the table before blasting the triangle of red balls in all directions. As they came to a rest, the pleasing symmetry of a moment earlier was replaced by a random chaos.

Apparently satisfied with his efforts, Drake offered 'All yours,' in upbeat fashion and picked up the chalk where Scarfe had left it, near the corner pocket.

Scarfe inspected the table. There was no hurry.

'Howard tells me one of your men is up at the castle,' he began casually. 'An accident or something, he said.'

Drake nodded, paying more attention to the lie of the balls.

Scarfe took his shot. A red rebounded awkwardly in the jaws of the middle pocket and stopped.

'Bit of a sitter there for you, Frank.'

Drake marched over. A pot was a pot.

'Sounded like a tricky case,' continued Scarfe, 'the way Howard described it.'

'Impossible, more like. That's why I gave it to that new Inspector I was telling you about.'

'The fast-tracker?'

'That's the one. Damn!'

Scarfe disguised a grin, stepping up to the table. 'Bad luck. Middle pocket's always a sod.' He began to rehearse the angle for a red in the corner. 'Why do you say impossible?'

'Don't you read the papers? All we've got is a skeleton from the fifties, some idiot who managed to fall in. Plenty of paperwork and no chance of a result. Good shot!'

Scarfe moved round for the black. 'No chance, you think? Shame for the family.'

'Never had you down as the caring type,' said Drake dryly.

'Means a lot, Frank, having a proper burial. I remember my dad. You'll have to keep me up to date with what happens.'

Drake shrugged. 'If you like. Are you going to take that shot?'

'What? Oh, right.' Scarfe tactfully missed. 'Another sitter for you.'

Drake pocketed a red.

‘Talking of being kept up to date,’ said the Superintendent, ‘where are we at with StreetEye?’

Scarfe Technologies, Harry’s core business, provided all the electronic surveillance for the city, but a recent upgrade to the software was proving unstable. Knowing how important Drake’s influence was on police budgets (not that this influence came free), Scarfe reassured him that the necessary fixes were going through their final testing and would be ready within the week.

The Superintendent looked unconvinced. ‘I pushed hard for you, Harry. Don’t make me look a fool.’

Scarfe looked him straight in the eye.

‘You have my word,’ he said.

19

Brian Finch had the first of the results from his tests.

'Polymorphisms?' repeated Inspector Morello.

'Genetic polymorphisms, to be exact. They're what gives each population its unique DNA profile.'

'And by population, you mean...?'

'Around the world, there are about two hundred and fifty, genetically speaking.'

'Each one with a different profile to the other?'

'Exactly. The profile from the ribcage correlates to a person of European extraction, Continental and white.'

'Not British?'

'No. Not in the sense we mean it here, anyway. When I've completed the isotope testing on the bones, I'll be able to narrow it down a lot more.'

'A tourist, then, by the sounds of it.'

'Seems that way.'

Morello looked around the room. With its faint chemical odour, it wasn't too dissimilar from other forensic laboratories he had been in, the main difference being that here, there was no sense of urgency. There seemed little point in asking his next question, particularly as Finch would surely have already answered it if he could. Just then there was a knock at the door, and Howard Kingsley entered.

'Morning all,' Kingsley greeted them both jauntily. 'I got a message you were already here, Inspector.' Morello had arrived early, wanting to talk to Finch without interruption. 'Have I missed much?'

‘Polymorphisms,’ said Morello, enigmatically.

‘Pardon?’

‘Mr Finch can explain on our way down.’

On his first visit, Morello had been satisfied with simply standing over the well, unnerved as any other visitor by the peculiar sensation. Now he wanted to take a look at the underground room the well passed through. Not much to see in terms of the investigation, if it could be called that, but all he had waiting for him back at the station was paperwork.

The three of them began making their way to the Great Hall, Finch explaining his results again, his enthusiasm undiminished.

‘Interesting,’ commented Kingsley. ‘Sounds like a tourist, then.’

‘That’s what the Inspector and I thought.’

‘I was going to ask,’ said Morello. ‘Did you get a chance to run the profile through our DNA database?’

Kingsley glanced nervously at Finch.

‘I did. No matches, you won’t be surprised to hear.’

Morello gave a rueful look. ‘Would have been too easy, wouldn’t it?’ He stopped suddenly. ‘I didn’t know this was here.’

They were outside the Egyptian exhibit.

‘Like to take a look?’ Finch asked him.

Kingsley frowned at his deputy. ‘I’m sure the Inspector doesn’t want to waste time sightseeing.’

But it seemed Morello did.

‘I’ve always been fascinated by Egypt, watch it on Discovery all the time.’

‘It’s one of our star attractions,’ Finch enthused. ‘As it happens, there’s quite an interesting story surrounding the sarcophagus. I’ll go and get the key.’

When Finch returned, Morello had his nose pressed against the glass.

‘I was just saying to Mr Kingsley, it’s quite a stunning

collection you've got yourselves.'

'We've been very lucky in the past with donations from local collectors. Of course, there are no gentlemen archaeologists carting whatever they like back off to England anymore.' Finch sounded regretful that this was the case.

A young couple, followed by a family of four, appeared next to them.

'Sorry, this exhibit's temporarily closed,' Finch told them. 'If you'd like to come back in ten minutes?'

The young couple nodded amicably, but the boy holding on to his mother's hand began to cry.

Once they had disappeared, the boy persuaded with the promise of ice-cream, Finch turned his key in one of the large glass panels and pulled. A door of glass opened outwards. Morello stepped inside, followed by Kingsley and Finch. With the door pulled shut again, there was total silence.

The sarcophagus, the stone table, everything around Morello seemed far more real without the glass barrier. He turned slowly on the spot, taking in the symbols, the artefacts, the mummified bodies of all the various animals. But what struck him most of all were the eyes of the sarcophagus. They seemed to look straight through him, reading his thoughts. He imagined himself transported back thousands of years, to a river in the sands of North Africa, and a time when these objects were part of the landscape, not 'objects' at all. The shafts of bright blue light that lit the room reflected on every surface, on polished stone and precious metals, giving him the surreal sense he was standing underwater. He felt he could almost swim away from where he stood. Finch broke the spell.

'You don't know about the mystery of our priest then, Inspector?'

Morello smiled broadly. 'Always amazes me. Anything to do with Egypt, and there's a mystery attached. Is that what's in the sarcophagus?'

'That's right.' Finch went on to tell the story of the mummified priest, Ankh Hor, and of the Victorian brackets that held him down, despite the sarcophagus never having been opened. Morello looked bemused.

'As a detective, the solution is simple.'

'Really?'

Finch didn't sound pleased. Over the years he had spent many fruitless days, weeks and months trying to discover the truth, using all the technology he knew of, and all to no avail.

'These brackets are definitely Victorian?'

Morello wanted to be certain of the facts.

'Absolutely. Shape and detailing, no doubt. The magnetic scan proves it. The type has never been used before or since.'

'In that case, the only possible answer is that someone has opened it. They did whatever they wanted to do, put the brackets in, and then sealed it up again. Maybe the brackets were put there to hold the body together, after they'd disturbed it.'

Finch looked relieved. 'Not possible. The scan shows the seals are untouched. If they'd been cut or melted, we would have seen it. And the material the seal is made of is impossible to forge. Carbon-dated to over three thousand years old.'

Morello, perplexed, said 'If the brackets are genuine, then it's the only possible solution.'

'And therein lies the mystery,' intervened Kingsley. 'Shall we go?'

He seemed keen on the idea.

Morello noticed he was cold. The air inside the exhibit was designed to prolong the life of the dead, not the living.

Suddenly Finch leaned past him, to where a dagger was sat on a velvet stand. When he picked it up, it flashed and glowed. 'That's odd,' he said.

'Is that real gold?' asked Morello.

'It is. Priceless, to all intents and purposes. The priest's ceremonial knife.' Finch rotated it between his fingers, avoiding any unnecessary contact. 'We clean it once a year, which is usually enough.'

Morello scanned the object, dazzled by the red and green jewels embedded in its handle. They glinted and winked at him. What appeared to be rust spots were dotted across the blade.

'I thought gold wasn't meant to rust?'

'It doesn't. It's the impurities in the air, they settle on the surface. Once they do, they attract more dirt until you can see it. But I'm sure we cleaned this only six or seven months ago. I'll have to check my records.'

'I thought the climate control protected everything?' said Kingsley.

'Only slows down what would happen outside. Can't do more, not if we want people to see what's here.'

'Can I take a look?'

Finch passed Kingsley the dagger.

'Hold the ends,' he advised.

Kingsley did so, spellbound as the dagger gleamed magically in the blue light, despite the spots of discolouration. Then, without warning, he wiped a wet finger over some of the marks.

'Don't do that!' exclaimed Finch. 'You'll make it worse!'

Finch grabbed the dagger back.

'Sorry,' said Kingsley, clearly rattled.

Morello wanted to hold the dagger too, the desire to possess it almost overwhelming, but felt the moment had passed.

'Can you clean it up okay?' he asked Finch instead.

Finch took a small clear plastic bag from his trouser pocket. 'It'll be good as new when I'm done.'

'Good as new?' repeated Kingsley.

Finch was confident.

'Same as always. I'll even get rid of your spit.'

'That's all right then.'

What a pair, thought Morello to himself.

*

Standing in the Great Hall at the top of the well, Inspector Morello felt the same queasiness he had the last time he'd been there. The surface of the water looked so peaceful – impossible to imagine the dangerous currents encountered by Sergeant Lomax and his team.

Together with Finch, he followed Kingsley to a nearby spiral staircase, which they descended, coming out into an underground chamber attached to one side of the well. The air was cold and damp, causing Morello to shiver slightly. He walked over to a large metal grille set into the shaft. It was safely locked.

'Easy enough for someone to fit through the gap. You only unlock it to empty the bucket, you said?'

'That's right, Inspector,' answered Kingsley. 'And always with two people present, both tethered to this peg.'

Kingsley tapped a shiny metal hoop, four bolts holding it firmly to the wall, as if to prove its robustness.

'And this room, has it always been open to the public?'

'As far as we know.'

'What about that door.' Morello pointed to the opposite side of the room. 'Where does that go?'

'That's kept locked,' said Kingsley. 'Museum staff only.'

'What's behind there?'

'Storerooms, never used any more. I should imagine they got the worst of the flooding.'

'You can access the chalk works too,' added Finch.

'Chalk works?'

'And flint mines. Quite a maze under Norwich, Inspector. Not very safe though, tunnels collapse all the time. Bus fell in once, along the Earlham Road, didn't it Howard? Do you want to take a look, Inspector?'

Morello thought about his paperwork. 'If it's not too much trouble.'

'As Brian says, Inspector, it's not very safe. I'm not sure I'd advise it.'

'Just a quick look, Mr Kingsley. I'm sure we'll be fine.'

'I can't see they'll be anything of interest,' Kingsley persisted. 'We could take a quick tour of the dungeons, if you like. The entrance is on the other side of the Hall.'

But Morello's curiosity was aroused. He crossed the chamber to the door. Irregular in shape, it was beautifully carved to fit its rock frame.

'Have you got the key?' he asked Kingsley.

'I can go and get it – if you don't mind waiting?'

'No problem. Will we need a torch?'

Kingsley left to fetch the key. When he returned, Morello was stamping his feet to keep warm. Finch didn't seem so affected by the cold.

'Sorry to take so long, couldn't find the thing. Are you still sure you want to...?'

'If you don't mind.'

Kingsley held out the key he'd brought, large and ornate to the point of being comical, as if it were meant for a pantomime door. After several clumsy attempts, he managed to fit it into the lock. The door creaked slightly as it opened a few inches towards them.

'Could I have a look at that key, Mr Kingsley? It's quite a work of art.'

Kingsley handed it to Morello. 'Keep it till we get back, if you like.' He switched on the torch he'd brought, strapped to his head, and stepped forward, leading Morello and Finch into the darkness.

*

On the other side of the door was a passageway, quite

large, which sloped steeply downwards. The walls were a mixture of rock, light and dark, with thick white horizontal streaks running at intervals. Two dark recesses marked the beginning of other tunnels. The air was laden with moisture, making it more difficult to breathe. The earthy smell was nothing like that when digging a garden, instead having the slightly putrid tang of a place where the sun never reached.

'Like Brian said Inspector, it's quite a labyrinth down here, so don't wander off. Mobiles don't work.'

'Have you been down here before then, Mr Kingsley?'

Kingsley hesitated. 'I... yes, several times. Following the maps in our archives. I didn't get very far – they're not very accurate.'

Morello, his face starkly lit by Kingsley's torch, nodded slowly, saying nothing.

'I wanted to see for myself if there might not be something we could show the tourists,' Kingsley added, by way of explanation.

'Was there?'

'Not really. Storerooms, as I said. Nothing we could charge for. I'll take you along the bit I know.'

They followed the passageway deep underground, ignoring the other tunnels that led away from it. Small puddles had formed in places, whether from the dripping, which could be heard everywhere, or the recent flood, it wasn't possible to tell. The number of rooms surprised Morello. Some behind doors, others little more than niches carved into the softer, chalkier veins of rock. Kingsley supplied a little history to the place.

'A lot of these rooms were used to hold prisoners,' he explained, 'that is, if the castle was full. There are plenty of stories about inmates being conveniently forgotten.'

'Seriously?' Morello thought about some of the villains he'd be happy to see lost underground.

'And jailers not being able to remember where prisoners'

cells were.'

'You mean those prisoners are still down here? What's left of them?'

'Unlikely, I'd say. When the castle stopped being a prison, back in the Victorian era, they had a purge. There were some gruesome stories circulated at the time in the scandal sheets, but no proper evidence. Not that I've ever come across, anyway.'

'What about these other tunnels?' Morello had counted at least a dozen, leading off from the one they were in. One or two seemed to be continuations of each other, dissected by the passageway Kingsley had led them down. 'Do they go anywhere on your maps?'

'The Cathedral, several of them, some to other churches. Not that I've ever put it to the test. You heard what Brian said about the tunnels caving in.'

'And Guildhall, don't forget,' said Finch. 'That's one of the best known of all the tunnels.'

'Why's that?' asked Morello.

'It was used for prisoners when the Guildhall was a courthouse.'

'Straight from there to the dungeons?'

'Exactly. One way ticket for most of them.'

'Especially if they got left in a storeroom, eh, Mr Kingsley? I would have thought people would pay to see that. Following in the footsteps of the prisoners, hearing what happened to them? People love a bit of torture.'

'What you have to remember, Inspector, is there are probably hundreds of tunnels under the city, mostly uncharted. They were never meant to be used again, once the chalk and flint had been taken. Only the people that dug them knew their way back out. Imagine if we lost someone down there.'

Morello conceded that this would be an unfortunate circumstance.

'Can we go back?' asked Finch, trying to read his watch. 'I've got an appointment I don't want to be late for.'

'Have you seen enough, Inspector?'

'I think so, Mr Kingsley. What about this tunnel? The one we're in?'

'How do you mean?'

'Where does it go? Do you know?'

'Er, the Roman Catholic Cathedral I think, if memory serves. Past City Hall.'

'Shall we?' said Finch, moving back up the slope, slipping slightly on some loose rock.

Morello gazed beyond the single beam of light coming from Kingsley's head torch.

'City Hall... As you say, Mr Kingsley, quite a labyrinth.'

*

After Inspector Morello had left, and Finch had gone to keep whatever appointment he'd had, Kingsley returned to his office and picked up the phone.

'Hello, Tracy. Can you put me through to Mr Scarfe, please?'

Ten minutes later Kingsley replaced the handset, which had clicked annoyingly throughout the call. Harry had of course been very pleased by the fact that the police database had failed to give a DNA match, though like himself, not surprised. How could it have done? Finch's forensic work was impressive, but as they both knew, ultimately it would lead nowhere.

He hadn't considered the dagger being taken for cleaning important enough to mention. Although he had sterilised it thoroughly himself, having Finch clean it also, using whatever specialist methods he employed, could only be a good thing. All in all, Kingsley thought, it looked like everything was going to work out.

20

For the first time in years, Harry Scarfe was feeling nervous. He wasn't in control, and the sensation was not a pleasant one. He had often imagined the grandeur of the occasion, but the reality was proving quite different.

The shabby room was seldom used by the Conservative Club. The question as to why it had been pressed into service for such an important announcement had set Scarfe's mind racing. Was it paranoid to think that the Party grandees wanted to tone down his highly anticipated success? Not being able to stop him, were they instead making it clear what they thought of him in their choice of venue? As if to reinforce this point, many of the chairs set out for Party members were empty. Some of the board had also chosen not to attend, including the Chairman. Scarfe's face hardened. Whoever was here to witness the event, he was about to be declared the Tory candidate for the Norfolk South by-election.

Next to Scarfe stood the two other nominees, also nervous, looking like schoolboys awaiting the arrival of a particularly strict teacher. With their floppy hair and college ties it couldn't be that many years since they *were* at school. A boarding school of course, thought Scarfe. All toast with the masters then back to dorms for a quick wank over the mag Chumley Minor had smuggled in. Or over Chumley Minor, more like. Arseholes.

'I think we're ready to start, gentlemen,' spoke an officious looking man, seated behind the long bench facing the room.

He twitched his moustache. Scarfe had always thought Jack Veal a pompous prick, but today he had excelled himself. Wearing a boldly checked suit, a gold watch chain hanging from one side of a mustard waistcoat, he looked like Mr Toad had walked into a Dickens novel.

The room went quiet, all attention focused on Veal. Beside him sat seven other men, just half the full board. They looked at the three nominees sternly, as if it were only now to be decided who should be selected, rather than their true task of simply announcing the outcome of the vote. Scarfe wanted to tell them all to get on with it, having more to do with the rest of his day than drink cocktails and wait for dinner to arrive, but he held his tongue. After what seemed an eternity, Veal continued.

'Looking at the results, gentlemen, I think we are in for a surprise.'

He eyed them dolefully.

'Surprise?' Scarfe felt suddenly faint. All his work, the time spent away from his business, the fortune he'd spent, had it all been for nothing? Was he destined to be kept where he was, a self-made man, successful but not quite the ticket if you know what I mean? Had Kingsley let him down after all?

'I don't like surprises,' said Scarfe flatly.

*

Harry Scarfe walked out into the fresh air, his head spinning. Veal had taken five years off his life. The man's words were still buzzing in his ears, chaotic, nonsensical.

'With all the votes in, I declare our candidate for the forthcoming by-election to be – Harry Scarfe.'

A spattering of applause went up.

'Well done, Harry!' called out one man raucously.

Veal scowled, causing his moustache to droop.

Scarfe felt a surge of elation. Ignoring the outstretched

arms of the other two nominees, he punched the air.

'Yes!'

He didn't have a tie to indicate his attendance at some famous school or college, but he'd won anyway. Won through hard work and low cunning – two things you couldn't teach.

'If I might have your attention?'

Scarfe faced the bench. He looked forward, once he had won the election, to telling Jack Veal exactly what he thought of him.

'I mentioned a surprise. It's a little unorthodox, but the board has agreed, in the circumstances, that it might be wise to field a second candidate.'

It took Scarfe a moment to take in what Veal had said. 'A second... what circumstances?'

'A back-up, if you like. In case your electoral appeal, Mr Scarfe, proves too, er, narrow, shall we say.'

Scarfe looked at him, uncomprehending.

'Technically, our second candidate will have to stand as an Independent. Julian, we decided you should take on that responsibility.'

Julian Fairbrother stepped forward to shake Veal's hand.

'Thank you sir. I won't let you down.'

'Won't let him down?' Scarfe was incredulous. He had won, but they couldn't accept it. 'Have you gone mad? What you're doing will divide our voters!'

A few members seated behind Scarfe muttered their agreement.

'I'm sure you understand the position, Mr Scarfe.'

With nothing more to say, Veal rose from his chair and left the room, the men either side of him following suit.

*

Scarfe walked towards his Council office as if in a trance, thinking. Veal and his co-conspirators would rather risk losing their safe seat to Labour (or worse, the Liberals) than see him take power. As he passed the market square, he dropped a ten-pound note into a busker's suitcase, as if this charitable act might earn himself some good fortune.

By the time he reached City Hall, the first wave of shock had begun to wear off, to be replaced by anger. Whatever it took, he told himself, he was going to win the election. When the Norwich Eye was finished, complete with a brass plaque showing his name, the initials MP would be there too.

Whatever it took.

21

'YOU'RE VERY QUIET,' said Penny Henderson. 'Nothing I've done, I hope?'

She laughed uncertainly.

Caroline Scarfe played with the lavender that ran along the edge of the grass. She shook her head. 'If there's one person I can rely on, Penny, it's you.'

Penny was glad to hear her say that. She often wondered if her intense dislike for Caroline's husband was an obstacle to their friendship. She tried to disguise it, but with limited success.

Raising her head, Penny breathed deeply, letting her eyelids droop. It was a beautiful day. They were sitting in the kitchen garden of Blickling Hall, an historic stately home run by the National Trust. The sun was shining on the soft brick walls that enclosed them, the smell of herbs mixing with the heady scent of late-flowering roses. It was one of their favourite places. But not today. Something wasn't right.

'You seem a little distant, that's all.'

Caroline smiled apologetically, speaking in a soft voice.

'I'm tired. Can't seem to get much sleep.'

Penny had noticed the dark rings under her eyes.

'Is it Harry?' she asked abruptly.

Caroline tensed. 'How do you mean?'

'Caroline, I'm your best friend. The last time I saw you together he was treating you worse than I've ever seen. Why do you put up with it?'

Caroline bowed her head, shoulders heaving, trying to

stifle her sobs. Penny put out a hand to comfort her.

'I'm sorry, I don't mean to make things worse. You've got me worried, that's all.'

'It's not Harry,' Caroline managed to say. 'I know we've got our problems, but it's not that.' She sniffed noisily and wiped her eyes. 'Really, it's not,' she reassured, seeing Penny's expression. 'To be honest, we hardly seem to see each other these days, anyway.'

Normally Penny would have considered this to be a bad thing in a marriage, but where Harry was concerned, she wasn't so sure. She refused to believe he wasn't behind her friend's unhappiness either.

'You're such a strong person, I don't understand it.'

'Not as strong as you think,' confessed Caroline. 'Penny – can I tell you something?'

'Of course you can.'

'You promise you won't say a word, no matter what I tell you?'

Penny pondered this for a moment. What could Caroline have to say that meant so much? She had to know.

'I promise.'

If Harry were beating her, she would have to tell someone.

'See,' said Caroline, looking at Penny anxiously, 'I spend all my time coping. Where Harry's concerned.'

Penny nodded non-committedly. That wasn't difficult to believe.

'Months go by, years, and I cope. Except that I'm not coping, not really. It all gets bottled up inside, you see. The affairs, the arguments. Then something happens, and it all comes out at once – I get so angry I can't control myself.'

She went back to stroking the lavender.

'Why don't you leave him?'

Caroline just shook her head. Penny felt sympathy and frustration battling inside her.

'Is that all you wanted to tell me?'

'I... yes. It all gets bottled up... I get angry...'

Not angry enough, thought Penny. 'I'm always at the other end of the phone, if you need me. You know that.'

Caroline burst into tears again. Penny hugged her, wondering at the same time why her friend wasn't being completely truthful. There had been more Caroline had wanted to say, she was sure of it, but for some reason she had changed her mind. Fear of Harry?

A short time later, they were back at the car park. It was a day Penny wanted to put behind her.

'We still have a bond, Harry and I,' Caroline said, as if apologising for something.

The only bonds Penny could picture were those of a hostage.

22

The elderly man sat the other side of Harry Scarfe's desk had lost the Councillor's interest the moment he had walked in. Worse, he had begun to repeat himself, his pickled walnut of a face becoming more indignant the longer he continued. Scarfe shifted his buttocks in an attempt to keep the blood flowing.

Some had called Scarfe arrogant in setting up a constituency office before being elected, but he had decided it was a good idea anyway. His publicity advisor had agreed. It would give an impression of him as Norfolk South's MP-in-waiting, and offer the opportunity to talk to voters and persuade them that their concerns were top of his to do list. Which could make all the difference, so the advisor advised, when the time came for filling in the ballot papers. As something of a bonus, Scarfe had heard that Jack Veal and his cronies were beside themselves with rage at his presumptuousness.

In the lobby outside Scarfe's surgery, a queue of people sat waiting, as if he were some twenty-first century King Solomon. The elderly man was over-running his slot.

'So I said, that's shocking. Having to pay to park, when I'm here to visit my sick wife? I'm a pensioner, I said, how am I meant to afford it? There's no buses go past us, I told him. And do you know what he said?' Mr Woodford tapped a large and gnarled finger on Scarfe's desk. 'Do you know what he said?'

Scarfe shook his head woodenly. He expected the man

would answer his own question, as he had every other.He understood Woodford's dilemma; the way hospitals were run now was ideal, but only if your purpose was to make an easy profit out of the 'customers' who had no choice but to be there. First with the car park, and then with other services like phones and TVs. Scarfe Technologies did very nicely out of the electronic add-ons, which was not something he would be mentioning in his manifesto.

'He said, if you don't like it, go somewhere else. Go somewhere else! I said, we live here, this is where we live, I said. So he only had the nerve to say...'

Perhaps a buzzer could be installed, thought Scarfe, like the one he sometimes used at his business office. When pressed, two large men would be alerted to the fact that another good and honest citizen had outstayed their welcome, and would come to his rescue, dragging the unfortunate person away to bore the pants off someone else.

The man had finished talking.

'I shall certainly look into it, Mr Woodford. I'll make it a priority to speak to the hospital board myself about the parking, and several other issues that have come to my attention. Of course, I hope I can rely on your vote, in order to be able to do that?'

Scarfe raised his eyebrows, smiling ingratiatingly.

'Good God no. I vote Labour, always have done. But they never get in, do they? That's why I'm here.'

Scarfe looked dumbfounded at this sudden burst of reasoned eloquence.

'But I thought…'

The old man shook his head. 'I could never vote for your lot. If you're not swindling the taxpayer out of what's theirs, you're up to your necks in tarts and rent boys.'

'Rent boys! Mr Woodford, I can assure you –'

'Save it for them that's listening,' said Woodford, suddenly more cheerful, and with surprising agility, he made for the door and left, before Scarfe could respond.

'You ignorant fucker,' Scarfe muttered after him.

'I'm sorry Mr Scarfe, what was that?'

It was his secretary, standing in the doorway. The half dozen or so people sat behind her leaned inwards, the better to see.

'Nothing, I… I'll close this window, there must be noise coming in from outside.' He got up to wrestle with the sash arrangement behind his desk. 'Er, who's next, Mrs Green?'

*

'Well,' said Scarfe, feeling far more motivated, 'it's nice to see the younger generation taking an interest in politics.'

Despite her dingy clothes, outsized rucksack and cheaply bleached hair, the young woman couldn't disguise her attractiveness. She spoke with an accent rooted in privilege, but Scarfe ignored this, moving his chair closer and adopting an interested expression. Felicity (Filly to her friends) looked vaguely offended by Scarfe's tone, as if half-expecting him to add, 'And how can I help you, young lady?'

'And how can I help you – Filly?' Scarfe smiled encouragingly, baffled by the stormy expression over the desk.

'I'd like to know what you're going to do for the puppets,' Felicity finally said.

Scarfe looked blank. 'Puppets?' he repeated, dumbly. 'Are they – that is, do they – what?' He backed into his chair, grinning idiotically. He wondered if the girl was all there.

'When I say puppets, I mean of course the Puppet Theatre,' Felicity explained.

'Oh, I see!' Scarfe's expression turned to one of bewilderment. 'What Puppet Theatre? Why the hell would anybody want a Puppet Theatre?'

Felicity was indignant, clutching the arms of her chair,

knuckles whitening. She had passion.

'That's exactly the sort of attitude we need to change!'

She bent down suddenly, rummaging in her rucksack, taking from it a mass of coloured wood and fabric, wrapped in string. Standing up, she proudly announced, 'Meet Shintu, the Oriental Master of Verse.'

Scarfe sat stunned. Before him Felicity waved a large doll, dressed in silk, suspended on strings attached to a lattice, presumably used to control it.

'Would you like me to show you how he comes alive?'

'Alive?'

Felicity smiled at Scarfe's look of concern. 'He's quite harmless. His only ambition is to bring light into the world.'

A minute later, Scarfe was holding one of the control rods, while Felicity expertly manipulated the others. He could smell her hair, as he contorted himself around her. The puppet lurched crazily along the floor, like a drunk miraculously held aloft.

'Master of Verse, eh? So what can he sing?'

'Anything. Say whatever comes into your head.' Felicity looked at him sternly. 'Free your mind, Mr Scarfe.'

'Please, it's Harry.'

'Keep your hands on the control rod, Harry. Both hands.'

'Oh, I see, yes. Sorry. It's all a bit tricky.'

'Sing, Harry!'

'What?'

'Sing!'

'I don't know any songs,' Scarfe croaked.

'Then follow my lead.'

Together they began to move slowly around the room, Shintu staggering in front of them. Felicity began to hum loudly before bursting into song.

'I am the sea,
I am the wind,
I am –'

'I don't think I know that one, Filly.'

'Just repeat it after me – I am the sea…'

Felicity waited.

'I – I am the wind,' Scarfe stammered.

This had better be worth it.

'The sea, I am the sea!'

'Haven't we done that bit?'

'You've moved your hand again.'

'My mistake.'

'Mr Scarfe?' a third voice enquired.

'What –' Scarfe dropped everything, spinning round towards the door. 'Mrs Green! What is it?'

Shintu's arm slumped ape-like to the floor.

Mrs Green had worked in the Tory office for nearly twenty years, so there was little which still surprised her. The sight of Mr Scarfe with one hand on a constituent, the other on a bizarre-looking puppet, was simply a variation on a theme.

'Sorry to disturb you sir, it's just there are several more people to see, and time's getting a little short.'

'Of course, Mrs Green. Very diligent of you. Er, give me a moment would you?'

Mrs Green nodded understandingly and closed the door. Scarfe heard her explaining to the people still waiting that he wouldn't be long. A man asked if he had heard singing, but Mrs Green assured him otherwise.

'Well, Filly, that was – most instructive.' Scarfe retreated back into formality. 'Perhaps we could discuss your puppet issues when time isn't so pressing? I'm rather busy at the moment during the day, as you can see... Maybe a drink instead? How does tomorrow evening suit?'

Attractive women produced a Pavlovian response in Scarfe, even when he knew what the answer would be.

'Okay,' said Felicity.

Scarfe took a few seconds to respond. As long as he lived, he would never understand the opposite sex.

23

Fisher Bayley was transfixed, gazing at the dagger in Brian Finch's gloved hands. The dagger of Ankh Hor. Under the laboratory's strip lighting, the jewels decorating the handle were less brilliant, and several specks of discolouration could be seen on the blade's scarred surface, but it was still a thing of beauty. A dazzling point of gold.

'Marvellous, isn't it?' said Finch proudly, seeing Bayley's expression.

Bayley nodded reverently. The dagger exerted a powerful spell. Ian Chapman was less moved, his work more often bringing him into contact with it.

'Strictly ceremonial of course,' Finch added, referring to the knife's probable use in animal sacrifices. And the more contentious belief that it may have been used to butcher human organs, before the donor was dead. All of which added to the priest's legend.

'Didn't we clean it not long back?' Chapman asked.

'We did, but it's dirty again. Good to keep on top of it if we can.'

Rather than simply clean it, however, as normally he would have done, Finch intended to satisfy his interest in what might have caused the early discolouration of the blade. Maybe the filters needed replacing. He hoped not – the budget, what was left of it, was already earmarked.

He placed the dagger carefully on a small stage in front of them.

'I'll take a sample, and then Ian, you can do the clean.

Show Fisher how we do it. We can put a small piece about it on the website.'

'No problem,' said Bayley. It made a change from bones.

Finch focused the optics above the stage, until a clear magnified image appeared on a screen next to him.

'What's that?' said Bayley. 'Right in the middle – can you zoom in?'

Finch fiddled with the controls.

'Yes, I see it. Pass me some tweezers.'

Bayley and Chapman watched the screen, as Finch carefully extracted what looked to be a tiny blue thread, caught where the blade met the hilt.

'That shouldn't be there,' Finch remarked.

He put it in a small plastic phial, doing the same with five tiny samples of the stain that had first caught his attention.

'Okay then you two, I'm done. When you've finished, Ian, take it straight back to the display. We don't want to upset Ankh Hor longer than we have to, do we?'

24

Divided from City Hall by a wide road, Norwich Library, known as the Forum, had been built after its predecessor was ruined in a devastating fire. Shaped like a giant horseshoe, the open end enclosed by a glass wall to form a huge atrium, its famous architect had succeeded in giving the building a light and airy feel.

Following the shape of the horseshoe was the library itself, while suspended halfway up the glass wall was a pizzeria, which looked out onto a large terraced square and St Peter Mancroft Church. To the left of this view could be seen the castle, a few hundred yards away, and further round, the market square. Beneath the pizzeria, connected by a spiral staircase, a coffee bar spanned the inner atrium and outside paving, catering for the best and the worst of the British weather.

Sat at one of the tables outside, lit by the late morning sun, Fisher Bayley, Phil Henderson, and Chris Stokefield were waiting. Sean Cooper had texted each of them in turn, asking them to meet him there, but intriguingly not saying why.

Fisher was not so much intrigued, as apprehensive. Were Sean and Penny really having an affair? Was that what Sean intended to tell them, in that frank and honest way people had which they seemed to think excused whatever they had done? The youths who were slouching moodily on the sweep of stairs leading up to the Forum's entrance seemed to reflect his own melancholy. Or, perhaps, they were still aggrieved by the ring of builders' hoarding that for months now had taken up most of their square.

Pictured along the hoarding was an artist's impression of how the completed Norwich Eye would look, while on the other side, amidst the noise and dust, tentacles of corrugated pipes and thick cabling spewed from the hole out of which the Eye would eventually grow.

Fisher's attention was brought back to the table by Phil, wanting to know if the modern art exhibition soon to be held at the castle would be worth seeing.

'Is it going to be any good? Penny wants to drag me along.'

'I'd say so,' said Fisher. 'Ginny's talked about it a lot – she's the one organising it. She said some of Damien Hirst's work will be there.'

'Really? I've always wanted to see that shark of his.'

'I don't think that's coming – something on a shelf, Ginny said.'

'A shelf?' said Phil doubtfully.

Chris pointed towards the other end of the Forum, where the BBC had their local base.

'Isn't that Sean, in that hat?'

Fisher watched, his stomach knotting as Sean approached. Whatever it was he wanted to say to them all, they were about to find out.

Close up, Sean looked tired and thin as he weaved between the tables to join them. After a brief 'Hi' that seemed to confirm Fisher's worst fears, he sat himself down as if exhausted.

Phil stood up. 'Coffee?'

'Cappuccino. Thanks, Phil.'

Phil went off to join the short queue at the bar.

'What's with the hat?' asked Chris.

It was a Homburg, wide brimmed with a black band.

'Eleanor picked it for me. What do you think?'

'I reckon she doesn't want anyone else fancying you.'

Phil returned with a cappuccino, which Sean took gratefully.

'So why are we here?' was Chris' next question.

Fisher braced himself.

Sean paused, then said, 'I wanted to invite you all to my wedding. Our wedding. Me and Eleanor, I mean.'

There was uproar. Fisher shook Sean by the hand, causing him to grin stupidly. Phil and Chris fired questions at him – when did you ask, where, what did she say? Did you go down on one knee?

'I think we need something stronger than coffee!' exclaimed Fisher. As much as the wedding, he wanted to celebrate the fact that he had been wrong about any affair. 'One bottle of bubbly coming up!'

Chris watched Fisher go. 'Leaves just me then,' he said bleakly.

Phil broke off from congratulating Sean. 'Fisher's not married,' he pointed out.

'Not exactly celibate though, is he? Ah, forget it. We're here to celebrate.'

Phil took it upon himself to give Chris the benefit of his wisdom.

'I was like you, before I met Penny. No one interested in me.'

Chris looked as if he could well believe it.

'So I stopped trying.'

'You gave up? Is that meant to be advice?'

'Worked for me. I don't know how, but –'

'None of us do.'

'*But*, when I stopped trying so hard, Penny turned up. Changed my life.'

'You got lucky. That's what I need. A bit of luck.'

Fisher arrived back, carrying a gold-topped bottle and four glasses.

'Here we go! Didn't think we'd need a cooler.' He filled

each flute and passed three round. 'To Sean and Eleanor!'

Not yet midday, Fisher nevertheless downed half his glass, stopping only when the bubbles fizzed up his nose.

'While you're all in the mood,' said Phil, wiping his lips, 'I've got some news of my own – I've started seeing a hypnotherapist.'

Fisher's eyebrows shot up.

'You're kidding!'

'Penny wants me to give it a try, see if maybe this guy can sort out my problem – you know, with getting old. Old*er*.'

'Question is, can he sort out all your other problems?' said Chris. Phil's advice hadn't gone down well.

Ignoring him, Phil continued to explain. 'He stopped a friend of Penny's from smoking in six weeks. Twenty a day, she was on. Got to be worth a try, hasn't it?'

'Is it safe?' asked Fisher, doubtfully.

'This bloke has been practising for nearly fifteen years. Wouldn't be in business still if he wasn't any good, would he?'

It sounded a reasonable enough argument, but as Fisher knew, where Phil was concerned, reasonable wasn't always enough to keep him out of trouble. Something told him it might not be too long before Penny regretted taking up her friend's recommendation.

'Good luck with it,' said Sean. He had hardly drunk a drop of his champagne. 'Thanks for coming, all of you, but I've got to go.' He rose to his feet, somewhat unsteadily.

'Wait a minute,' said Fisher, with sudden realisation. 'You haven't told us when the big day is.'

'Just before Christmas, right over there at St Peter's.'

'Before Christmas! How are you going to get sorted out that quickly?'

'Where there's a will... actually, you've reminded me, Fisher. Phil – will you be my best man?'

Phil stood and shook Sean's hand, pumping it vigorously.

'Course I will! And I'll sort you out a stag night you won't forget!'

Sean left then, skirting around the builders' hoarding to cross the square, entering St Peter Mancroft Church on the other side.

Fisher put down his empty glass, strangely unsettled. For a man about to be married, he thought, Sean didn't seem all that happy.

25

Waiting patiently in Brian Finch's laboratory, Detective Inspector Felix Morello leaned on the workbench in the centre of the room and took another mouthful of coffee. Brought to him by a colleague of Finch's, the brew was to his taste rather weak. Must be his Italian heritage. As a boy, instant coffee, instant anything, had almost been unheard of.

The high wooden stool he was seated on wobbled uncomfortably, putting him in mind of the science lessons of his schooldays. In a glass enclosure nearby, four flasks containing a blue-green liquid of some sort were bubbling away, smoking slightly, though there seemed to be no source of heat.

Nearer to hand, sharing the bench with him and supported by several hard foam wedges, the ribcage lay. Scattered around it were several dog-eared folders, the title of their contents crossed out and re-written each time they had been used. The bubbling sound of the four flasks had a therapeutic quality, and Morello found his gaze shifting out of focus. Then with a bang the door swung open and the Deputy Curator strode in.

'Apologies, Inspector. Difficult getting out of the staff meeting. I think Howard wanted me to wait for him.'

'Not a problem.'

'He said he'd join us, soon as he could.'

'We'll crack on anyway, shall we? Your email said you had the rest of the tests done?'

'I have. And I've found something else since I sent you

that message – something I think you'll agree is incredible. Means a rethink, I would say, about sending your divers back down.'

Morello felt suddenly alert.

'I'm all ears,' he said.

*

Howard Kingsley was becoming more anxious by the minute. The meeting was over-running.

'Shall we put it down for further discussion, Howard?' asked Stephen Brent, the museum's Liaison Officer. 'Next month's meeting, say?'

The agenda item Brent was referring to was one Kingsley felt very strongly about. The Joint Museums' Committee, the regional body that controlled every museum in Norfolk, had put forward the idea of replacing the castle's art galleries with a virtual 3D "experience". What would be done with the originals they hadn't said. Kingsley's opposition was all the more fierce as Scarfe Technologies were mentioned as the preferred supplier. Was there any pie Harry didn't have his grubby little fingers in, Kingsley wondered. He was prepared to do whatever it took to prevent Scarfe Technologies coming anywhere near his precious collection. With that in mind, more time to consider his defence seemed prudent. He looked at the clock on the wall.

'Makes sense,' he said. 'We're already fifteen minutes over. Any other business can move to next month too.'

'With all due respect, Howard, I don't think the photocopying issue can wait that long.' Brenda Richards from accounts spoke with conviction. With her braying voice and thick helmet of hair, she always brought to mind in Kingsley an impression of a drill sergeant in drag. He sometimes wondered if others thought it too. 'If something isn't done,' she warned him, 'the admin budget will run out before Christmas.'

'That's a risk we'll have to take. I've some important business to attend to.'

Richards continued to object, but Kingsley over-ruled her. With the meeting disbanded, he rushed from the room, hoping the Inspector hadn't yet left.

*

'How definite are you?' asked Morello.

'Hundred percent, near as I can be. She was female. The PCR test is very reliable, never known it to fail. The difference in the amelogenin gene from the male version is quite clear.'

Finch had open one of the card folders, passing to Morello a ten-page printout, headed **Polymerase Chain Reaction – Test Results**. The body of it was peppered with words and graphs unintelligible to the Inspector. There were more papers in the folder still to go through.

'It's a complicated procedure, analysing that part of the DNA, that's why it's taken a little time. Different, of course, if we'd had the pelvis.'

Morello added another entry into his notebook, quickly scanning his previous scribbles before moving on.

'I've got here, once you knew the sex, you'd be able to tell me the age. Her age.' It sounded less clinical.

'Between eighteen and twenty-four, when she died. If you look at this,' Finch handed over another sheaf of papers, 'you'll see the Īşcan test came in at phase two or three.'

'I'll take your word for it.'

Morello made another note, confirming with Finch what he had just written.

'So let me get everything straight. What we've got is a woman, aged eighteen to twenty-four, and according to her DNA, white European, but not British.'

'That's right.'

‘Wasn’t there something else?’

Morello could normally rely on an excellent memory for the details of a case, details that often gave the lie to the bigger picture. But with all the scientific mumbo-jumbo Finch had been throwing at him, he was finding it difficult to keep track.

‘Bone composition, that’s what you’re thinking of. The isotope test. I’ve got it here.’ Finch retrieved another report, laying it on the bench in front of the Inspector.

‘That was it. And what was that going to tell us again?’

‘Where she lived for the last twenty years or so, within a few hundred square miles. I found the location.’

The location could wait, thought Morello. In over fifteen years on the force, he had never before seen this particular forensic method used. He asked Finch for the gist of how it worked.

‘In layman’s terms, let me see... Oxygen, it comes in different forms, which we call isotopes, yes?’

Morello nodded. ‘If you say so.’

‘Well, in water, the ratio of those isotopes varies, according to where in the world you are. Most of the oxygen present in bone comes from water, so analysing the ratio tells us where you drank it.’

‘Very clever.’

‘All I had to do was compare the ratio to a distribution map. The map only covers Europe and America, but that was enough in this case.’

Morello was impressed. ‘Quite the detective yourself, aren’t you?’

‘There is one proviso. Like I said, the test is only good for tracing a person’s whereabouts for the last twenty years or so, which means of course it doesn’t necessarily reveal where an adult was born or grew up – where they come from, if you like. Not with today’s migratory patterns.’

Using the term ‘migratory patterns’ to describe human

activity seemed to Morello more than a little strange. Like the time he'd been to America with his wife, New York on a shopping trip, and had had to fill in a form describing himself as an alien. Both amusing and alarming at the same time.

'But as we're dealing with a woman less than twenty-four years old, I'd say we're pretty safe. And it ties in with the DNA results.'

'I see. Good. So what location did you come up with?'

'Statistically speaking, I'd say it's highly likely that the woman we have here is from Eastern Europe. To the north. I've marked out the area on page four of the report.'

Morello turned to the relevant section.

'Remember, the test is based on geography, not nationality. That's why the area crosses over three borders.'

'Hmm. Came a long way, didn't she, just to fall down a well?'

Morello made several more notes in his pad and then closed it. To all intents and purposes, this was the end of the case. He couldn't help thinking that Kingsley had maybe been right. It was a lot of effort to go to for nothing. For all the scientific wizardry that had been brought to bear, he still had no ID, or even a definitive cause of death. Somewhere, a family would be forever in mourning, never knowing the fate of their loved one.

Though it was small consolation, at least Drake wouldn't be able to haul him over the coals for some minor procedural error. Unlike his usual style, he had conducted this investigation by the book. To the letter. Now it was over. With a little luck he might be taken on by the team looking into the double murder at Horning, a holiday let somewhere out on the Norfolk Broads. Sergeant Lomax's unit in action again.

'That's it then,' he said, standing up and stretching. The wobbling stool had cut off the circulation to his legs, numbing them. 'No more we can do. Thanks for all your help, Mr Finch. Our lab boys are backed up for months on non-urgent cases. I'll be able to get this typed up today.'

'Aren't you forgetting something, Inspector?'

Morello recalled the Deputy Curator wanting Lomax and his team to return to the castle.

'I can't sanction searching the well again, Mr Finch. Not based on what we've got, as much as I appreciate all your efforts.'

Finch took the last sheet of paper out of the card wallet, a shine of excitement in his eyes.

'I think you can. I told you I'd found something incredible, didn't I? Take a look at this.'

26

The coincidence struck Finch suddenly.

'Same part of the world your scholarships are from, isn't it?' he asked Kingsley.

Sat where Inspector Morello had been not ten minutes earlier, Howard Kingsley conceded the truth of this, while adopting an expression designed to dismiss the coincidence as irrelevant. Having listened to his deputy repeat all he had told the Inspector, he was ready to believe it was over. He was safe. There was only one thing more he needed to know. He passed the Isotope Report back to Finch.

'That's it, then. What did the Inspector say, before he left?'

'Wait a minute, I've saved this until last.' Finch handed Kingsley a transparency. 'I think you'll find it changes everything.'

A chill wave curdled Kingsley's stomach.

'Are you going to look?' Finch prompted him.

On the transparency were three circular colour photographs. In each, tiny flecks of silver and yellow were scattered against a dull white background. It was impossible for Kingsley to tell what he was looking at – the images were distorted in some way, slightly pixelated it seemed.

'What's this?'

'That was my question, so I ran some more tests. You won't believe what I found.'

'I mean, what is it? What am I looking at?'

‘Micrographs. The break in the ribs.’

Kingsley looked again at the grainy images. He had a bad feeling about this. The ribcage itself lay across from him on the bench. How glad he'd be to see it gone for good.

‘What you’re seeing there are tiny scraps of metal embedded in the bone – two metals, in fact.’

‘I... did you tell the Inspector about this?’

‘Of course. He agreed with me.’

‘He did? Agreed about what?’

‘Well, we know how strong the currents at the bottom of the well are – the body would have been broken up against the rocks or anything else lying around down there, like the arrowheads and sword fragments Tom found.’

Kingsley stared at Finch uncomprehendingly.

‘That’s what the silver in the micrographs is – steel from the weapons still lying at the bottom of the well.’

A sense of relief swept over Kingsley. Finch could only see what he wanted to see.

‘Arrowheads... Yes, I’m with you now.’

Finch’s next words were spoken with zeal.

‘But it’s the second metal that really matters. It’s gold!’

Kingsley’s heart nearly stopped.

‘Real gold, almost pure. We must go back in and do a proper search for whatever’s down there.’

‘Is that what the Inspector said he was going to do?’

‘This could be the biggest discovery ever made at the castle, Howard.’

‘What did the Inspector say? Is he sending a team down again?’

‘He can’t, can he? Not with the case closed. They’re not treasure hunters.’

Case closed! That was what Kingsley had been waiting to hear. Why couldn’t Finch have just said it? Stupid question, he thought. He stood up.

‘Where are you going?’

'I've got things to do, Brian. Can't sit here all day, dreaming about treasure.'

'Dreaming! Howard, this is proof! Right in front of you!'

But Kingsley was already making his exit. Finch chased after him, arguing all the way back to Kingsley's office, but without success. With a huge smile, Kingsley entered his room and closed the door.

27

THE NEXT DAY Howard Kingsley arrived at work late, and with a hangover. Scarfe had insisted on celebrating when told the news.

'The exhibition's off to a good start then, Mr Kingsley. You all right sir?'

'Morning Barry.'

Barry Cleaver, the security guard, would normally have had Clive Dunlop in tow, but Dunlop had been off sick now for nearly a week.

'Mind you, modern art,' Cleaver went on, pacing alongside Kingsley as he headed towards the Great Hall, 'never understood it myself.' He shook his head, as if in wonder at his own ignorance. 'Prefer your traditional stuff. You know – paintings that look like something? Since when was a bog a piece of art?'

Kingsley knew that Cleaver was referring to the installation entitled "End of a Dream". His own tastes ran similar to those of the security guard's, but he believed the castle galleries needed to cater for as wide an audience as possible. Even if a segment of that audience liked to think of "bogs" as a work of art.

'Ten of 'em, all in a row, proud as you like! All different colours. Don't make it art. My Veronica, she'd have a fit. She likes your Turners, you know, Constable. Proper stuff. Talent, that's what they've got. Bogs!'

'Each to their own, eh?'

Nothing could dampen Kingsley's spirits today.

‘Talking of proper paintings, I see one of your favourites has gone. Having a clean-up, is it?’

Kingsley paused.

‘What do you mean? Which painting?’

‘One of the Cotmans. Can’t remember what the card said. Cotman’s the one you give lectures on, isn’t he?’

Kingsley’s interest in the Norwich School was well known amongst the staff. Sometimes he was invited by local art groups to give a talk on the subject, and, on occasion, by the Norwich University of the Arts.

‘Thought you must be doing a bit of restoration work, like you do. That not right then? Mr Kingsley?’

Striding off in the direction of the galleries, Kingsley didn’t reply.

*

Kingsley entered his office, mystified. Ginny had allowed two men to take *The Baggage Wagon*, a rare Cotman oil. For what purpose, they hadn’t been able to tell her, but their paperwork was all in order, signed by the Museum Committee itself. She’d assumed he knew all about it. This worried him greatly. Preparing himself to make what would undoubtedly be an unpleasant phone call, he noticed on his desk a letter, not there when he’d left his office the day before. He recognised the logo in the top left corner. Ripping it open, he read the contents. His hands shook. The Museum Committee had ignored him and gone right ahead.

‘You’ve gone too far this time,’ he said to himself, crushing the letter and throwing it across the room.

*

Arriving at the reception desk of Scarfe Technologies, Kingsley was given a pass by a pretty woman with long red hair.

'If you'd like to take the lift to –' she began.

'I know the way, thank you.'

Scarfe wasn't in his office. His PA directed Kingsley to the second floor, the StreetEye monitoring centre.

Finding it, without knocking he walked in. It took a moment for his eyes to adjust. The long room was in semi-darkness, banks of computer monitors blinking silently, watched over by a small team of staff. Most of the images he recognised, well-known roads and buildings within the centre of Norwich. Scarfe stood with a young woman, discussing whatever it was she had attached to her clipboard. Seeing Kingsley, his expression turned to one of alarm.

'Howard? What are you doing here? Give me a moment, would you Barbara?'

In the corridor outside, Scarfe's immediate concern was whether Inspector Morello had changed his mind. Kingsley assured him his visit had nothing to do with the Inspector but rather the rare Cotman oil his men had taken. Scarfe relaxed.

'Ah. Not a fan of virtual reality, then? You don't surprise me.'

'Where's the painting?'

'Our research facility. We're using it in our final trials.'

'I want it back.'

'It takes weeks to digitise all the information, and when it's done we've been asked to keep it in storage.'

'By who?'

'Your Museum Committee, who else?'

'Why the Cotman oil, Harry? You could have used any painting, we've got hundreds.'

'Start at the top, don't they say?. No point in creating a 3D image no one wants to see, is there?'

'You're not taking anything else. And I want the Cotman back.'

'No-can-do. You need to talk to your Committee. My guess is they'll want to sell it, could be worth quite a bit.'

Exactly what Kingsley had been afraid of.

'I'm telling you right now, don't try taking any more of my paintings.'

'*Your* paintings? This is an important trial for us, Howard. Could be a big income stream.'

'People come to my museum to see the real thing, not some trick of the light.'

Scarfe slapped him on the back.

'Ah, who cares about all that? Have you forgotten? We're in the clear. No more policemen.' He studied Kingsley's face. 'Go get yourself a fry-up, you look like crap.'

And with that, Scarfe disappeared back into the monitoring room to continue his discussion with Barbara.

Driving away from the business park on which Scarfe's office complex stood, Kingsley's mind was racing. He couldn't stand by while his galleries were systematically stripped and replaced piece by piece with technical gimmickry – he had to do something. At the very least, protect the star pieces. Hide them away somewhere, while he came up with a way of reversing the Committee's decision. If anyone asked, he could say they had been taken for restoration. But where? By the time Kingsley had reached his parking space at the castle, he knew the answer. It was perfect.

*

'Found you!' exclaimed Ginny Carmen. 'Can you spare a minute, Howard? I need you to sort something out down in the exhibition.'

'Right now? I've just walked in.'

'It's urgent. And I think you'll want to see the problem for yourself.'

'Nothing else is missing, is it?' said Kingsley, as if he

couldn't cope if it were.

'No, nothing like that. Can you come, please? Now?'

Kingsley followed Ginny as she set off at high speed towards the inter-connected set of galleries in which the modern art exhibition was taking place. As they neared, they came across a gaggle of visitors milling about the entrance, blocked off by a red cord. Some were laughing and joking, others wore a more contemplative expression. Ginny and Kingsley threaded their way through the crowd, stepping around the red cord and into the first of the galleries.

To most visitors, at first glance, the clean white space looked devoid of any kind of art at all. On closer examination, however, what appeared at first simply to be shelving was revealed as in fact one of the installations. The various objects placed upon it were arranged in what the artist considered to be a meaningful way. Further inspection exposed other well disguised works – a pile of loose bricks, painted white; an old-fashioned television screen, endlessly repeating the same three-minute video, and a crack in the floor, which Ginny had promised Kingsley would be made good later. The only object Kingsley recognised as art, as he understood it, was a huge piece of polished wood, unsculptured in favour of its natural shape. As he and Ginny passed it, however, several penguin heads could be seen, protruding inexplicably the other side.

In a small annexe to the main space, and housed by itself, was the exhibit *End of a Dream*. It consisted of ten toilets lined up in a row, each one moulded from a different shade of brightly coloured perspex. Bayley, Finch, and a few others were stood in an arc at one end of the installation.

'Howard!' Finch sounded relieved. 'Thank the lord. What do you suggest?'

'About what?'

'Didn't Ginny say?' Finch stood to one side, breaking the human shield. Kingsley stopped dead.

‘Have you come to help too?’ asked a frail-looking lady, grey-haired, sat second from the end on a lime-green toilet.

Her thick skirt was hitched up around her waist. Clearly visible through the opaque bowl was a large unbroken turd, resting in an inch or so of liquid. Kingsley picked up a strong, deeply unpleasant odour.

‘I can’t stand any more!’ Ginny rushed from the room, clutching her mouth.

The grey-haired lady, a Mrs Burbage Kingsley was informed, seemed unaware of the pathos of her predicament.

‘There doesn’t seem to be any loo roll.’

Kingsley rubbed his forehead. ‘Fisher, go and get one of the stockroom lads to bring a trolley and a sheet.’

Five minutes later, Mrs Burbage and the lime green toilet were together loaded onto a cargo lift and transported out of sight, the trolley beeping its progress.

‘You’ve all been very helpful,’ Mrs Burbage called out to Kingsley and the other staff as she disappeared around the corner. ‘Thank you most kindly.’

‘What do we do with the gap?’ asked Finch.

Kingsley slid the red toilet bowl standing on its own at the end to join with the others.

‘Didn’t know you were an artist, Howard.’

Kingsley gave his deputy a look and walked off.

28

'ARE YOU READY?' asked Fisher Bayley.

Following the episode in Snap, Ginny had been somewhat distant. Only to be expected, Fisher supposed, having had to wash his sick out of her hair. Ginny answered his question with another.

'Notice anything different?'

Fisher ran his eyes hastily up and down her.

'Your hair, you've had it cut. Looks nice, suits your –'

'Not me, the room.'

'Oh.'

It was early evening, and the exhibition was closed for the day. They were in one of the castle's permanent galleries, where paintings and sculptures sat behind glass-fronted walls, an archway at one end leading through to another, similar room.

'Looks the same as normal, doesn't it?'

Ginny shook her head. 'Two more of our most important paintings have been taken. It must be the same men that took the Cotman. Howard told me on no account to let them take anything else, but they must have come when I wasn't here. Why didn't they check with me first? What's Howard going to say?'

Ginny looked as close to tears as Fisher had ever seen her.

They left the castle and headed towards Fisher's car. Autumn had properly set in, and the silver Golf had a fair covering of red and gold leaves. He tried to reassure her.

'You said these men had all the right paperwork last time,

so they will have this time. You just didn't happen to be there when they came. Howard can't blame you for that. These blokes should have made an appointment.'

'I wouldn't be worried so much,' said Ginny, climbing into the passenger seat, 'but the two paintings they've taken are even more valuable than the Cotman.'

'What were they?'

Ginny stared forward out of the windscreen. 'A Rembrandt and a Crome.'

29

Brian Finch was troubled. He kept telling himself it was mere coincidence, but experience had taught him that coincidences were seldom simply just that.

He had rung security and spoken to Barry Cleaver, requesting he find Ian Chapman as soon as possible and send him to his laboratory – his lunch break would have to wait.

The door opened. Chapman was accompanied by Bayley, who had assumed he too was needed. Finch apologised for the misunderstanding, but allowed Bayley to stay while he questioned Chapman about the priest's dagger. Bayley sat down at the work bench to one side of the Deputy Curator, while Chapman sat the other. Bayley could sense Finch's unease.

'Everything okay?' he asked.

Finch nodded meaninglessly. In front of him lay a blank card. His laptop was open, several document tabs ready. 'Why don't we start with the thread?' he began enigmatically.

Chapman was at a loss. 'Er – what thread is that, Brian?'

'Sorry, I'm not explaining myself. It's all I've been thinking about. I mean the thread on the dagger, caught in the hilt. Remember it?'

Bayley and Chapman confirmed they did indeed remember, as Finch maximised one of the documents on his screen.

'Well,' continued Finch, 'it turned out to be silk, blue silk. The quality normally used for detailing on clothes – motifs, that sort of thing. Possibly lingerie.' He looked at Chapman.

‘The dagger wasn’t wiped on a shirt or something, was it? Last time it was cleaned?’

‘Or your thong,’ added Bayley, which earned him a sharp glance from Finch.

Chapman was adamant he had done no such thing, and Finch saw no reason not to believe him.

‘That’s what I thought.’ He gave a small sigh. ‘I can’t see how the thread got there, then. Anyway, never mind that for now. What I’m more concerned about is this.’

He brought up another document.

Bayley peered at the screen, running his eyes down the different sections of a table, trying to pick out key phrases. Near the end of the form, a box containing only one word caught his attention.

Blood

‘Blood!’ Bayley and Chapman spoke at the same time.

‘Blood,’ confirmed Finch. ‘That’s what was causing the stains on the blade. Obviously, it shouldn’t have been there.’ He looked at Chapman. ‘Can you explain why it was?’

Chapman stared at the screen, trying to think back to when he’d last cleaned the knife, several months previously.

‘Maybe you cut yourself on it?’ Bayley suggested. ‘Or had a nosebleed?’

Chapman shook his head. ‘I’d remember something like that. And I would have cleaned it again. Anyway, the blade isn’t sharp enough to cut through skin. Not unless you really tried.’

Finch agreed. ‘Or,’ he added, ‘did you already have a cut? On your hands, maybe?’

‘But I always wear gloves.’

‘Ah, of course,’ said Finch, though he didn’t seem in any way reassured.

Chapman didn’t share the Deputy Curator’s concern.

'Does it really matter how the blood got there, Brian? Is there any permanent damage?'

'No.'

'Then I'll just make sure I'm extra careful next time. Maybe I did have a cut.'

'Maybe. But there's still one question I want answering.'

*

'Howard, I'm glad you're here,' said Ginny, not sounding as if she meant it.

She was stood in the gallery next to where Cotman's *The Baggage Wagon* should have been. A lesser work hung in its place, though its depiction of the Cathedral cloisters was attractive enough.

'Another two paintings have gone. I had no idea those two men from –'

'A Rembrandt and a Crome?'

'You know about it. Thank God.'

'I should apologise, I meant to come and speak to you. I've decided to go ahead with the virtual reality pilot we talked about at the meeting.'

Ginny looked disbelieving. 'Really? I thought you were dead against it?'

'I was, but I've thought about it some more, and I think we should hold off judgement until we see the results.'

'Oh.' Ginny had been in favour of the experiment anyway – the idea of a virtual gallery quite excited her. 'I think that makes sense. How long before they send us one of the 3D versions to look at?'

'Difficult to say. I was told a few months, but we'll see. I offered a few more paintings too, so don't worry if you notice them gone. Anyway, enough of that. How's the exhibition going? No more hiccups?'

The modern art exhibition Ginny had organised was

proving to be a big success.

'We've got record visitor numbers, and no more trouble with the toilets, you'll be pleased to hear.'

'Excellent.'

'One of the penguin heads did fall off. I only got it stuck back on by leaning it against another penguin – looks like they're kissing. Someone said it contrasted with the alienation in society – I didn't have the heart to tell them it was just the wrong sort of glue.'

*

Finch pressed the return key. The laptop's screen faded, leaving behind only a revolving egg timer, which tracked slowly to the edge, where, trapped, it changed direction. 'It might take a while, it's a large database.'

'You still haven't said why you think there might be a match,' insisted Chapman. 'What's the coincidence?'

'Let's see if I'm right first.'

Bayley had his own thoughts about why Finch might be running the blood's DNA through a police database. Was someone who worked here known to the police? Someone who had handled the dagger without the Deputy Curator's knowledge? If they had a criminal record, was there a chance they might be planning to steal it? The dagger was, after all, extremely valuable.

They waited in silence. Finch seemed unusually fidgety, as if dreading the outcome. Finally, the computer bleeped, and the egg timer vanished. A row of header data appeared, confirming the source as the blood sample, and the search parameters. Underneath this was a grey box, filled in with neatly arranged text. Bayley and Chapman leaned forward.

'You were right!' exclaimed Chapman. 'It has found a match.'

Bayley re-scanned the screen. 'Does it give a name? Is it someone who works here?'

Finch ignored him. For some reason he looked nervous.

'Read me the ID number in the top left.' He touched the screen to indicate the number he was referring to, then picked up the card lying in front of him, turning it over to look at what was written on the other side.

Chapman called out the digits. 'One, zero, three, four, nine, eight, eight, double zero three.' He scrolled down the page. 'No name, though. Is that normal?'

Finch was pale. He took a moment to answer. 'Only if the person is unknown.'

Bayley was confused. 'So what have we found, then?'

'Do you recognise this?'

Finch dropped the card he was holding onto the bench. It was the tag normally tied to the ribcage, neatly summarising what was known about it, including the number Chapman had just read out. The number generated when Finch had run its DNA through the same police database.

'I still don't... that doesn't make any sense.'

'No, Fisher, it makes no sense whatsoever. Not until you accept our young woman from Europe never had an accident after all.'

The realisation of what Finch meant by this stunned Bayley.

'Are you saying...?'

'That's right. She was murdered. And we've just found the weapon.'

PART II

There is no fortress so strong that money cannot take it.

Marcus Tullius Cicero, *Ad familiares*

30

Superintendent Frank Drake waved impatiently at Inspector Morello to sit down. Pacing behind his desk, he smiled thinly into a cordless phone, his pasty and heavily fleshed face like a peeled spud.

'That's right, Fergie. Don't forget to say who's running it... no problem. Thought you might appreciate being one step ahead of the nationals. Absolutely. Right, I'd better go, duty calls and all that…yes, I'll be there. See you then.' Drake put down the phone, the Masonic emblem on his cufflinks clearly visible.

Morello had no time for senior officers with a hunger for media attention, particularly when they stopped him from getting on with his job. He was anxious to get over to the castle as soon as possible.

'You got my message,' said the Superintendent matter-of-factly, looking at his newest recruit with mild hostility.

'Yes sir.'

Why Drake had wanted to see Morello again, so soon after their briefing together the previous evening, hadn't been a part of the message. But Morello was learning not to expect any of the usual courtesies from this boss. Fortunately, so rumour had it, Drake intended to retire at the earliest possible opportunity, which wouldn't be long, judging by the deep lines and tufts of grey sprouting from his nose.

'I've talked with the Chief. Now this castle affair's become a murder inquiry, she was concerned you had too little experience to head it up. I persuaded her otherwise.'

‘Thank you sir.’

‘I’d save your thanks, if I were you. I want a result.’

‘I understand.’

‘Your deputy is Sergeant Robbins. He’ll sort you out a team. Find his desk and get him up to speed.’

‘I will sir – is that all?’

‘For now. Keep me up to date – I want a daily report, nine sharp.’ Drake eyed Morello coldly. ‘This is your chance to show us why they made you Inspector, eh? Well, what are you waiting for? Move it!’

Morello jumped up. ‘Sir.’

Descending the staircase from the Superintendent’s office, Morello was perfectly clear on why Drake had persuaded the Chief not to replace him with someone more senior. The case was going to be a difficult one, and if anyone was going to fall flat on their face, Drake would rather it was him.

*

‘So from what you’ve said, anyone could have got in, if they knew where to find the key?’

Morello was irritated by this lack of even the most basic of precautions. The Egyptian display next to which he and Kingsley were standing contained dozens of artefacts, all of which were irreplaceable. And yet one of the keys to the only lock protecting them was left hanging on a hook in the staff lounge. It could have been taken and returned without so much as a signature. The other keys were held by the Curator, his deputy, and the security desk.

‘That’s right, I’m afraid,’ said Kingsley. ‘It’s always been like that. We’ve never had an issue before, not until now.’

Kingsley smiled apologetically, producing a handkerchief and wiping his nose, though there seemed no need. Displacement behaviour, thought Morello – something to do at a time of stress. And being told an apparent accident had become a murder investigation was definitely one such time. Added to which, inside the display that morning, dressed in what looked like surgical attire, a photographer and three Scene of Crime Officers were going about their business, examining the room and all its contents with minute precision. Kingsley had asked to join them, but the display was now a crime scene, as was the area immediately surrounding the well, also cordoned off until further notice.

'Not likely to have been a visitor though,' Morello thought out loud. 'More likely one of the staff.'

'Staff?' Kingsley looked stricken. 'Impossible.'

'Why do you say that?'

'Well – it just is. Only Brian and I ever go in there. Sometimes Ian.'

'I'll need to interview everyone again. And if you wouldn't mind speaking to my Sergeant, we'll need to set up an incident room. Anywhere you can squeeze us in will be fine.'

'Inspector! You can't ask my staff if they're murderers!'

'I won't be quite so blunt, Mr Kingsley. It might help if you could tell me now anything that might be of interest.'

'I'm not sure I understand.'

'Have any of your colleagues been acting in an unusual manner? Is there anything different about anyone, anything that stands out? Anything at all?'

'No. No, I'm sure not.'

'What about the victim? Has anybody worked here who would fit their description?'

Kingsley shook his head. 'Inspector, this is ridiculous. Why would anyone here want to kill anybody?'

'The victim was a young woman, Mr Kingsley. More often than not, that's motive enough.'

*

Having dismissed Kingsley, reminding him at the same time

of the need for himself and all other staff directly involved to keep their knowledge of the case confidential, Morello watched the SOCOs inside the display. He had already seen to it that the dagger, blood samples, and the ribcage itself, along with other evidence found by Finch, were moved to a police forensic laboratory. He'd also ordered further tests on the steel scrapings embedded in the bone. Mounted fragments of silk thread, metal, and blood, he allowed to remain at the castle, so that Finch could be called upon if necessary to provide additional forensic support.

There was still the problem of the victim's identity, he thought, without which progress would be difficult. To that end, he'd arranged for Sergeant Tom Lomax and his team to return to the well, much to the delight of the Deputy Curator, Brian Finch.

Finch had provided him with a useful timeframe – seven months since the dagger had last been cleaned. Together with the victim's age and gender, he had enough information to make it worthwhile sifting through the missing persons list, though his hopes were low, the victim being in all likelihood a foreign national. Another problem was that without a precise time and date of death, ruling any potential suspect in or out based on any alibi wouldn't be possible. It was going to be a struggle to get a result. Footsteps brought him out of his reverie. It was his deputy, Detective Sergeant Grant Robbins, who had been directing a second Scene of Crime team at the well. He seemed a quiet man, not yet thirty, well built, with a shaved head and thoughtful eyes.

'Any progress, sir?'

Just then one of the SOCOs stepped out of the display room next to them. Her two colleagues and the photographer were packing their equipment.

'That's everything we need, sir.'

'Anything interesting?' asked Morello.

'Plenty of prints, but not many are clean. Dust samples

might have some organic matter in them, but don't let me raise your hopes.'

Contamination would be even worse around the well, thought Morello.

'And no sacrificial blood,' she grinned at him.

'That's a relief,' replied Morello drily. 'Okay, if we find another site, I'll let you know. We can't search the whole castle.'

The SOCO re-entered the display to help pack the equipment.

Morello turned to his deputy.

'Seems our killer was quite a risk taker.'

'How so, sir?'

'Using this dagger. Could have easily been spotted taking it. Then they took another risk putting it back, so it wouldn't be missed – or suspected, if the body was found.'

'See what you mean.'

'Why go to the trouble? Any knife would do.'

'Maybe it was spur of the moment. Act of passion – didn't think.'

'Possible. My next question is, where might this act of passion have taken place? Has to be inside the castle.' Morello believed it unlikely the murder was committed outside the building, given the murder weapon. The logistics involved made no sense.

'You don't think in there?' Robbins nodded towards the display room.

'Helpful if it was. Thing is, wherever it happened, the killer would still have had to get the body to the well and then open the grille. Meaning a second key. And without being seen.'

'Unless it was at night.'

'Good point. That's a very good point. All of which makes me think our killer must be someone who works here.'

'Almost set himself up, hasn't he? Could have used any

knife, dumped the body anywhere. Instead he chooses his own backyard.'

'Know what puzzles me most, Sergeant?'

'Sir?'

'The Curator's right. I've already interviewed the staff once, and in my entire career, I've never come across such an unlikely group of suspects.'

31

THE SOCOs SERGEANT Robbins had instructed had had little luck. In the underground chamber attached to the well, the grille that secured the opening to the shaft was covered in countless fingerprints, including those of the journalists who had got there before them. Which also meant that a meaningful DNA hit would be impossible. Morello and Robbins climbed back to the Great Hall, busy with tourists.

'Inspector!' a voice called out. It was the Curator. 'I've found you some space. The office next to the cafeteria's not being used.'

'Thank you, Mr Kingsley. That's much appreciated.'

'I'll have a desk put in. Are you off?'

'I think so. Paperwork doesn't write itself, unfortunately. We'll set up tomorrow.' Morello could see Kingsley had something on his mind. 'Was there anything else?'

'I... there is. I hardly like to mention it, but you said if I were to think of anything...'

'I did. Fire away. Don't worry if it seems insignificant.'

'Okay. Well. One thing did occur to me.'

The Curator seemed reticent to go on.

'And what was that?'

Kingsley looked embarrassed. 'The sarcophagus,' he said.

'You think the killer used it in some way?'

Morello hoped he wasn't looking for a ritualistic murderer. They were notoriously difficult to catch.

'Not used it,' Kingsley explained. 'Is it.'

'Is – what?'

‘The legend of Ankh Hor,’ whispered Kingsley.

‘The legend of…’ Morello understood. He indicated to Robbins that he would explain later.

‘Mr Kingsley, this is a murder inquiry. Stories about mummified bodies roaming the castle are best kept for the tourists.’

‘But –’

‘I’m not disputing whether the legend is true. Shall we just say, the priest is low on my list of suspects.’

‘Works here though, doesn’t he?’ said Robbins innocently.

Morello smiled.

‘Makes as much sense as anything,’ the Curator insisted.

32

Staring unseeingly from the window of his business office, across to Whitlingham Park, Harry Scarfe clenched his hands, anger threatening to get the better of him.

What had started as a non-event had become a full-blown murder inquiry, and at a time when he needed to be focusing his energies on his election campaign. Polling day was looming near.

Thank Christ, he thought, he hadn't touched anything in that Egyptian room, except the dagger of course, which Kingsley had wiped clean. Why that arsehole Finch had been giving it the once-over in the first place was a mystery. Now the police believed it to be the murder weapon they suspected one of the castle staff, as he had threatened Kingsley they would.

His insurance had crumbled into nothing more than a bluff, and now it had been called.

On top of that, with the return of the police divers, there was every chance some other piece of evidence might be found inside the well, something to directly incriminate him, though he couldn't imagine what. But forensics were clever bastards these days – look at all the trouble they'd caused already.

Scarfe decided he needed to keep himself as close as possible to what was going on, which meant being in frequent contact with Superintendent Frank Drake. And if Drake suspected his motives, so what? The Superintendent had been on his payroll too many times to start talking now.

But far more urgently, he had to double-check his contingency plan was ready still to be put into action, if necessary at very short notice.

Using the pay-as-you-go mobile phone he had bought for the purpose, Scarfe thumbed in a number.

'Yes?' answered a voice.

'Doyle, it's me.'

'Thought it might be – saw the papers. Am I back on for Spain?'

33

The darkness was absolute. He switched on his torch. The roughly hewn passage that led away from the chamber to the well was starting to become familiar. A distant sound echoed faintly about him, and he froze. After a moment, having heard nothing more except for the ceaseless dripping, he continued towards one of the storerooms, some one hundred yards ahead. It was the only storeroom still with a lock. Maybe the sound was rats.

Reaching the door, Kingsley carefully put down the parcel under his arm, sealed in plastic. The large bunch of keys he carried clanged noisily on their ring, two modern Yale-types mixed incongruously with blackened steel. Choosing the Yale marked with a small blob of red paint, he unlocked the door and pushed it slowly open, leaving the bunch dangling from the lock.

Inside was a large room, several other parcels similar to the one he was carrying stacked in one corner. He walked over and placed the new addition next to them. Another Crome. The floor and walls were slippery, damp from the flooding caused by the well. It was a risk leaving the paintings here, no matter how well he sealed them, but a risk Kingsley felt he had to take. As he stood up, another noise made him pause, sounding nearer than before. He listened intently. Nothing but silence.

Closing the door, he turned the key again, locking the parcels in the room. The only known key, he thought with satisfaction. Returning to the well chamber, he switched off his torch and climbed back up to the Great Hall. He began to breathe freely again. Another success.

*

As Kingsley made for one of the side exits to the castle and out into the cold November night, far beneath his feet a hand reached out. It pushed against the door protecting the parcels. The door remained firm. The small square cut into it, crossed with three metal bars, didn't allow for a view of the whole room. Doyle considered picking the lock, easy enough for him, but there seemed little point. Instead he turned away, not following Kingsley this time but moving off in the opposite direction, while the map given him by Scarfe remained folded in his pocket. The Private Investigator was familiar enough now with his route not to need it.

34

Fisher Bayley was glad of Jane Meadows' company. They had been in the tunnels now for nearly an hour, and he was beginning to worry they might never find their way back out.

As part of the murder investigation, police divers were once again searching the well. Their activities had already caused it to rise and fall several times more, which seemed to have distressed Kingsley almost as much as the first time it had flooded. Rather than the public dungeons, however, this time the Curator seemed far more worried about the effect this might be having on the tunnel that led from the well, seeming to believe it might disappear altogether underwater. His concern made little sense to Bayley. No one ever came here, and there was nothing much to see if they did. Nevertheless, armed with a faded map, compass, and chalk, Kingsley had sent him to take a look at least twice a day, and it was getting tedious.

The only thing Bayley found of interest about his task was the chart Kingsley had given him. It showed an underground maze, linking a whole host of buildings around the centre of Norwich. As if anticipating his curiosity, Kingsley had expressly instructed Bayley not to stray beyond the area he had marked out for him on the map. In the spirit of adventure Bayley had decided to ignore those instructions, and had persuaded Jane to join him in trying to reach one of the buildings shown. There was no way Ginny would have gone along with it. But their initial excitement was beginning to turn sour. If they were lost...

'I'm not sure that last bend we counted was a bend,' said Jane.

'You could be right,' Fisher agreed. 'We've definitely passed three tunnels on the left though. Wait a minute!'

Up ahead, the passageway began to climb. The map had been accurate after all.

Putting on a spurt, he and Jane scrambled up the slope, where the floor suddenly became drier. They came to a door.

'This must be it!' said Fisher excitedly.

A large bolt seemed to be all that was holding the door in place. Fisher began to slide it open.

'Stop!' whispered Jane, her hand on his. Fisher tingled at the touch.

'What is it?'

'We don't know what's on the other side.'

'It should be –'

'I don't mean that – I mean, what if there are people?'

Fisher realised Jane was right. To anyone who saw them, it could appear as if they were trying to break in. But after coming all this way, he had to know what was there.

'Go on then,' said Jane. 'But be quiet.'

With the bolt fully retracted into its housing, Fisher pulled gently on it, there being no handle. The door moved, then cracked loudly. Loud enough to attract the attention of anyone standing the other side.

'Close it!'

Fisher did, wincing as it made the same cracking noise. He just managed to force the bolt home before Jane grabbed his hand and they raced off, back the way they'd come.

The chalk marks they had left behind gave them enough confidence to move faster, though twice they had to splash through several inches of water that hadn't been there earlier, slowing them down. Even so, in less than thirty minutes they were back at the well again, no one in pursuit.

In the tiny office he and Jane shared, Fisher folded up the

chart and tucked it safely once more into his drawer, before rushing off to find Kingsley. When he returned, Jane had reopened the map and had it spread on her desk.

'How was Howard?' she asked him.

'Doing his nut. Wanted to know why I'd been so long.'

'He's always doing his nut these days.'

'Where do you fancy next, then?'

'On here? I don't, to be honest. Howard was right, wasn't he? About there still being flooding. And I was just checking. The tunnel we took was fairly straightforward, same one pretty much all the way. These other places, you've got to branch off to get to them. Far too dangerous.'

Fisher glowed with reckless optimism.

'If we can find City Hall, I bet we can find anywhere.'

35

It was Monday morning, and Inspector Morello had chosen to interview the staff most closely linked to the ribcage himself, tasking Sergeant Robbins to begin working his way through the others.

Kingsley had had little to say he hadn't already heard, also repeating his fanciful speculation regarding the legend of Ankh Hor. Morello decided the next time Drake pissed him off (the next time he saw him, then, he thought to himself), he might bring up the theory.

A head popped round the door.

'Morning, Inspector. Ready for me?'

'Yes, Mr Finch. Take a seat.'

Morello didn't expect to learn anything new from Finch either.

'Before we start, Inspector, I've been meaning to mention something. Might be of interest, might not. Coincidence, I suppose you would call it.'

Morello's attention was always drawn by the word coincidence.

'Go on.'

'It's about where the victim came from – you remember my report?' Morello nodded. 'As it so happens, some of our students, the Scarfe scholarships, come from that same part of the world. Perhaps Howard has already mentioned it?'

Morello's gaze sharpened.

'No, Mr Finch. No he has not.'

After Finch had left, Morello recalled a story one of his

mentors had told him while still at Hendon College. It was about a fourteenth-century Friar called William of Ockham, and an idea credited to him that had since become known as Occam's Razor. It boiled down to a single principle, one that had helped him on numerous investigations – that simple explanations were preferable to complex ones. He intended to apply that same principle to what Finch had just told him. Why Kingsley hadn't mentioned these scholarship students, and whether that was significant, he wasn't sure.

A knock on the door interrupted his thoughts. It was Fisher Bayley.

'Make yourself comfortable, Mr Bayley.'

He would make this the last interview today. For the first time, he felt he had something to go on, and was impatient to make a start. Flicking through his paperwork again, he surmised Bayley was unlikely to provide any more information than he had the first time he'd interviewed him. He had been, after all, only an observer in Finch's laboratory.

For the second time that morning, Morello was to be proved wrong.

After going through Bayley's background checks with him and asking a few other questions, Morello could see nothing more to be gained. He reminded Bayley of his obligation not to discuss the forensic details he was party to with anyone else.

'I understand,' Bayley replied. He got up to leave, then hesitated.

'Was there something else?' Morello asked.

'It's something I overheard, it keeps coming back to me.'

Leaving out the more embarrassing details, Bayley explained as well as he could remember the conversation he had inadvertently listened to the evening he and Ginny had been occupied inside Snap the Dragon.

' "They can blame Ankh Hor"?' repeated Morello slowly. He couldn't seem to get away from the dead priest. And there was Scarfe's name again, a name he recognised from TV. Why would he be discussing with Kingsley the Curator's ridiculous theory about the mummified remains? Not only that, thought Morello, but discussing it *before* the dagger had been discovered. He was even more keen now to make contact with Kingsley's scholarship students.

'I didn't think any more about it at the time,' finished Bayley, 'but after what's happened... Strange thing to say, don't you think?'

36

Detective Inspector Felix Morello's parents had settled in England from Italy during the nineteen-sixties. It was a time when Britain had held a strong appeal for a twenty-something couple with little prospect of work in their home village.

Antonio and Adrienne Morello had tried to fit in with their adopted country as best they could. They attended language classes, naming their son Felix after a character in one of the books they were given to study. Morello knew this name made him stand out rather than blend in, but had become used to the expressions of amusement that usually followed his introduction.

Not long after Morello had joined the police force, his parents had moved back to Italy, both now at an age where they appreciated the slower pace of life. But plenty more ambitious young people from all over the world were ready to take their place, many choosing the University of Norwich as their ultimate destination. One such person sat before Morello now, in one of the University's lecture theatres, empty that Monday afternoon except for the two of them.

Kirsten Turnik was a very attractive girl. Long dark hair, wide brown eyes, and with a slight pout that some might have found suggestive. Morello tried to disregard all this as he began his questioning.

'I understand there are five of you, all here on the same scholarship. Is that correct?'

Kirsten tucked a stray lock of hair behind one ear. Her

English was excellent, with an accent that served only to add to her beguiling beauty.

'That is true. We didn't know each other before we came, of course.'

'Of course. Your Dean tells me that two of your friends are suspended for non-attendance. Do you know anything about that?'

For the first time, Kirsten looked apprehensive.

'You won't be getting them into trouble,' Morello reassured her. 'It might be useful for me to talk to them, that's all.' He didn't elaborate.

'They are not in trouble?'

Morello shook his head.

'Okay, I tell you. Sonia, she is working. I'm not sure where, she tells me on the phone. I haven't seen her for many months. I don't think she is coming back.'

'I see. And the other one?

'Odette. I haven't seen her either, not for a long time. I don't know what she is doing. Maybe she went home. It is easy to get homesick. I nearly went back myself, when we first came. She was a funny girl though, if you know what I mean?'

'How so?'

'She liked men, very much.'

'Any man in particular?'

'That was the problem. She liked lots of men, even the one who paid for us. Not pleasant to see a woman with a man so much older. Anneka wasn't much better. Sometimes the gap can be too big, don't you think?'

'The one who paid for you? Do you mean Mr Harry Scarfe?'

'Yes, that is the one.'

'Am I to understand Miss Novad had a – relationship, with this man?'

'This is right. She said they were going to live together,

but I don't know how serious she was. He did give her lots of presents though. Expensive jewellery.' Kirsten's eyes grew wider. 'Very nice earrings. Real diamond.'

Morello stared at Kirsten Turnik. So Scarfe and one of his scholarship students had been having an affair. He'd watched Scarfe on the local news, overplaying the family values card – what politician didn't? If his affair had turned sour... or he'd become worried he might be found out... It would give him motive, right there. The coincidences surrounding Scarfe and the victim's identity were mounting.

'That's very helpful, thank you.'

'There is another man I remember, but different this time. I liked him too, but Odette... she was always so fast.'

'What was special about him?'

'Nothing, really. It's just I still see him sometimes, when I go to the castle for lectures.'

Kingsley's lectures, thought Morello. For a moment, he didn't know what to believe.

'Can you tell me his name?'

'Of course – Fisher. Not such an easy name to forget, do you think?'

*

Morello drove slowly down the long drive that led away from the University campus, stopping as he reached the main road. The afternoon traffic was heavy. After several minutes he gave an exasperated stab on the accelerator pedal, joining the steady stream of cars that slowed reluctantly to accommodate him.

Beside him on the passenger seat was a short list, provided by the University's HR department. On it were the names and personal details of the two missing students, Sonia Arman and Odette Novad. Two leads to follow up, thought Morello, though if what Kirsten Turnik had told him proved to be true, it was Odette who interested him most.

And while it appeared that both Harry Scarfe and Fisher Bayley had been on intimate terms with her, if she was his victim, and he could prove it, then he knew who he would be treating as his main suspect.

37

'COME.'

The following morning, Inspector Morello opened the door to Superintendent Drake's office with little enthusiasm. It wasn't a place he enjoyed being. To his surprise, Drake already had company, someone he recognised but couldn't place. A short, strong looking man, hair slicked back greasily over his head.

'You're early,' remarked Drake. 'Let me introduce you. This is Councillor Scarfe.'

Of course, realised Morello. Looked different on TV. But why of all people was he here? Something didn't feel right. He shook hands as casually as he could, holding the Councillor's eye.

'I'm Inspector Morello. Would that be Councillor Harry Scarfe? Running in the by-election?'

Scarfe seemed pleased to be recognised.

'That's right. Seen my campaign, have you?'

'You were on Look East.'

Beneath the easy charm, Morello sensed a hardness about the Councillor. He was a man it would be unwise to get on the wrong side of.

'Take a look at this, Inspector.' Scarfe ushered Morello over to the window.

The Superintendent's office was on the top floor of one wing of City Hall, facing out towards the Forum. Between the library and St Peter Mancroft Church, Morello had an excellent view of the excavation for the Norwich Eye.

'Being built by Scarfe Industries – that's me. Not long now before it's ready. What do you think?'

Morello had read about the huge wheel being erected on Millennium Plain. It seemed a cramped spot for such a large machine.

'I imagine you'll get a great view from the top,' he offered diplomatically.

'Course you will, that's the point, isn't it!' exclaimed Scarfe jovially, slapping Morello on the shoulders. 'I'll see to it you get a ticket for the opening ride.'

'That would be – quite an experience.'

There was something contrived about the way Scarfe talked, as if he were giving a performance or selling something. Whatever it was, thought Morello, he wasn't buying.

The Councillor gave an oily smile. 'Well, I can't stand here chatting. Work to be done, and all that. Good to meet you, Inspector.' Scarfe shook Morello's hand again. 'And good luck with your murder. You look a bright fellow, I'm sure it won't be long before we get an arrest.'

Morello didn't recall himself or Drake mentioning why he was there – not while he had been in the room, anyway. But judging by the Councillor's handshake, he and the Superintendent had few secrets from each other. Given the direction his investigation was leading him in, he needed to be very careful about what he said.

After Scarfe had left, Superintendent Drake sat down, his tone changing abruptly.

'Robbins tells me you were up at the University yesterday. What have you got?'

'Possible lead on the victim's ID, sir.'

'Possible lead. *Possible.* Nothing else? Do we have a suspect?'

He'd been right, Morello thought to himself. The next time he saw Drake was the next time Drake would piss him off. Time then for Kingsley's theory and a little winding-up of his own.

'One possibility has come up, sir, but...'

'But what? Don't dither man, get on with it.'

Morello explained as sincerely as he could the legend of Ankh Hor, watching the Superintendent's astonishment grow, until finally it turned to suppressed fury.

'Let me get this straight. Are you suggesting the victim came over here to study, but instead was attacked by a homicidal priest meant to have been dead ten thousand years?'

The vein on Drake's temple was raised.

'Three thousand, I believe Kingsley said it was.'

'Morello!' shouted the Superintendent, standing up and leaning over his desk towards him. 'You are severely testing my patience! Three thousand, ten thousand, it doesn't make any difference, does it? What do you think the papers are going to say if I tell them our main suspect is wrapped head to toe in bandages and helped build the Pyramids? As well as the more obvious disadvantage that he is fucking-well dead!'

Superintendent Drake slumped backwards, wiping his forehead.

Morello decided he had pushed his luck far enough.

'Sorry, sir. Just thought I'd mention it so you're aware.'

Drake looked ready to renew his attack, so Morello moved promptly on.

'One of the lab reports came in this morning. We found a set of prints close to the dagger.'

'And?'

'We know who the prints belong to, and they shouldn't be there.'

'Have you questioned this person?' asked the Superintendent, squeezing a penholder on his desk.

Therapeutic maybe, thought Morello.

'I'm waiting on other enquiries to come back first. Soon as

I do, I'll update you in my report.'

The subject of fingerprints seemed to have calmed Drake down – traditional police work.

'Make sure you do, Inspector.'

'Sir.'

*

The Superintendent watched Morello leave, an ugly expression on his face. *Mummified priests.* He'd make sure that came back to bite the Inspector, and hard. Though it occurred to Drake he needed to be careful. If he gave Morello too much rope from which to hang, there might be enough left over for himself.

38

It had been the best possible news. Even Superintendent Frank Drake hadn't been able to hide his approval.

Sergeant Robbins crossed the canteen, joining Inspector Morello in the far corner.

'Here's your sandwich, sir,' he said, putting down a tray on the table.

Morello took a bite. Swiss cheese was his favourite.

Robbins sat down opposite, only salad and a skinny latte for lunch. His wife had been getting on to him about his weight.

Interpol had been remarkably efficient. Morello had requested that DNA tests be carried out on the parents of both Sonia Arman and Odette Novad only on the Monday, and by Friday morning the same week, today, the results had come back. What they showed was the biggest development of the case so far. With near certainty, Morello now knew the victim's identity – Odette Novad, a young woman from Petrova, in England less than six months and on a scholarship paid for by Councillor Harry Scarfe.

Not only that, the latest forensic report, also given to Morello earlier that day, had provided a solution to the problem that had been worrying him ever since his interview with Kirsten Turnik. Lying on the table next to his plate, Morello patted it with one hand, hoping that Robbins would agree with him its significance.

'This changes everything, Grant. Kitchen knives are a lot easier to come by than Egyptian daggers.'

‘Cheaper too.’

The report had concluded that the other metal fragments found embedded in the ribcage were stainless steel, of a type made with nineteen percent chromium. The same type, apparently, as that most commonly used in the manufacture of cutlery and kitchen knives – the sort of weapon everyone had access to. Morello had never been entirely happy with Finch’s assertion that the steel fragments must have come from medieval debris littering the well floor. The Deputy Curator had seen what he’d wanted to see, but it had been his own mistake to have allowed Finch to convince him too.

‘Very droll. What it gives us is the possibility that our killer wasn’t a castle employee, and that the murder didn’t happen there. The well would have seemed like a good place to hide the body, that’s all.’

Robbins munched discontentedly on a mouthful of leaves and grated carrot.

‘If that’s true, they still had to get the body into the castle.’

‘You’re right, which is why I think the killer must have had an accomplice. Someone who *did* work at the castle, and could let them in when no one was around. Maybe the night the security guard heard a noise.’

‘He was very vague, wouldn’t swear to it.’ Robbins frowned, not won over. ‘I can see the well looking like a good place to dump a body, but an accomplice, inside the castle? How would anyone there know a murderer, let alone want to help them? And what about the dagger? If the girl was already stabbed with a kitchen knife, why stab her again? Doesn’t make sense.’

‘I’ve been thinking about that. I think the dagger was used to throw us off the scent.’

Robbins nodded slowly.‘If the dagger was the murder weapon, then we’d be bound to suspect someone who worked at the castle. I see that.’

‘A precaution to protect the real killer, just in case the

body were found. It all fits.'

'Fits what?'

Morello had been withholding some of Kirsten Turnik's testimony, waiting to hear back from Interpol. If the DNA results had been negative, his theory would have been dead in the water. Now, however, together with the forensic report, he felt he had a case, though before going any further he wanted the back up of his colleague.

'There's something else you need to know about our victim. She wasn't just a Scarfe scholarship student – she and Harry Scarfe were also having an affair.'

'Jesus – are you sure?'

'According to her friend Kirsten Turnik, yes. Paints a whole new picture, doesn't it?'

'Scarfe has got a bit of a reputation,' agreed Robbins. 'Jesus, the dirty bastard. He must be twice her age at least.' His expression suddenly froze as he registered the full implication of Turnik's allegation. 'Hold on – are you suggesting –'

Morello nodded. 'Fits with everything else we know, doesn't it?'

'Jesus sir, I'm not sure... Harry Scarfe?' Robbins looked uneasy. 'What about the accomplice, then? Who would that have been?'

'Someone who knew Scarfe. The same person who conveniently forgot to tell us that some of his students matched the profile of the victim, despite the fact he saw them every week. The same person Bayley overheard.'

It took a few seconds for Robbins to realise that this meant Howard Kingsley. Morello admitted he couldn't answer why Kingsley would have wanted to help Scarfe, or why he would have given him access to the dagger. Robbins sat back in his seat, having been hunched up over the table.

'Scarfe and Kingsley...' he repeated. 'You really think?'

'I've met Scarfe, up in Drake's office.' Morello noted Robbins lack of surprise at this coincidence. 'Gave the impression, if you locked him in a room with a pack of wolves, he'd come out wearing a fur coat.'

Robbins didn't disagree, but was still reluctant to give his support.

'I think we're going to need some hard evidence before we go upsetting Councillor Scarfe. He's got powerful friends.'

'Friends like Drake, you mean?'

Robbins looked uncomfortable. 'Just saying. You're going to need more than what we've got so far, a lot more, before we go anywhere near him. He's running for MP, for Christ's sake.'

'Maybe that's what pushed him. Turnik gave the impression that Odette took their affair very seriously. Maybe he didn't, and she threatened to go public, a risk he couldn't take.'

'We still don't have any hard evidence though, do we?'

Something about the Detective Sergeant's resistance to the idea of Scarfe and Kingsley's involvement reminded Morello that Robbins, like Scarfe himself, and Superintendent Drake, was also a Mason. Did they belong to the same Lodge? Possible – likely, even. Had Robbins been chosen as his deputy for a reason? To protect a Masonic brother, a duty to be put before all others? He made a quick reassessment of his position.

'Maybe I'm adding two and two and making five,' he said, as if doubting his own logic.

There was relief on Robbins face.

'Very possibly, sir. If we do turn up some real evidence, that's different, we can follow it up. At least that way we get to keep our jobs.'

'Makes sense. We'll put the idea on the back-burner, unless, as you say, something turns up.'

'Wise move, I hope you don't mind me saying, sir. And anyway, Bayley is the one we should be concentrating on.'

Robbins had a point, thought Morello. In many ways, Bayley presented the simplest solution. Not only did he work at the castle, he had known the victim intimately, and had yet to answer some awkward questions regarding evidence found by the Scene of Crime team. With an appointment at the castle at two, he would hear what Bayley had to say then. It couldn't be ignored either that Scarfe and Kingsley had first popped up on his radar together because of a conversation Bayley claimed to have overheard. Was he telling the truth? There was no doubt he needed to know more about Fisher Bayley than he currently did.

'You're right, Grant. He has to be top of our list.'

Robbins nodded, seemingly satisfied. He stood up and put his unfinished salad and Morello's empty plate back onto the tray, before carrying them over to a hatch by the serving counter.

As Morello watched him, he came to a decision. There were two investigations to pursue. One would be official, with Bayley as the main suspect. Bayley may yet prove to be guilty, though he had great difficulty in seeing him as a killer. What possible motive could he have had? Not that monsters always needed a motive, any more than their appearance gave away who they were inside.

Unofficially, he would dig deeper into the lives of Scarfe and Kingsley, to see what came up. Though he felt more confident of their guilt than Bayley's, as Robbins had made clear, it wouldn't be wise to make a mistake where Scarfe was concerned.

To do the digging, he would need some outside help – he didn't want Scarfe warned, and neither did he want to risk being taken off the case by Drake. The kind of help, then, that very few could provide, in fact only one man, a man he would trust with his life – Ronnie, a friend he had left behind in the Met.

'Ready for the castle?' asked Robbins, returning to where Morello sat.

Morello looked out of the window.

‘We’ll walk, shall we?’ he suggested.

‘Good idea. I can get some chips on the way.’

*

Leaning against the sink, Harry Scarfe’s reflection in the mirror was fragmented. Shards of glass lay on the bathroom floor from where he had punched it only a moment ago, right hand still bleeding.

His thoughts were racing.

The Inspector knew who she was. And when he came to realise the girl was known to Kingsley, as surely he would, then the link to himself would be made, if it hadn’t been already – those scholarships. He could easily play down the coincidence, shocked as anyone, but when the Inspector focused in on Kingsley, it would be a case of when he cracked, rather than if. Everything had become too messy, too unpredictable, the risks to himself too great.

Part of Scarfe’s anger stemmed from the fact that the decision he needed to make was being forced upon him, and the knowledge that he may be eliminating one risk only to be taking on another, potentially far more dangerous.

But what choice did he have? It all boiled down to one thing – either Kingsley suffered, or he would.

Scarfe looked again at his reflection, the parts of his face he could see.

It’s not going to be me, he thought.

He picked up the mobile phone from the vanity unit that ran along the wall, his pay-as-you-go, untraceable. As he punched in the number, the keys became smeared with his own blood.

Doyle answered immediately.

‘Yes?’

‘Do it,’ Scarfe ordered.

39

THE CASTLE'S LECTURE theatre was situated on the first floor, just off the central atrium. Howard Kingsley and Fisher Bayley were inside, discussing the layout of a PowerPoint presentation being projected onto a large white screen. Morello and Robbins walked between the theatre's plush blue seating, down the central aisle. Kingsley saw them approach.

'Inspector – Sergeant.'

'Afternoon, Mr Kingsley, Mr Bayley. You remember I called, to say we would be here at two?'

'Of course. Shall we go to my office?' Kingsley turned to Bayley. 'Do slides three to fifteen for now, then. We'll take a look at the rest later.'

'Actually, Mr Bayley, I'd appreciate it if you could join us too.' It suited Morello to interview both men together – it would appear less formal, take each off their guard. And he might learn something from the way they reacted with each other.

Bayley nodded amicably, leaving his notepad in the storage cupboard cum workspace masked behind one side of the screen.

In his office, Kingsley went through the motions of making drinks for the four of them, the radiator burbling as noisily as ever, the fluorescent strip light high above, softened by the myriad of colours refracted through the stained glass window.

'Thank you, Mr Kingsley,' said Morello, accepting a mug of coffee. 'Very kind.'

'You're welcome.' Kingsley took out his handkerchief and wiped his nose nervously. 'So, you said you wanted to see me, Inspector? I'm sure I've told you everything I can think of.'

'It's interesting you should say that. If I may, I'll come to your statement in a moment. First of all, Mr Bayley, there's something I need you to explain for me.'

'Okay. If I can help.'

There was nothing in Bayley's demeanour to suggest he was in any way concerned. He either had balls of steel, thought Morello, or he was innocent. For now, it suited him to treat Bayley as guilty.

'I've been led to believe that only Mr Kingsley and Mr Finch ever go into the Egyptian room.'

'And Ian Chapman, don't forget,' interrupted Kingsley. 'If Brian asks him to, of course.'

'And Mr Chapman,' continued Morello. 'So what I'd like to know is, why have we found your fingerprints in there?'

Bayley swallowed. 'Mine? Are you sure?'

'Quite sure.'

Morello was intrigued. He had clearly caught Bayley out. Now he appeared very worried indeed.

'I can't think.'

'We suggest you try,' said Robbins meaningfully.

'I – yes. Wait a minute. When I do think about it – I was with Ginny, and... I wanted to take a closer look, so I took the keys.'

'Ginny?'

'Ginny Carmen.'

'Our Art Curator,' added Kingsley.

'How does she come into it?'

'She doesn't, I just – she was there when I went in to take a look.'

'And Miss Carmen will verify that, will she?'

'Definitely. That's all it was.'

'Sergeant, would you mind...'

Robbins left to find Ginny Carmen.

Although uneasy about the sudden change in Bayley, Morello decided to move on. Corroborating his story would be easy enough. He focused his attention on Kingsley.

'In your statement, Mr Kingsley, you said you'd disclosed everything you knew that might be of help in the case. Are you still absolutely sure about that?'

Kingsley wiped his nose again. 'Positive.'

'You see, I'm finding that very difficult to believe. Bearing in mind what was known about the victim at the time.'

'I'm not sure...'

'A young woman, Eastern European, white? Does that description not remind you of anyone you know?'

Morello allowed the silence to intensify, before carrying on.

'Part of the group you lecture, they're from Eastern Europe, isn't that so?'

'Our scholarships...' Kingsley's voice cracked slightly. 'You're right. I'd forgotten. I only see them once a week.'

'You'd forgotten.'

'It just didn't occur to me. I'm sorry.'

'To me, Mr Kingsley, it seemed quite a coincidence. Too big a coincidence to ignore. So I followed it up. Two of your scholarship students haven't been attending for quite some time, have they?'

'I could check...'

'Mr Kingsley, you must have noticed. The University did. They suspended them. One of the two, Sonia Armen, is working somewhere, though I haven't been able to establish where. The other I could find no trace of.'

'Returned home?'

'That was a possibility. So I had Interpol look into it for me.'

The mention of Interpol had the desired effect. Kingsley paled, taking off his glasses and wiping them with his hanky.

If he was right, thought Morello, and Kingsley was the killer's accomplice, then there was every chance he could break him. A confession naming Scarfe as the murderer, as he strongly suspected him to be. All he had to do was pick his moment. Hopefully he would have more ammunition when Ronnie got back to him. That would be the time to strike.

'Was she there?' asked Bayley, his interest seemingly innocent.

'No, but her parents were. They gave a sample of DNA, which we had analysed.' Morello paused. 'It matched the ribcage.'

'Surely not!' exclaimed Kingsley.

Morello could see the Curator was suddenly frightened.

'A perfect match. Our victim, as it turns out, was from a small village outside Petrova. A young woman by the name of Odette Novad – her parents' only child.'

Now it was Bayley who looked stunned.

'That can't be!'

'I can understand why you say that, Mr Bayley, but unfortunately I have to inform you that the victim is indeed a woman you had a relationship with.'

Kingsley gaped at Bayley, who sat speechless.

At that moment, Robbins returned.

'Ah, Sergeant. What do you have for us?'

Robbins gave Bayley a hard look before replying.

'I've taken a quick statement from Miss Carmen, sir. I think you're going to find it answers everything.'

40

HARRY SCARFE RE-READ the email for the fifth time.

Someone who worked at the castle, someone called Fisher Bayley, was the Inspector's main suspect. Not only had his prints had been found inside the Egyptian room, he'd also had a relationship with Odette.

Slut, thought Scarfe.

His luck had returned. Using the gold dagger to ensure Kingsley's silence may have been a flawed idea, but it seemed to have proved very useful in implicating this Bayley instead. Not something he could possibly have anticipated. A born opportunist, fresh possibilities whirred through Scarfe's mind. An altogether less risky option than paying for Doyle to retire to Spain was now suddenly available. One where he needn't fear an investigation into Kingsley's apparent suicide, or worry that Doyle would return from the Costa Brava in a few years time asking for more money. With people like Doyle, the money always ran out. Superintendent Drake was a safer bet.

He had a choice.

Scarfe found his pay-as-you-go phone and hit the redial. No answer. He tried again. He must speak to Doyle right away.

Kingsley had a stay of execution.

*

Doyle approached the door, having waited until he was sure the two policemen had left.

This was it.

He didn't intend wasting any time, once he was done. There was no way of knowing how long it would be before the body was discovered. In an hour and a half, he was booked on a flight from Norwich Airport direct to Schiphol, his only luggage his ticket and passport, both safely zipped under his shirt. From there, he would fly to Barcelona, hire a car, and drive. The password and ten-digit number he would need to access the Lichtenstein bank account in his name would reach him by text.

In his jacket were a pair of latex gloves, and, in a plastic sleeve, a typed note – the Curator explaining why he had killed one of his students. A crime of passion, rage brought on by unrequited love. And how he couldn't live with the guilt any more.

All very emotional.

Lying against the plastic sleeve was a small glass phial, filled with a liquid – pentobarbital, drug of choice for any tortured soul intent on ending it all. Originally bought from a pet shop in Tijuana for thirty US dollars, its official use was to anaesthetise animals prior to surgery. If the surgery failed, a larger dose was injected, euthanizing the creature instead.

The price Doyle had paid was five hundred pounds, quite a mark-up. But there was no paper trail, or digital one, and Doyle hadn't had to fly to Mexico, one of the few places where it could be bought over the counter.

The bitter taste of the drug could be hidden by coffee, which was how Doyle intended to administer the deadly chemical. Half an hour after drinking it, Kingsley would fall into a sleep from which he would never awake.

Doyle went through his cover story again, murmuring aloud the names he needed to remember – Cotman, Crome... At last he was ready. Out of habit, he checked his mobile phone one more time before knocking. Typical, he thought.

No reception.

41

THE KNOCK ON the door was unexpected. Had the Inspector changed his mind and come back to arrest him for withholding information?

'Come in,' he called, his voice unnaturally high-pitched.

'Mr Kingsley?'

Kingsley didn't recognise the man. He wore an unremarkable, somewhat shapeless suit, brown hair neat and tidy, military almost. With a puce-like pallor and round, bland features, he looked as if someone had started to rub him out.

'Do we have an appointment?'

'Mr Kemp? John Kemp? The office told me I'd be expected.'

Kingsley flicked over the page in his diary. 'Can't see you. Where did you say you were from?'

'Scarfe Technologies? We're running the 3D trials.'

Kingsley's expression hardened. 'That's you, is it?'

'Something of a mix up last time, I was told. We assumed you were aware of what was going on. That's why I'm here. Mr Scarfe was anxious not to repeat the mistake.'

'Repeat?'

'Yes. What we –'

'Over my dead body.'

Mr Kemp had the decency to look embarrassed.

'Could we discuss it? Three more paintings is all we're requesting, exactly which ones isn't important – entirely up to you. Your Cotmans and Cromes are quite safe, Mr Scarfe wanted me to specify that.'

The phone on the desk rang. Kingsley i

'That's not my understanding.'

'The information given to me, Mr Kin have hundreds of paintings in storage, m rarely seen. We'd much rather negotiate with

Kingsley eyed the man with distaste. If minor significance were taken, it would leave the rest of the collection relatively safe, for the time being at least.

'Why don't you take a seat,' he offered grudgingly.

'Thank you.' Doyle sat on one of the chairs facing Kingsley's desk.

'Coffee?'

'That would be great.'

42

'YOU'RE VERY QUIET,' said Jane Meadows, sat at her desk.

'Got a lot on my mind.'

Since his interview with Inspector Morello an hour or so ago, Fisher Bayley had been feeling highly subdued. Although he and Odette Novad had been together for only a short time, the thought of her dead at the bottom of the well while he worked close by made him feel sick. And on top of that, Ginny had denied being with him in the Egyptian room, making him a suspect in her murder. Totally ridiculous.

'Want to talk about it?' asked Jane.

Fisher did. He found himself confiding everything, while Jane listened without interrupting.

'Dull life you lead,' she said, once he'd finished.

'Get a lot duller if I go to prison.'

'I don't think there's much chance of that.'

'Really?'

Jane laughed, and despite himself, the sound cheered Fisher up.

'Will you come visit?' he asked.

'Fisher – you didn't murder anyone, I know that.'

'How?'

'I just do, okay? I bet this Inspector does too – you're all he's got, that's all. Have you spoken to Ginny?'

'Tried to. She doesn't seem as convinced about my innocence as you are. I think that's why she didn't tell that Sergeant the truth. I might drag her down with me.'

Jane absorbed this before making a suggestion.

'What are you doing Saturday?'

Fisher shrugged.

'Fancy coming round for a bite to eat? I do a good chilli. Hot enough to take your mind off anything.'

Fisher smiled.

'Sounds good. Yeah, that would be great, thanks. I'll bring a bottle, shall I?'

'Perfect.'

43

THE PHONE RANG again.

'Do you need to get that?'

'It can wait.'

Kingsley passed Kemp his drink and sat back down, his own mug in front of him. Appropriately, it was emblazoned with a painting by Van Dyke, an image that ranked amongst his favourites.

'Could I have a splash more milk?' asked Kemp.

With ill grace, Kingsley returned to the fridge next to the sink. As he did so, Doyle took from his pocket the small glass phial, leaned across the desk and emptied its contents into Kingsley's coffee. He hurriedly dropped the phial back into his pocket, just as Kingsley turned towards him holding a carton of semi-skimmed.

'Say when.'

'Thank you.'

Settling behind his desk once more, Kingsley had an important question to ask, one which to date he had received no satisfactory answer to. There would be no further discussion until he had.

'What I would really like to know from you, Mr Kemp, is what sort of arrangement you've made with the Museum Committee. It's all very well me giving you three paintings that won't be missed for a while, but am I to expect another visit from you in a few months time, asking for more? Where does it end?'

'I can absolutely assure you, Mr Kingsley, this is the only

time you will receive a visit from me.' Doyle swallowed several mouthfuls of coffee. 'I needed that. Long day.'

Kingsley held his mug in both hands and raised it to his lips.

The phone rang once more.

'For the love of God.' Kingsley picked up the receiver. 'Hello...? Harry. Is it you who's been ringing for the last – what?' The Curator listened. 'Does it have to be straight after work? Can't it wait?' It couldn't. 'Okay. Mr Kemp? Yes, he's here.' Kingsley passed Doyle the receiver. 'Mr Scarfe wants a word.'

Whatever Harry was saying to Kemp, it appeared not to please him. He even looked angry. Good, thought Kingsley. Kemp replaced the receiver.

'Bad news?'

Kemp gave him a funny look. 'Looks like we won't be needing those paintings after all. Sorry to waste your time.'

'Really? Excellent.'

'Before I go, could I take a look at your mug? That painting, who is it by?'

Kingsley allowed him to pick it up. 'Van Dyke. It's one of his –'

There was nothing he could do. The mug slipped through Kemp's fingers and smashed onto the floor.

What Kingsley found even more extraordinary than Kemp's clumsiness, was that the man didn't bother to apologise. Instead, he simply turned and left his office, leaving him to pick up the pieces.

44

'So you and Ginny are really over?' said Ian Chapman.

Fisher Bayley nodded, somewhat morosely. 'Said she didn't appreciate the police asking questions about her private life, just because I was in trouble. I told her, it's more than just "trouble"; the police are treating me as a suspect for murder!'

'Her private life? All they wanted to know was...' Ian paused. 'You weren't just taking a closer look at our bandaged friend, were you?'

Fisher looked away. Ian grinned.

'You dirty bugger. The Egyptian room. You were lucky no one saw you.'

'Yeah, lucky, that's me.'

The Lamb Inn was quiet for a Friday night. The wind whipping around outside the building was cold, carrying with it the first hint of winter. Even the music sounded subdued. A portrait of a cocktail jug, full, was chalked up on a blackboard, underneath it the phrase "HAPPY HOUR – 5 'til 7". The irony wasn't lost on Fisher.

He began his first pint.

Ian looked at him appraisingly. 'You don't look like a murderer.'

'Thanks a lot.'

'Mind you, they say you can never tell.'

'Thanks again. When it goes to court, I'll call you up as a character witness. Should add five years.'

'Ten, when I tell them where you've been shagging. That's

a thought – what about Ginny's fingerprints? They must have been there as well.'

'She had gloves on, so no.'

'Gloves? Don't think I've ever seen Ginny wear gloves.'

'Not ordinary gloves. They were... doesn't matter.'

Ian had another question.

'How did those Detectives know they were your fingerprints anyway? I don't remember being asked to give dabs.'

'Dabs? You watch too much Sweeney.'

'How did they know?'

'It's a long story.'

'It's a long night.'

'All right. I was living in London. Me and another guy got locked up for a few hours, too much to drink. That's it.'

'What did you do? They don't lock you up just for being drunk.'

'Peed in someone's garden.'

'Disgusting.'

'I was desperate, Miss High and Mighty. The police drove right past and saw me.'

'Capital punishment, only thing that works.'

'I think that Sergeant would probably agree. Anyway, who cares? What I can't deal with, Ian, is that all Ginny was worried about was not getting herself into trouble. She wasn't bothered what might happen to me.'

'Course she was bothered.'

Fisher puffed his cheeks out philosophically, taking another large swig from his pint before ordering another round.

'It'll blow over,' said Ian, starting on his fresh beer. 'They can't arrest you for murder just because of a few fingerprints, can they?'

'Who knows?' Fisher sighed. 'Thing is, it's not just the fingerprints.'

Ian paused, his glass halfway to his mouth. 'What do you mean?'

'Turns out I knew the person who was killed.'

'You're kidding! Who was it?'

Fisher told him. Ian became suddenly sombre.

'Odette. I remember meeting her. Poor girl. Can't believe it.'

It was a moment before either spoke.

'The Sergeant reckons we split up, and I couldn't take it,' said Fisher at last.

'So you killed her?'

'Exactly. Except I didn't, of course. I told them, I was with Ginny, so why would I? Then Ginny makes me look like a liar...'

'She really has shat on you, hasn't she?'

'Not keeping you from your shift at the Samaritans, am I?'

'Sorry.'

Fisher drained his second pint, the effect pleasant. He decided it was time to change the subject.

'Jane's invited me to dinner tomorrow night,' he said. Too late, he remembered Ian's feelings towards Jane. 'I think she thought I needed cheering up.'

'How very nice for you,' said Ian, a little stiffly. 'No period of mourning, then?'

'Why don't you come too? Make a party of it?'

'No thanks. Anyway, I'm going away this weekend. I could do with a change of scenery.'

'Where are you off to?'

'Stay with a mate in Cambridge. Get hammered, probably.'

'Sounds like a plan.' Fisher glanced around the near empty bar. 'Let's go. This place is depressing the hell out of me. Can you give me a lift?'

'What's wrong with your own car?'

'Nothing. It's just my keys have gone missing.'

45

'I DON'T LIKE it,' said Howard Kingsley, his expression pained.

Across the city in another pub that Friday evening, Harry Scarfe had expected a more appreciative response.

'You don't have to like it. They want Bayley, so I'm giving them Bayley. All that matters,' Scarfe pressed home his point, 'is that you've got nothing to worry about. Remember that, next time you see the Inspector, and keep your mouth shut. You should be grateful.'

'For what?'

'Grateful they do want Bayley.'

'But planting evidence... he's innocent.'

'Not for long.'

'I work with him, Harry.'

'Can you hear yourself? Do you *want* to go inside?'

'Go inside...?'

'Prison, Howard. Jail. Know what they'll do to you?'

'Who?'

'The other inmates. They'll love you.' Scarfe eyed Kingsley's slender frame. 'You're practically a woman as it is. You'll get buggered to kingdom come.'

'What about you?'

'People like me don't go to prison.'

'Harry –'

'For the love of Christ, will you shut the fuck up?' Two women sharing a bottle of wine nearby looked round. Scarfe lowered his voice. 'Just do as you're told, and everything will be all right. It's not difficult. You should think yourself lucky.'

‘Lucky, grateful. Why exactly am I lucky?’

Lucky because you emailed me when you did, thought Scarfe, or you wouldn’t be here to argue, or have another moan earlier about missing paintings. He drank his whisky. Kingsley’s attitude bothered him. He decided it would be prudent for Doyle to continue with his surveillance of the Curator, probably right up to the point of Bayley’s conviction.

‘Is it Drake?’ Kingsley asked, meaning who it was would plant the evidence to frame Bayley. ‘It must be.’ He was clearly scandalised at the thought. ‘No door your wallet won’t open, is there?’

Scarfe supposed it didn’t take a genius to work out. He hadn’t actually yet acquired Drake’s co-operation, but didn’t expect there to be a problem – money had changed hands too many times before. It was just a matter of scale. He would make the arrangement tomorrow evening, at the Lodge.

‘I wouldn’t try taking the moral high ground when it comes to money.’

A look of resignation fell across Kingsley’s face. Scarfe smiled. It seemed after all that Kingsley wasn’t so noble he would put himself in prison before another man, innocent or not. Who was?

‘So what happens now?’ Kingsley wanted to know.

Scarfe thought of the text he’d received from Doyle. He’d accepted his new instructions with commendable poise, and already carried them out. Next was Drake. ‘Just sit tight. The way I’ve got things worked out, by next Friday, your friend Fisher Bayley will be behind bars, for a very long time.’

46

WITH A MURDER to investigate, Detective Inspector Felix Morello didn't get a weekend. Which meant many others didn't either. He sat in the interview room, waiting. It was stark at the best of times: a table, three chairs, and a voice recorder. It seemed worse somehow on a Saturday, like part of an empty house.

At last the door opened and Fisher Bayley came in, escorted by Detective Sergeant Grant Robbins.

'Good afternoon, Mr Bayley. This won't take long. Would you mind taking a seat?'

Having been brought to the police station in a marked squad car, the Sergeant refusing to speak, Bayley was apprehensive. What more could they possibly want to ask him? He sat down in silence, while Robbins joined Morello the other side of the table.

'Before I begin, Mr Bayley, is there anything you want to tell me?'

'You mean about the murder? That is why I'm here, isn't it?'

Morello nodded.

Bayley felt at a loss. 'I've told you all I can. There isn't anything else.'

'Fair enough,' said Morello. Bayley's relief was to be short-lived. 'Do you recognise these?'

The Inspector slid a plastic wallet across the table. Bayley took a few seconds to realise what he was looking at.

‘They’re my – I think these are my car keys. How did you know they were mine? Where were they?’

‘Let’s leave that, for a moment. How long ago did you lose these keys, Mr Bayley?’

‘Yesterday. I had to get a lift home – Ian dropped me off.’

‘So that’s sometime on Friday, is that correct?’

‘That’s right. Wait a minute – has someone stolen my car? I left it at work.’

‘No, your car is quite safe. That’s how we were able to establish the keys were yours.’

Thank God for that, thought Bayley. He really didn’t need any more grief right now. In search of solace, his mind leapt forward to the coming evening. Jane’s chilli.

‘And you’re absolutely sure it was yesterday you lost these keys?’

‘Positive.’

‘Can anyone verify that?’

‘Verify it?’ Bayley didn’t understand. ‘I asked a few people if they’d seen them, but no one had. I’ve got a spare set at home, so I thought I’d leave it until Monday.’

‘And they’d turn up?’

‘Well – yes. And they have. Was it the cleaners who found them?’

Robbins eyed him coldly, but it was Morello who answered.

‘No. That would have been beyond the call of duty. It was one of our divers who found them.’

‘One of your…’ An unpleasant sensation squirted through Bayley’s insides. The accusation behind the Inspector’s statement was perfectly clear. This was the real reason he had been brought to the police station on a Saturday. They were going to lock him up. The walls of the interview room seemed suddenly to close in on him. He needed to get out. Instead, all he could do was shake his head in denial. Trapped.

Robbins leaned forward. ‘And what we’d like to know, Mr

Bayley, is this. How did the keys to your car come to be at the bottom of the well?'

47

Grey instant in hand, the polystyrene cup scorching his fingertips, Inspector Morello sat at his computer. The vast open plan office around him was busier than when he'd first arrived that morning. He did his best to ignore the distractions and organise his thoughts. The evidence against Fisher Bayley, whom he'd released less than half an hour earlier, was mounting.

But did it make any sense?

First there were the fingerprints. If Bayley had entered the Egyptian room to take the dagger, why then were his prints only found around the stone table, several feet away? Forensics had discovered nothing to suggest the victim was killed there, and anyway, the dagger was most likely a decoy. The real murder weapon was a kitchen knife, of that he was convinced. Even more compelling, why wouldn't Bayley have worn gloves?

Having said that, the explanation given by Bayley as to why his prints had been there at all had been seriously weakened by his girlfriend, Ginny Carmen. Why had she denied being there with him? A natural desire to avoid trouble, which murder undoubtedly was? Or because it was true? And as an employee, Bayley had every opportunity to take the dagger – the key was easily available to anyone who wanted it.

Bayley's relationship with Odette Novad was more problematic. In his experience, matters of the heart were frequently the motive for murder. The vast majority of victims he'd come across in his career were killed by someone they knew, usually someone close. But in this respect, Carmen did provide Bayley with an alibi of sorts. It was unlikely that a man in a happy relationship, which according to the staff at the castle Bayley was – though not so happy now, he suspected – would make advances towards an ex, and, when turned down, go to such elaborate lengths to kill her. His impression of Bayley, gained from the victim's friend Kirsten Turnik, did not fit with the sort of psychopath who might do such a thing. Nor did it fit with his own impressions, or Bayley's history.

Not that that was proof of anything.

Bayley's car keys had an element of the absurd about them. So convenient. Robbins had put it to Bayley that they were dropped into the well as he struggled to dispose of Odette's body, an allegation he had vigorously denied. It was Tom Lomax who had found them, the lead diver, directly under the mouth of the well and trapped in a small gully of water, where they were protected from the worst of the powerful currents further in. Lomax had been surprised, as that area had been thoroughly searched already, and was routinely passed by all three of the team to reach deeper water. In other words, supporting Bayley's account that he had lost his keys only yesterday. Undermining this was Bayley's own contention that he had not been near the well all day Friday, a puzzling claim to make considering he was under suspicion of murder.

After continued questioning, pushing Bayley for a mistake that never came, he'd released him without charge. Even Robbins had had to accept that the evidence against him remained circumstantial. Nevertheless, he'd directed his Sergeant to arrange the immediate collection of Bayley's clothes and shoes, and to conduct a search of his house, before he was allowed to return home. Continuing to treat Bayley as if he believed him to be their main and only suspect was useful cover, in his pursuit of Scarfe and Kingsley.

Morello's computer pinged.

One new email.

The Inspector opened it, and the attachments, reading avidly for the next ten minutes as his coffee went cold.

Ronnie had excelled himself.

Morello knew all about Scarfe's politics, but hadn't realised that Kingsley was also an active member of the Tory party, and a fellow Councillor. Worth looking into, he thought. Scarfe's conviction for violence when he was nineteen didn't come as a surprise. When he'd met him, despite his charm, the man had practically radiated inner rage. Did his political friends know about that conviction? Might be useful somehow, somewhere along the line. But the most interesting documents Ronnie had unearthed were those regarding Kingsley's finances.

The Curator had been in bad financial trouble, until he'd begun to receive what were described as consultancy fees, related to a trust fund set up by Scarfe. The fund was to support students like Odette Novad, but Kingsley's fees took the lion's share, amounting to tens of thousands of pounds, all cleverly wrapped in perfectly legal transactions. Legal, but hardly credible. And not long after the payments had begun, they had been increased by a substantial amount.

Morello double-checked the dates. Something was wrong. The first payments had taken place before Odette had set foot in the country. That meant Scarfe had been paying Kingsley before she was killed. Why? A deposit for services about to be rendered? Didn't make sense. More reassuringly, the date from which the payments had been increased was significant. It would fit with the likely time Odette was killed and the body hidden. Kingsley was greedy.

He closed the email and the documents. He was now even more certain that it was Scarfe and Kingsley who were responsible for Odette's murder. But how best to play the information Ronnie had provided? He wasn't yet ready to go public with it, not when there was every chance Drake would fight Scarfe's corner rather than his.

Instead, thought Morello, he would take the path of least resistance – Howard Kingsley. Bring him to the station, the same interview room Bayley had found so intimidating. Isolate him, create maximum stress, scare him with conspiracy to murder. Paint a picture that would leave him in no doubt – the pretence was over. If he wanted to be treated with any kind of leniency, then this was his only chance. Offer the possibility of a deal in return for a confession, a simple piece of paper that he could take and hold up in front of Drake's supercilious face.

How sweet that moment would be.

With any luck, by the end of next week, Kingsley, and more importantly Scarfe, would be spending the first of many nights behind bars.

48

'Can I ask you something, Harry? In confidence?'

Scarfe potted the blue.

'Of course, Frank. Put that back on the spot would you, there's a good chap.'

Drake replaced the blue ball on the baize. 'That's six, isn't it?'

'Not bad for me. So what did you want to ask?'

It was Saturday evening, and the familiar room felt cosy. Three pools of yellow light lit the snooker table, its huge expanse like an altar under a misshapen halo.

'It's about the castle murder, these questions you keep asking me. Why are you so interested?'

Scarfe shrugged, making a show of concentrating on his shot. He missed.

'All yours.'

The game continued, but the atmosphere had changed.

Drake wandered around the table, clearly distracted. Scarfe felt his pulse race, knowing the moment had come. He wasn't expecting there to be a problem, but even so... He had a lot to lose if things didn't go his way. His dealings with Drake went way back, to when he'd been a mere Inspector. Very useful having a tame policeman, if somewhat expensive. But this was different. Murder was different. Would the Superintendent's malleability stretch that far? He was treading a tightrope, and there was no safety net.

They played on in silence, until Scarfe spoke again.

'There is a problem.'

Drake stood up from the table. 'I knew there was something.'

'Can I talk to you as a Brother?'

'You're asking a lot.'

'I know, but hear me out. This murder – there's an eyewitness.'

Drake's expression turned dour. The bags under his eyes looked heavy. 'Be careful what you say, Harry. I'm still a policeman. I haven't been told of any witness.'

'You wouldn't. Your Inspector doesn't know. That's because this person doesn't want to be named.'

'Why?'

'Sensitive issue, murder. Not something you want to be associated with, if you hold a certain position.'

'And what position would that be?'

'No need for detail, is there? The point is, this person saw who did it.'

'Who?'

'Fisher Bayley, your suspect. You've got the right man. So it's up to you to see he pays for what he's done. Can't be allowed to get away with murder, can he?'

'I see.' Drake had great difficulty keeping the sarcasm from his voice. 'And can we expect a statement from this "witness"? Because without it, all we've got is circumstantial.'

'As I said, murder's a sensitive issue.'

'Then there's nothing I can do. And for the record, I'm not happy with this conversation, not happy at all. You're putting me in a very difficult position.'

'None of us are happy, Frank. Not with a killer on the loose. That's why some hard evidence is needed.' Scarfe looked meaningfully at the Superintendent. 'Evidence Bayley can't argue with.'

Drake stiffened. 'Are you suggesting what I think you are?'

'He's guilty, Frank. What does it matter how you catch him?'

'It would matter in court.'

'Who would suspect?'

'Know what happens in prison to ex-policemen?' Drake walked over to a small side table and picked up his gin and tonic.

Scarfe watched as the Superintendent, his eyes distant, finished his drink, before saying, 'How long have you been on my payroll, Frank?' The question was asked in the same tone as if he were enquiring after his wife.

Drake strode right up to him. 'Don't you dare talk to me like that!' He was shaking.

Scarfe held his ground. Of the two, he was the bigger bully. 'A long time, I'd say. I'd have to check my books.'

Drake was still shaking, his face red like raw liver. But he backed off a little. 'This isn't a contract we're talking about,' he said, less aggressively.

Scarfe felt his confidence rise. Time to close the deal.

'You retire soon. Be good to go out on a big win, wouldn't it? Have a nice little villa waiting for you, like you're always talking about. Close to the golf club. Portugal isn't it?' What was it about the Iberian peninsula, Scarfe wondered. Give him Barbados every time.

'Harry... what you're asking...'

'Swimming pool. No worries about your pension. My eyewitness is a generous man.'

'If I go down –'

'No one's going down except Bayley.'

Drake remained silent for some moments. When he did finally answer, the words seemed to stick in his throat.

'The best places overlook the sea.'

Scarfe clapped the Superintendent on the shoulder, smiling broadly.

'Then a villa overlooking the sea is what you shall have. I knew you wouldn't let me down.'

Drake pulled away. 'The last time, Harry,' he said, laying

down his cue and making for the door. 'Remember that. This is the last time.'

49

'It is not a request, Inspector.'

Something didn't add up, thought Morello.

'I understand that sir, but I can't see what's changed. The evidence is too circumstantial, I thought we'd agreed.'

Superintendent Drake wore the superior expression of a man who held all the cards.

'We've found his prints, his keys, and he had a relationship with the victim. And the alibi he tried to use denied all knowledge.'

'But that doesn't add up to –'

'It's clear what happened, Inspector. Wouldn't be the first time jealousy got the better of a man, would it?'

Morello searched the room wearily. His eye settled on a small plastic pot, from which a spindly stem grew, supporting two spiked leaves, brown and curled at the ends.

He couldn't believe his luck. Kingsley had just returned from a three-day conference in London, so he'd decided that today, Thursday, he would bring him in for questioning. He could hardly do that at the same time as arresting Bayley. What was behind Drake's change of heart?

'I can see the logic, but at the risk of repeating myself –'

'Yes?'

Morello was feeling less and less comfortable. By this point, he would have expected Drake to be shouting at him, or at least to have raised his voice. Instead, he seemed totally at ease.

'As I've said before, Bayley's fingerprints in that room

were found nowhere near the knife. Why make such a careless detour? And the keys – why didn't Sergeant Lomax find them sooner? They were easy enough to spot.'

'So Bayley made a mistake. Criminals do. Same as he made a mistake trying to use his girlfriend as an alibi.'

Morello let the issue of the alibi go. He believed Ginny Carmen had acted out of fear, denying being with Bayley – fear of being implicated in a serious crime.

'And the keys?'

'No one's perfect. Lomax missed them, that's all there is to it.'

'When they were right in front of him, all that time? And his team? With all their experience?'

All this got from the Superintendent was a shrug.

Morello saw no point going over again the fact that the murder weapon was anyway in all probability a kitchen knife, and not the dagger from the castle. Drake had already made it clear he was willing to believe that Bayley, in a frenzied state, had used both.

Superintendent Drake drew a folder from a tray on his desk and looked at Morello with hard, beady eyes.

'If you've finished, Inspector, perhaps you'd like to take a look at this. I received it this morning.'

Morello opened the buff folder and pulled out a sheaf of papers stapled together. It was from the forensic department. He flicked through the various data, scanning it, until he came to the conclusion. As he read, the colour drained from his face.

'I was told when you came here you had good instincts, Inspector. On this occasion, however, they seem to have deserted you, wouldn't you say?'

*

After Morello had left, Superintendent Drake went to stand

at his window, where he watched the men working on the Norwich Eye. Sometime in the New Year it would be finished, and every gawping tourist with a ticket would be able to see straight into his office. Luckily, he wouldn't be around to put up with it.

50

Driving the short distance to the castle by himself, Inspector Morello was in turmoil.

His plan to prise a confession out of Howard Kingsley had been sabotaged. Difficult to apply pressure when at the same time arresting somebody else.

The forensic report had been damning. It meant either Bayley was guilty, which he didn't believe, or that someone involved in the investigation was bent. How else could those tiny specks of Odette Novad's blood have found their way onto Bayley's jumper? Evidence strong enough to put him away for life.

Was it Drake, Scarfe's friend and fellow Mason?

Robbins, whom he'd sent to collect Bayley's clothes, and who was also a Mason?

Dr Briton, author of the report?

All of them?

There was no other explanation. All had opportunity, and with the size of Scarfe's wallet, motive.Trouble was, thought Morello, he had no way of proving it. Not unless money could be found to have changed hands. Another job for Ronnie, though he held out little hope of a result.

From somewhere deep inside him, a knot of doubt emerged. What if Bayley was guilty? How certain was he of his innocence? What if his instincts had let him down, as Drake had said? No wonder the bastard had been so cool – payback for winding him up about the mummified priest.

Superintendent Drake had also made it clear that once

Bayley was in custody, all lines of enquiry were to be halted. He had argued against this, knowing that to convict Scarfe and Kingsley, he needed more evidence. If Tom Lomax and his team were called off, there would be little chance of that. There was the blue silk thread, which most likely had come from a motif stitched into clothing, Dr Briton had said. But searching through Scarfe's wardrobe for a match wasn't an option open to him.

He turned onto the bridge that linked the cobbled road with the mound on which the castle stood. The short trip from the station had felt like hours. With the castle looming above, doubts over Bayley's innocence surfaced in him again. Was he about to arrest the right man after all?

*

Bayley sat at a desk, squeezed into the large store cupboard situated behind the front podium of the castle's lecture theatre. He was searching through an old microfiche, one of the many that were still the only record the castle had of some of its collections. The light was off, making it easier to read the screen in front of him. It was a good place to work undisturbed, but not today. He was finding it difficult to concentrate wherever he was, as he had been every day since last Saturday.

Dinner with Jane.

A chaste evening, but no less exciting for that. This weekend it would be his turn to play host. The thought of it billowed through him like a summer breeze.

'Doesn't look like he's in here.'

Bayley pricked up his ears. Kingsley, and the footsteps of another person coming towards him.

'Where else might he be?'

Bayley's mood changed instantly. Inspector Morello. Not another trip to the station. He couldn't stand it.

'I'm not sure. He's usually about somewhere.'

Bayley remained silent. If the Inspector wanted him, he would have to look harder.

'Um... Inspector. Arresting Fisher. I... don't you think you might be making a mistake?'

Bayley froze. Arrest? The store cupboard swam out of focus.

'Why would you say that, Mr Kingsley?'

A long silence followed.

'No reason. Sorry. You know your business better than I do.'

'Is there anything you want to tell me?'

'No... hard to accept, that's all.'

The footsteps retreated.

Bayley got to his feet, struggling to bring himself under control, his insides a sickening whirlwind of panic.

'This can't be happening,' he said out loud.

But it was. He tried to think clearly, rationally.

What should he do? Give himself up? But if he did that, wasn't there a chance this time they wouldn't let him go? Could they do that? Did they have enough evidence? Had something else unexpectedly turned up, like his keys?

'Fuck.'

He was in big trouble.

A loud noise made him jump. It was his mobile. He looked at the display. It was Jane Meadows.

'Jane, is that you?'

'Course it's me. Why are you whispering?'

'Are you on you own?'

'I am now. Howard and that Inspector have been up here, asking to see you.'

It was real. The thought paralysed Fisher. Things like this didn't happen to people like him.

'Hello? Fisher? Are you still there?'

'He's come to arrest me.'

'Come again?'

Fisher explained as best he could. Jane suggested he go with the Inspector and clear up what was obviously a misunderstanding, but Fisher rejected the idea outright.

'You've seen the news. Every year they let someone out who should never have been put away.'

'That's not going to happen.'

'How do you know that? No one knows. I'm not risking it.'

'What else can you do?'

Fisher fought back tears of frustration and fear. Why was this happening to him?

'It's okay,' said Jane. 'We'll find a way out of this mess. They've made a mistake, that's all.'

'Howard said that.'

'I still think that for now it's best to go along with it. Let the Inspector –'

'No! If they're arresting me, they must think they can prove I did it.' Fisher stared around him, at the darkened cupboard. 'I'm... I'll hide somewhere.'

'Hide? Where? Fisher, you're starting to scare me. If you do that, it'll look like you're guilty.'

'Don't you see? They already think I'm guilty. I need to get out of here.'

Jane was silent for a second. 'Where are you?' she said, her tone decisive.

Fisher hesitated. 'Are you going to tell them?'

'No. If you really want to get away, then I'll help you. Till you see sense. Now where are you?'

Fisher told her.

'Wait there, I'll be two minutes.'

It was a very long two minutes. Would she be alone, Fisher wondered? He switched off the microfiche. Eventually he heard the door open at the far end of the lecture theatre and light footsteps hurry towards him. He peered cautiously into the room. The sight of Jane lifted his spirits.

'Why have you got a torch?'

Jane was also carrying a large piece of thick paper, roughly folded.

'You're going to need it.'

She explained her plan to get him out of the castle undetected. As frightened as he was, Fisher couldn't help but admire her quick thinking.

'Sure you don't want to change your mind?' she asked him, once she'd finished. 'It's not too late.'

'I'm sure. Let's go.'

He switched off his mobile phone. Every member of staff in the building was probably on the lookout for him by now.

With Jane leading the way, the two of them left the lecture theatre and moved warily down the corridor outside, towards a back set of stairs. Tiptoeing, they descended the creaky wooden treads, arriving thirty seconds later at a small stone archway, situated near one corner of the Great Hall. There were several visitors milling about, but no one either of them recognised as staff. The door they wanted, the one that led down to the well chamber, was in the opposite corner.

There was nothing for it but to trust to luck.

Walking as fast as they dare, they made it to the far side without attracting attention and stood next to the door, under the wide balcony that ran around most of the Hall.

'Take the keys and the map.' Jane pushed the roughly folded sheet into Fisher's hands. 'I'll wait outside here at seven, in case you can't get out of the tunnels anywhere else.' She looked at him, unable to keep the worry out of her voice. 'I don't want you to get lost.'

Reaching out, Fisher took Jane's hand and pulled her towards him. This time it wouldn't be a goodnight peck on the cheek. The plan of the tunnels crumpled on Jane's waist as they kissed.

A voice called out from the balcony above them, hidden from view.

'Ian, have you found Fisher yet?'

It was Kingsley. Simultaneously, Jane and Fisher twisted their heads. Not twenty feet away was Ian Chapman. The look on his face was a mixture of surprise and dismay. Fisher let go of Jane, widening his eyes and shaking his head in silent appeal.

Ian's response was slow in coming.

'Not yet. I'll try the cafeteria.'

'Good idea,' Kingsley's voice rang out.

Ian smiled sadly at his two friends, then turned and walked away.

Fisher wanted to go after him, to say he'd never meant for it to happen, but knew he couldn't. He looked at Jane.

'If I make it out, I'll head for Phil's.' He told her the address. 'Wish me luck.'

They kissed again, briefly, before Fisher opened the door and carefully made his way down the steep staircase to the chamber below, Jane watching until he was out of sight.

'Don't get lost,' she repeated softly.

PART III

There is a time with all passions... when they drag their victim down with the weight of their folly.

Friedrich Nietzsche, *Twilight of the Idols*

51

Alone and afraid, the thought of the Inspector close on his tail, the hidden maze of tunnels beneath the city took on a whole new feel for Bayley. Unfriendly and menacing. Very different to when Jane had been by his side.

Only five minutes after leaving her behind, he stopped.

Water, as far as he could see.

Dark, and totally still. No telling how deep.

Summoning what courage he could, Bayley began to wade through it, wary of any sudden drops. With the water reaching half over his knees, his foot found a loose stone and he fell. He cried out in shock, a spatter of icy coldness stinging his face. For a few seconds he was unable to regain his balance, trying desperately to keep the map and torch above the surface. When he did get back to his feet, he could feel himself soaked to the skin, his clothes weighing him down – but the map and torch were dry.

Eventually, without further incident, he reached the other side, the water having got no deeper. It continued to slop in his wake, making an unearthly, echoing sound.

Shivering, he stumbled on. When the passageway came to an end, it split into three. His first test. Jane's words echoed in his ears. Don't get lost. Bayley knew that if he did, he might not be found for a very long time.

Maybe never.

Holding the map against a smooth section of wall, he played his torch over it. The left tunnel was the one to take. He marked the map with a stub of pencil and the wall where he stood with a small piece of chalky rock. Then, eyes straining, he started off down the left passageway, slipping slightly as it took him deeper underground.

*

'What do you mean, gone?'

Morello was glad he'd decided to phone. Superintendent Drake was furious.

'He arrived as normal to work, but since I've been here, no one's seen hide-nor-hair of him.'

'Gone on the run, you mean. How did he know we were taking him in?'

'No idea, sir,' said Morello belligerently. 'Don't see how he could have.'

'You don't know. Why didn't you take Robbins with you?'

'I wasn't expecting any trouble.'

'Well trouble is what you've got. Find him, or you'll be directing traffic in the biggest shithole I can find.'

The phone went dead.

Morello's dislike of Drake took on a new intensity. We'll see who ends up in the biggest shithole, he thought angrily. If I can prove you're the one on the take...

He took another walk around the castle, in case he got lucky, but Bayley was still nowhere to be found. Somehow he had got wind of what was coming and had decided to make a run for it. Not a clever move – made him look more guilty.

Which, Morello had to accept, the little knot of doubt inside him making itself felt again, maybe he was.

*

Bayley could feel his wet clothes clinging to him, his shivering all the time getting worse. Then, at last, the tunnel began to work its way upwards again. If his map-reading was accurate, he shouldn't have much further to go. To his enormous relief, the passageway began to level out, the ground becoming less slippery, until finally he was stopped from going any further by a small but sturdy door.

There was no lock, just two large bolts rusted in place, denying access to anyone who might be stood the other side. He worked at the bolts until they were free, and, listening carefully, pulled on the door. It swung towards him quite easily, well balanced on its hinges. He switched off the torch.

From the other side crept a cold, weak light. There was no sound. Entering, he was met by a different kind of mustiness to the one he'd become used to. As his eyes adjusted, suddenly they widened in horror. Against the walls, running from floor to ceiling, were dozens of alcoves, each opening the size of a large oven. And in nearly every one lay a skeleton, like some kind of grotesque hive. He swallowed drily. Where were the coffins? Irrational voices came to life inside him, and it was all he could do not to turn and run.

But run to where?

Doing his best not to look either side of him, Bayley moved cautiously between the remains, towards a set of steps leading up to a narrow grille close to the ceiling. It was from this grille that the light came. Climbing, he peered out. He had a worm's-eye view across the floor of St Peter Mancroft Church, the nearest place he could find on the map to Phil Henderson's house. The altar must have been close, as most of the church was laid out before him, empty.

With a start, Bayley remembered that Sean would be married here soon. But would he be there too, free to attend his friend's big day? Would he be free ever again?

The idea that he might not terrified him.

Descending back to the floor of the Crypt, surrounded by the alcoves of bones, Bayley began to search for a way out. Half an hour later he was standing beside the steps once more, in despair. There was no way out. The thought of trying to find another exit route through the tunnels filled him with dread. He was cold, tired, and thirsty. He sat on one of the steps and lay back to rest, exhausted. Immediately he fell into a shallow sleep.

When he awoke, he noticed the light had changed. Artificial. Someone must be in the church. How long he had been asleep, he had no idea. He felt stiff from lying in such an unnatural position, and the penetrating cold from his wet clothing had begun to numb his limbs. Then something caught his attention. With almost superhuman effort, he leapt up. Two hinges directly above him glinted dully in the light that filtered through the grille, virtually invisible from any other angle. A trapdoor?

Bayley climbed the steps and tilted his head upwards. On the ceiling he could now see a dark broken line, in the shape of a square. Using his fingers, he searched for any sort of catch. There was none. He tried again, more carefully, running his fingers in slow, methodical sweeps. This time he brushed against a metal ring, held flush to the surface with dirt. Digging in a wet finger, he managed to lever the ring out of its recess. He pulled on it, gently at first, then harder. It wouldn't budge. He pushed instead. Still no movement. Sweat ran down his back. Was it locked the other side? He tried rotating the device. It moved with a precise click. Hardly daring to breathe, he pulled, then pushed at the square above him. With a creak it lifted. It was open!

Pausing, Bayley wondered who it was had switched on the church lights. The Reverend, perhaps, or would the Inspector be there, amused at his futile attempt to escape?

Whoever it was, he wasn't going back into the tunnels.

He pushed at the trapdoor until it was upright, before hauling himself up and out of the Crypt.

The pews were empty. Whoever had switched on the lights must be occupied elsewhere. This was his only chance. He quietly lowered the trapdoor back into place, then darted to the aisle on his right. A draught was coming from somewhere, cold but fresh. Open air – freedom! He ducked along the pillars, heading for the exit, constantly on the lookout for danger. Thankfully, there were no signs a service was about to begin. This close to Christmas, the congregation were paying homage at the tills.

When he came to the main doors, they towered formidably above him. Even if unlocked, he could hardly expect to prise one open without being noticed. Fitted within the left side, however, was a much smaller door, held fast by a latch. With his fingers barely able to grip, Bayley lifted the latch and leaned hard. The door swung open readily, almost causing him to fall. There was an immediate rush of frosty evening air, freezing the clothes to his flesh.

Through the door Bayley could see out onto Millennium Plain, teeming with shoppers. The other side of the Plain, past the Eye's hoarding, the Forum was brightly lit, a welcome sight under the starry ink-blue sky. Inside, he could see the crowded pizzeria, suspended behind the building's glass face.

'Can I help you?'

Behind him, the man's voice was surprisingly close.

Yelling out, Bayley jumped through the doorway and pelted across the square, never once looking back. The man didn't give chase, and nobody else gave him more than a fleeting glance.

Hurrying past the Theatre Royal, busy with an early evening performance, he raced over the road that ran along one side of Chapelfield Park, close to Ginny's flat. Entering the park, he dodged through the trees, towards Phil's house and sanctuary.

How long that sanctuary would last, he preferred not to think.

52

While for Fisher Bayley the day had led to him becoming some sort of suburban fugitive, a hundred miles to the south, Harry Scarfe contemplated a very different kind of future.

His newly appointed chauffeur gently braked, allowing the tourists to part. Scarfe smiled benignly at the camera flashes and pointing fingers. As a matter of routine, most MPs entered Parliament via a tunnel, linking it to their purpose-built accommodation nearby. Scarfe, however, had felt that this was no occasion to be shy. The Bentley saloon made its stately way through the entrance to the first checkpoint, then rumbled on another fifty yards or so before coming to a halt.

Scarfe stepped out onto an expanse of cobbles, slippery from the wintry sleet blown in by a bitter easterly wind. December had begun cold, and looked like staying that way. He turned to bask in the onlooker's curiosity but their attention had already moved on, a well-known minister pedalling through their midst, covering the two hundred yards from his flat to the House in media-friendly fashion, followed at a discreet distance by his official car.

Scarfe approached one of the building's doorways. He breathed deeply, savouring the moment. He had spent the night in his private apartment, attached to the Dorchester, unable to sleep. Unable to have sex even, despite the best efforts of Sade, his PA.

'Can I have your name, please sir?'

The two policemen manning the covered entrance both wore body armour, loaded weapons at their sides. No one got past them without their permission.

Harry Scarfe gave his name and showed his pass. Although in order, he was asked to face a lens embedded in a side wall, which took a time-stamped picture.One of the armed officers handed him back his pass card and he was allowed through.

For Scarfe, it was a dream realised. The epicentre of power. For a thousand years, the elite of society had ruled from this site, the modern Parliament's Gothic architecture simply its most recent incarnation.

The Central Lobby was an octagonal reception area, busy with smartly dressed men and women. Scarfe's heart raced. As he entered the Members' Lobby, the discordant sound of braying voices came to him from the House of Commons Chamber itself. Only one more set of doors separated him from that hallowed place.

The Members' Lobby was dominated by statues of former Prime Ministers, the greats of history. One plinth remained unfilled, waiting patiently for a new colossus of the age. Scarfe dreamed. The sense of occasion threatened to overwhelm him. Suddenly the door to the Chamber swung open, and a televisual young woman hurried past him to some unknown, but clearly urgent, destination.

He had been told to remain in the Members' Lobby and wait. Having been returned to Parliament through a by-election, he couldn't take the Oath of Allegiance to the Crown until oral questions were over. When that moment arrived, only then would he be led into the Chamber to the Table of the House, where he would swear the Oath before a Clerk, and any members present. The Test Roll would be signed, and the Clerk of the House would introduce him to the Speaker. From that moment on, he would be able to take his seat and join in the business of Parliament. His name, like all those before him, would be recorded in Votes and Proceedings, and the Journal.

His final ascent.

'Scarfe? Harry Scarfe? Norfolk South?'

Startled, Scarfe nodded dumbly. After the strain of the last few months, after all the setbacks he had suffered, he'd finally made it. He was here. They knew his name. Standing in the shadow of Churchill's statue, he followed tradition, rubbing the foot of the great man for luck. At that moment, sounding from a distance, the deep boom of Big Ben's chime reverberated in the air around him.

Heart pounding, Harry Scarfe MP followed his new colleague through the arched doorway, and out onto the Commons floor.

53

Fisher Bayley awoke to a low voice in the darkness.

In an instant he was fully alert. Asleep beside him in the Hendersons' spare room was Jane Meadows, breathing gently, her soft shape silhouetted in the moonlight. The voice wasn't hers – it was that of a man.

He sat up, rigid.

The man called out again. It was Phil. Bayley looked at the display of the radio alarm, next to him on the bedside table. Five twenty. He sank back onto the pillows, exhaling heavily. Trust Phil to talk in his sleep. Or maybe, like himself, he'd been having nightmares. His were of Odette Novad – so full of life, so beautiful and clever. Why had she been killed, and in such a brutal way?

Awake now, Bayley continued to listen, but the house was quiet, no more sound coming from Phil and Penny's bedroom. Outside, the pre-dawn was also silent, save for the call of an owl. Wanting to wake Jane, instead he stared at the ceiling, going over yet again how nonsensical it was that he was here, lying in the spare room of his friend's house, rather than at home, everything normal. Disbelief, anger and fear came to him by turn. He reminded himself that he was innocent, but as the slow minutes passed, the fact did nothing to lessen his torment. Rather, it made it worse. The owl's call stopped.

His thoughts turned to giving himself up. That was what Jane wanted. But that meant a police cell, and whatever else might come after that. Not a gamble he was ready to take, not yet anyway, though he knew he couldn't hide forever.

At least Howard Kingsley had seemed to believe he was innocent. Strange, that time he'd heard him talking with Harry Scarfe about the Egyptian priest, himself and Ginny hidden inside the dragon. Bayley sat bolt upright again. It wouldn't be strange at all, not if Howard knew already about the dagger. He checked himself. No. That was impossible. He rested his head back on the pillows, pulling up the thick duvet. But inside him, the idea began to take hold. Coincidences fell into place. He asked himself repeatedly, could it really be true? And if it was, what was he supposed to do about it?

Wrestling with this problem, he suddenly found himself faced with another, more urgent dilemma – how was he to escape from this Crypt? One by one, the skeletons were climbing from their dark holes in the wall, lining up to face him. Their eyeless sockets were angry, and from nowhere, in each tight bony fist, a gold sword appeared. They advanced in short, jerky movements. Suddenly the one with sharpened yellow teeth ran forward and lunged at him. Bayley screamed in agony.

'Fisher!'

'Wha –'

'Fisher!'

It was Jane, leaning over him, deep anxiety in her eyes. 'Are you all right? You were talking in your sleep.'

*

A short time later, Fisher was sat downstairs at the kitchen table with Phil and Penny, Jane taking a shower. Breakfast aromas of toast and coffee gave the illusion that the day was like any other. The Hendersons looked exhausted, having had very little sleep. Hardly surprising, thought Fisher, given that last night he'd turned up on their doorstep to tell them he was wanted for murder.

Neither Phil nor Penny had questioned his innocence, which secretly he'd been nervous about, but both had made it clear they were put out at not having been taken into his confidence earlier. They'd had no idea he was a suspect. Given the circumstances, when some time later Jane had also arrived at the house, rather than Ginny, little notice had been taken of the fact.

Jane came into the kitchen now, her dark hair still damp, and was soon putting forward once more her view that Fisher should give himself up.

'There's no other way of sorting out this mess,' she said, with blunt finality.

But Fisher felt he had enough reason now to delay the inevitable, other than just his blind fear.

'I need time to get my head around it. Think what I'm going to say to the police.'

'All you've got to say is the truth. Whatever reason they've got for wanting to arrest you, they'll work out eventually they've made a mistake.'

'That could mean months in prison. And what if they *still* think I did it?'

'They won't.'

'But what if they *do*?' said Fisher, his fear spilling over into anger. 'It happens. I need to work things out before I go handing myself in.'

'What things?' demanded Jane, exasperated.

'Things, all right?'

He wasn't yet prepared to tell anyone who he thought Odette Novad's true killer might be. Not until he had fully untangled his ideas and made sense of them. When the Inspector interviewed him, he wanted to be able to put forward his theory in as convincing a way as possible – it could make all the difference.

Instead, he asked Penny, 'Can I stay here?'

'You know you can, but I agree with Jane.'

‘I know. It’ll only be for a short time.’

Hiding Fisher put the Hendersons at risk of arrest themselves, but as they didn’t doubt his innocence, the thought never occurred to them.

Quarter of an hour later, Jane made to leave for work. Standing in the hallway, holding Fisher, she was reluctant to go.

‘I’ll speak to Howard, find out what I can.’

Fisher nodded. ‘I didn’t mean to have a go at you earlier.’

‘I know. We’ll get through this, don’t worry.’

And with a final kiss, she left.

Fisher watched the front door close after her. With Jane gone, spending the rest of the day inside the Hendersons’ house felt to him as if he were already being imprisoned. The long hours alone stretched ahead.

He returned to the kitchen, his shoulders aching, eyes bleary, tired. He needed some time out from thinking about what lay ahead, however false and fleeting that time might be. He looked at Phil and Penny.

‘Can we talk about normal stuff for a while?’

Penny seemed to understand.

‘Did you get any sleep?’ she asked him.

‘Some,’ said Fisher. He sipped his coffee, cold now.

Hearing the newspaper fall onto the doormat in the hallway, Phil went to fetch it. As he crossed the kitchen, Fisher couldn’t help noticing his somewhat peculiar attire, hidden up to that point by the table. Already tall, Phil’s Cuban heels and tight-fitting trousers accentuated his height still further.

‘Don’t ask,’ said Penny, noting Fisher’s startled look. ‘I’ve told him those trousers are indecent, but he says anything a teenager can wear, he can too.’

‘Nothing to do with his age thing, is it?’

Penny didn’t reply, as at that moment Phil returned to the kitchen, sitting himself down again at the table and unfurling the local newspaper in front of him.

'Let's see if you're in here,' he said, and began flicking through the pages, scanning each one.

'Anything?' asked Fisher, thinking at the same time, what if his parents saw?

'Nothing. Too soon, I suppose.'

'Should we put the news on?'

'I don't think you're on Britain's most wanted list just yet,' said Penny, in an attempt to dispel some of Fisher's anxiety. He gave her a brief appreciative smile.

Phil turned to the sports section, as if the lack of news indicated all was well.

'Another draw,' he snorted, seeing the report on City's latest away game. 'We'll be lucky to stay in the Premiership at this rate.'

Penny looked at the clock.

'You'll be late. Don't forget to ring –'

She never finished her sentence. The three of them froze.

At the front door, somebody had just knocked.

54

It was a nice house, thought Inspector Morello. Small, but very cosy looking. Cared for. The young woman who answered his knock suited it perfectly.

'Mrs Penny Henderson?'

'That's right. And you are...?'

'I'm Detective Inspector Morello, and this is Detective Sergeant Robbins.' Robbins nodded. 'May we come in?'

'Detectives?' parroted Penny loudly, holding the door close to her. 'Can I help you?'

Morello smiled inwardly. Their third port of call, after Bayley's own house and his parents, and it looked like they had found him. A master criminal he wasn't.

'If we could come in, Mrs Henderson, perhaps I could explain. It's rather cold on the doorstep.'

Robbins briefly stamped the ground with his feet, as if to confirm this.

'Of course, sorry. Would you mind taking your shoes off?'

Morello and Robbins dutifully obliged. Robbins sported a striped pair of socks, which contrasted brightly with his rather sombre grey suit.

'Come through to the kitchen and I'll pour you a coffee. You both look like you could do with one.'

In their stockinged feet, Morello and Robbins allowed themselves to be led through the brightly lit hallway and towards the rear of the house. Several framed pictures decorated the walls, originals it looked like to Morello. Either the Hendersons had plenty of disposable income, or one of them could handle a brush.

That Mrs Henderson hadn't immediately asked why he and Robbins were there, knocking on her door at this hour of the day, confirmed to Morello that she already knew the reason for their visit. It also meant there was every reason to suspect that Bayley had spent the night. The Hendersons being close friends, so his parents had said, it was an obvious place to run to.

The kitchen smelt like a kitchen should, first thing in the morning. All that was missing for Morello was the salty tang of bacon. Sat at one end of the table in the middle of the room was a man he took to be Mrs Henderson's husband. He stood as they entered, unusually tall and wearing unusually tight trousers. Couldn't be comfortable, Morello thought, or good for the circulation.

'These men are policemen, darling. Inspector Morello and Sergeant Robbins.'

'Really?'

'Mr Henderson?'

'That's right. Is anything wrong?'

He lacked the composure of his wife, thought Morello. Nervous, as he had every right to be. He considered the best approach to take, while Robbins took out his notepad

'Could we sit down?' he suggested.

The four of them sat at the table. Morello took a sip from the small white cup given to him, before asking his first question.

'Is there anybody else in the house? Children maybe?'

'Only us,' the husband and wife answered in unison.

Robbins made a short scribble.

Mr Henderson gave a puzzled frown. 'What's this all about, Inspector?'

An attempt, it seemed to Morello, to appear mystified by the presence of himself and Robbins. He put down his already half empty cup. 'Is it correct that both of you are friends of a Mr Fisher Bayley?'

Each nodded without speaking. Robbins made another note.

'And has he tried to contact you, in the last twenty-four hours?'

Mrs Henderson answered firmly. 'No. We haven't seen him for, oh, I don't know – maybe a week? Is he all right?'

Quite a woman, thought Morello, but not a good liar. Which was probably a good thing. He decided to cut to the chase.

'Not exactly. We need to talk to him as a matter of urgency, in relation to an ongoing enquiry.'

'Really? What enquiry is that?'

'I'm afraid I can't answer that question. What I can say is, if Mr Bayley does contact you, I would like you to inform either myself, or my Sergeant, immediately.'

In the silence that followed, Morello gave out his card. He could see that Mrs Henderson had lost some of her colour, her husband too. Shock, Morello recognised. He knew from experience that whatever Bayley had told them, hearing it from a police officer often brought home the reality.

'Sir...' began Robbins.

Acknowledging his Sergeant's prompt, Morello made a quick calculation. Standing on the front doorstep when they had first arrived, there had been no sound like a back door opening or closing. And through the window, he could see that the back garden was enclosed on all sides. If Bayley was here, then he was most likely upstairs. For some reason, whenever people tried to hide, they always went upstairs, trapping themselves. King Kong syndrome, his friend Ronnie in the Met had called it.

'Before we leave, Mr and Mrs Henderson, and with your permission of course, we would like to make a search of these premises.'

'You think he's here?'

‘It would help a great deal if we could eliminate that possibility. Routine, that’s all.’

‘Is there any reason you wouldn’t want us to?’ asked Robbins, his tone a little more forceful.

The couple exchanged glances.

‘No... no reason.’ Mr Henderson’s worried frown was very much at odds with this statement.

‘Good,’ said Morello. ‘Much appreciated. Sergeant, if you start in the garden, I’ll begin upstairs.’

The stripped wooden staircase had a soft cream carpet running up the middle, held in place with slim brass rods. Reaching the landing, Morello glanced into the bathroom opposite the stairs. Nothing. Two bedrooms also revealed no clues, except perhaps one. A single bed that had recently been slept in. Marital strife, or somewhere for a man on the run to bed down for the night?

The third room he entered he took to be the master bedroom. Minimally furnished, a large rug covered most of the polished floor. A traditional iron bed had on it a flowered duvet, telling him that Mrs Henderson most likely took charge of the décor. As with most things, he imagined. Two doors on the far side probably led to an en-suite bathroom and a wardrobe.

He crossed the room and opened one of the doors. Inside was a neatly appointed walk-in shower, all chrome and glass. Empty. He opened the other door. Behind it was a deep cupboard, crammed with clothes hanging from a rail that bent alarmingly towards the middle. Mainly female clothing, judging by the colours. Towards the right of the cupboard, the dresses and tops were twisted out of line. Morello bent down. At the back, clearly visible, were a pair of legs. For a heartbeat, the only sound was of his own breath.

Then a noise made him look round.

‘Nothing downstairs, sir – any luck up here?’

55

The rain outside had refused to stop, pattering away relentlessly as night had fallen. During the day Fisher Bayley had tried to catch some sleep, but was too agitated, eaten up with frustration and anger. Downstairs, he could hear Penny asking who wanted what to drink.

Everyone was waiting for him.

Fisher looked at his reflection in the teary window. His features were drawn but alert. Changing focus, he peered out into the garden, where dark shapes moved in the wind that whistled past the glass. Normally, he enjoyed the weeks that led up to Christmas, with their bonfires, the novelty of wrapping up against the cold, cosy pub lunches. And the chance over the festive season to catch up with friends, culminating in the promise of a New Year.

He looked at his reflection again. What promise was left for him now?

'Fisher!' Penny called up the stairs.

He jumped involuntarily. 'Coming.'

Pulling on a jumper of Phil's that was too long for him, he made his way down to the hallway and into the sitting room.

As soon as he entered, Jane rushed to put her arms around him.

'How have you been?' she asked, not letting go.

'Okay... Hi, everyone.'

Chris, Sean, and Eleanor were also in the Hendersons' front room. Phil had asked them over, saying only that Fisher was in trouble and needed his friends. They all now greeted him at once, Chris as forthright as ever.

'So, are you two an item?' he asked, casting a glance in Jane's direction.

Jane arched her brow at this lack of discretion.

'That's right,' replied Fisher simply.

Eleanor looked radiant, clinging to Sean, who sounded as if he had a sore throat. His face was thin and his eyes were deep in their sockets, giving him the appearance of not having slept for about a week. The Homburg hat had been replaced by a New York Yankees baseball cap. Fisher thought it looked out of place on him – more casual than was his usual style.

'Are you really in trouble then?' Sean smiled, 'or is this your way of introducing us?'

'I think we can call it trouble,' said Fisher.

'Why don't we sit down?' Eleanor suggested, and she led Sean back to his seat.

The room was barely large enough to hold them all. Jane sat next to Fisher on the carpet, her thigh warm against his, the others squeezed onto the sofa and two armchairs. Behind the thick curtains the rain intensified. The fire had been lit, flickering warmly in its grate and casting rich shadows. Fisher took the whisky Penny offered him and immediately drank a measure, giving Jane time to speak.

'I saw Howard first thing,' she reported, 'asking if I knew where you were.'

'What did you tell him?' Fisher asked.

'I said you must be ill. He wouldn't admit why the Inspector had been looking for you yesterday.'

'Did you see Ian?'

Jane nodded. 'We had a chat. He hasn't told anyone he saw you – us. He doesn't seem to know what's going on, I don't think anyone does. The place is just like normal.'

'What *is* going on?' interrupted Chris. 'Who's this Inspector?'

Fisher gave a small sigh.

'His name's Inspector Morello. He came here this morning to – well, to arrest me.'

Sean and Eleanor stared in shock, while Chris' mouth gaped open before he could speak.

'Arrest you for what?'

'Murder.'

There was a tense silence for a moment, the only sound that of the fire crackling in the grate. Then all at once came a cacophony of questions, of which Fisher could hear nothing but a torrent of words, mixed and meaningless.

'Quiet, quiet, let me tell you.'

And, clutching his whisky, he did. Every detail, right up to that morning when the Inspector had knocked on the Hendersons' door. When he finished, there was a brief silence, then Phil spoke.

'The whole thing's crazy.'

'Crazy doesn't begin to cover it,' said Chris.

'Poor girl.' Eleanor was holding Sean's hand tightly. 'You must have felt terrible, Fisher, when you found out who it was down the well.'

Fisher nodded, biting pensively on his lip, avoiding eye contact with Jane.

'Have they mixed you up with someone else?' asked Sean.

Fisher thought about this, but not for long. 'No. It's definitely me they want. Like I said, I was a suspect from the moment Ginny lied about being in the Egyptian display with me.'

'If it's you they want,' reasoned Chris, 'then why didn't you get arrested this morning? The Inspector can't have seen you.'

'He must have done,' said Fisher. 'Couldn't have missed my legs.'

'So why didn't he arrest you?'

Fisher had spent much of the day going over the same question.

‘The only way I can make sense of it is, he doesn’t really think I did it.’

‘That makes no sense either. Why bother coming to arrest you in the first place?’

‘We can’t work it out,’ said Phil.

‘And neither the Inspector nor his Sergeant were fools,’ Penny added to the mystery. ‘I think they saw straight through me and Phil right from the start.’

Chris seemed annoyed by this absence of logic.

‘He didn’t see you, it’s obvious. Stupid place to hide anyway, a cupboard.’

‘You’re right,’ said Fisher, his tone heavily sarcastic. ‘I should have used Phil’s secret hideout, down in the basement. No, wait, even better – used my special CIA skills to kill Morello and escape over the rooftops. This is real, Chris, not the fucking Bourne Supremacy.’

‘All right, sorry. Calm down.’

‘You try –’

‘Boys, that’s enough,’ commanded Penny.

Sean had been thinking.

‘If they think you’re innocent, wouldn’t you be best to give yourself up? Running from the police can’t look good.’

‘That’s what I’ve been saying all along,’ said Jane.

Fisher brought his temper under control. ‘I am going to give myself up. Soon.’

‘Soon? Why wait?’

Fisher bit on his lip again. ‘An idea I’ve got. Thing is... I think I know who did kill Odette.’

56

For a few heartbeats, no one said a word. It was Chris who asked the question.

'Who?'

Fisher told them. Having thought of nothing else all day, he now had his ideas straight, strengthened by the possibility that Inspector Morello might think him innocent. And he had a plan. It was a relief to get everything off his chest.

'I think it was Harry Scarfe.'

Phil looked dumbfounded. 'Harry Scarfe? That's – you mean Caroline's husband?'

Fisher nodded gravely. 'I'm sorry, Penny. I know Caroline's a good friend of yours.'

Penny didn't reply. She was muttering the name Harry under her breath, as if to herself.

Fisher continued.

'But I think he had help.' He looked at Jane. 'From Howard Kingsley.'

'Howard?' Jane eyed Fisher worriedly.

Sean, like Chris, looked sceptical.

'Are we talking about the same Harry Scarfe who's just become an MP?'

'That's right.' There was a touch of defiance in Fisher's voice.

Chris was not impressed. 'I've seen him on telly. Fisher, MPs don't go round murdering people. You're going to end up in prison for slander. And isn't Kingsley your boss?'

'He is.'

'And you want to accuse him of murder too?'

'Not exactly. I know how it sounds, but hear me out.'

And with the fire weakening, doing his best to appear confident, Fisher tried to convince everyone how he must be right. After all, he thought, if he couldn't persuade his friends, what hope did he have with the Inspector?

'Think about it. The dagger that was used to kill Odette came from the castle's Egyptian room. And she was hidden down the castle well, which is always kept locked. What does that tell you, to start with?'

He banished from his mind the graphic images this conjured of Odette's horrific death, only partly succeeding.

Jane grimaced too, but understood what Fisher meant. 'That whoever used the dagger knew it was there, and how to get to it. And they could open up the well.'

'Exactly! In other words, someone who worked at the castle.'

'Making Kingsley the murderer,' said Chris. 'Not that he is. Why are you dragging Scarfe into it?'

'For a start, Chris, I don't think Kingsley's the murdering type. Scarfe, I can easily imagine.'

'Your imagination's not evidence though, is it?'

'Let me finish. A while back, Scarfe used to hang around the castle with Kingsley. I overheard them talking. Kingsley said to him, "They can blame Ankh Hor". I thought it was strange at the time. I only remembered when Inspector Morello interviewed me.'

'He must have been joking about the legend,' said Jane.

She then had to explain the mystery that surrounded Ankh Hor's sarcophagus, and the fact that the murder weapon had belonged to the mummified priest, while Fisher waited as patiently as he could. When she had finished, the consensus seemed to be that Kingsley had indeed been making a joke, though his humour was in poor taste.

'Trouble is,' Fisher responded, 'I heard Kingsley say that

before anyone knew about the dagger.'

This caused a ripple of unease around the room. Even so, the prevailing wisdom was that it was nothing more than an unfortunate coincidence. Or, Chris suggested, perhaps Fisher had misheard.

'I did not mishear. Can't you see? Kingsley and Scarfe knew about the dagger because they were the ones who – did what they did.'

'You'd have a hard time making that stick in court,' Chris told him. 'They'd just say you were making it up. Besides which, it makes Kingsley look more guilty than it does Scarfe.'

'I know. Maybe that's why the Inspector didn't do anything about it when I told him.'

'Course he didn't. And think about it – why would someone like Scarfe, and he's an MP don't forget, wanted to have killed Odette in the first place? He wouldn't even have known her.'

'That's where you're wrong. He did know her.'

Chris looked taken aback.

'According to Brian – Fisher explained who Brian Finch was – Odette was here on some sort of scholarship, and it was Scarfe who was paying for it. Odette and some others. They had a party for them. Brian didn't get invited, but Scarfe was there.'

Penny gritted her teeth. 'You're saying Harry and Odette had an affair, aren't you?'

'He has got a bit of a reputation at work,' said Phil.

Fisher jumped on this piece of information.

'You see? And people kill over affairs all the time, don't they?'

'What about Howard?' asked Jane. 'Are you saying he had an affair with her too? Why would he have got himself involved?'

'He's not the sort who would have an affair,' agreed Fisher. 'But if Scarfe wanted Kingsley to get the dagger for him, God knows why, and help him afterwards to hide the body down the well, I bet he could be pretty persuasive.'

'You're being naïve,' said Chris. 'Scarfe is rich – he's Scarfe Technologies, isn't he? He would have paid Kingsley, simple as that. If any of it was true, of course.'

'Scarfe Technologies!' exclaimed Jane, looking at Fisher excitedly. 'That's the company that took the picture from the Art Gallery, isn't it?'

It was a connection Fisher hadn't thought of. 'You think there's a link?'

Jane hesitated.

'I'm not sure. Howard was angry about them taking the picture, wasn't he... so why would he have done any favours after that... doesn't make sense...'

In Penny's view, it didn't matter.

'Fisher, let's say you're right – right now it doesn't make any difference. You still have to hand yourself in and sort this mess out. Tell the Inspector what you just told us, if he hasn't already worked it out for himself. They can't keep you, there's been a misunderstanding somewhere along the line, that's all.'

'Since when did the police let something like that get in their way?' muttered Chris.

'That's not helpful,' said Penny sharply.

'I am going to give myself up, I never said I wasn't. But there's something else I haven't told you yet. Not even Kingsley knows about it.'

The long day had allowed Fisher to recall the tiny blue silk thread, caught in the hilt of the dagger. The kind often found in the logos of clothing, he remembered Finch saying. The clothing Scarfe had been wearing when he'd killed Odette? His shirt? What if that shirt could be found? The logo could be matched with the thread from the dagger, which would then tie Scarfe to the murder. Fisher's faith in the ability of the police to perform such a feat was matched only by his complete lack of knowledge as to how they would do it.

He explained this, while everyone listened attentively. When he'd finished, Chris was dismissive.

'You're clutching at straws,' he said. 'Not saying it isn't possible, but that thread's probably got nothing to do with the murder. And even if it did, it's more likely to have come from Odette's clothes, isn't it? Where the knife went in.'

Fisher hadn't considered this possibility, and nor did he want to. Why had such an obvious flaw in his logic not occurred to him?

'And, think about it,' Chris continued. 'If everything you've said is right, then Scarfe's clothes would have had blood on them, so –'

'So he would have thrown them away, or burnt them,' finished Sean. 'I think Chris is right, Fisher.'

Fisher looked around the room, and could see he was in a minority of one. Which meant that what he had in mind to do was not going to be very popular.

'You can't say that for sure. Anyway, I've been working out how I could find that logo.'

Earlier, he'd decided there were two locations where he could realistically search. Both had their dangers, but with his liberty at stake, he'd convinced himself he had nothing to lose if he got caught.

'You?!' exclaimed Chris.

'Fisher, that's the Inspector's job,' said Jane gently.

'Then why isn't he doing it? Why isn't he already after Scarfe, instead of me? Maybe he never did see me in the cupboard. Maybe he thinks I did it. How can I be sure?'

The spectre of having a life sentence wrongly handed down to him had been haunting Fisher all day. And once in police custody, the possibility was there. Right now, delaying that moment was all that mattered to him, and searching for a logo that probably didn't exist was as good an excuse as any. And what if, despite the odds, he did find it? Then the

Inspector would have to take him seriously.

'What exactly have you worked out?' asked Penny, sounding as if she already knew the answer and didn't like it.

Fisher looked at her.

'I've got a plan,' he said. 'But I'm going to need some help.'

57

Fisher's plan was not well received.

'You're living in fantasy land,' was Chris' judgement. 'There's no way you'll get away with it. Or find anything.'

Nobody disagreed.

'If it doesn't work, I'll go straight to the police. But I've got to try, even if there's the smallest chance I'm on to something. You understand, don't you? I only need a few days.'

'You keep forgetting,' said Jane, 'you're innocent.'

'That doesn't always guarantee you're safe though, does it?'

'He's right there,' agreed Chris, earning himself a sharp look from Jane.

'And I'll be in the papers,' Fisher went on. 'People will think I did it, whatever happens. No smoke without fire.'

There was a hint of panic in the way Fisher spoke, as if he were being abandoned to his fate.

'I'll help you,' said Penny suddenly. 'If that's what you really want.'

'So will I,' Phil was quick to follow.

'You will?' Fisher felt relief wash over him. Without the two of them, he had no plan. 'You don't know how glad I am to hear you say that. I really am. You won't regret it.'

Jane tried to keep Fisher focused on what she firmly believed he would nevertheless eventually still have to do.

'If you go ahead with this plan of yours, will you at least promise you'll hand yourself in afterwards?'

'I will.'

'Definitely?'

'Promise.'

This went some way to appeasing her, though Chris maintained the whole venture was both risky and pointless, before becoming distracted by Sean fidgeting next to him on the sofa.

'Can't you sit still?'

'Sorry.' Sean moved his leg. He held the same view of Fisher's plan as Chris did, but seemed to want to move on. 'While we're on the subject of promises, there's one I made myself tonight.'

'Not to wear stupid hats?' said Chris, reaching out and snatching the baseball cap from Sean's head.

Instantly everyone, including Fisher, forgot all about the murder, staring instead at Sean's patchy scalp. The cap fell from Chris' hand, and with a rush Fisher understood the embrace he had witnessed at the hospital.

*

Much later, everyone except Jane had left. Cleaning his teeth with the new brush she had brought him, Fisher felt oddly calm. Learning of Sean's illness had effected everyone the same way. Whatever trials lay ahead for himself, they seemed trivial by comparison with what his friend was going through. He rinsed out his mouth and spat into the sink.

He joined Jane in bed, and in the darkness lay silently in her arms. He tried to visualise Sean fit and healthy and himself vindicated, wishing he could see into the future.

Fortunately for Fisher, he couldn't.

58

'DID YOU HEAR something?' asked Caroline Scarfe, perched on one of the cream leather stools in her huge kitchen. She put down her wine glass onto the granite worktop beside her.

Penny Henderson swivelled in her seat and cocked her head. 'I don't think so,' she answered, trying to sound as natural as possible.

The deception of her friend made Penny very uncomfortable, something she hadn't accounted for when last night she'd agreed to take part in Fisher's plan. Her sense of betrayal wasn't helped by the fact that not for one moment did she believe Fisher would have any success.

Penny also felt bad for not being able to discount entirely the idea that Caroline's husband might be an adulterer and a killer. Added to the distress of Sean's illness, it was, all in all, proving to be a difficult evening.

Fisher's plan was a simple one, Penny thought – to search the Scarfes' bedroom for clothes belonging to Harry, and which bore a logo stitched with the same blue silk as that on the dagger. Simple, that was, providing he didn't get caught. Didn't he realise the noise he was making upstairs? If Caroline found him going through her wardrobe, it would be obvious who had let him in. How would she explain herself?

'Sounded like the wardrobe in our bedroom. It's been squeaking like that for months.'

A dull thud followed, impossible to ignore.

'Penny!' Caroline spoke in an urgent whisper. 'I think there's someone upstairs!'

'Don't be silly. Have you left a window open? It's pretty windy outside.'

'I don't think so... I'd better check. Come with me!'

Together, the two women cautiously made their way out into the entrance hall and up the flight of stairs that swept away to the first floor. When they reached the door to the master bedroom, Caroline hesitated.

'What if there is someone in there?' she said, her voice low. 'Should we call the police first, just in case?'

'No, don't do that. It'll be a window or something, I'm sure.'

As if to show how convinced she was she was right, Penny boldly opened the door and strode in first. If Fisher hadn't already hidden, hopefully he would still have time. It was like a repeat performance of the Inspector's visit.

The room was empty. Despite its size, to Penny the room seemed cluttered and over-elaborate. 'There's no one here,' she announced.

Caroline crossed the threshold and looked around her bedroom. 'But the window's shut. I definitely heard something.'

Caroline began a more careful search, heading towards a built in wardrobe that took up nearly a whole wall.

Thinking quickly, Penny spotted a stack of CDs, piled loose on a small ebony table. Using her body to shield what she was doing, in one movement she sank to the floor.

'Found what it was.'

Caroline retraced her steps to stand behind Penny, who held up a few of the CDs in her hand, the rest lying in a neat pile on their side.

'These had fallen on the floor. You need to get yourself an iPod.'

They carried the CDs back downstairs, storing them in their proper place in the sitting room. Penny rifled through the collection, picking one out.

'God, I haven't heard this for ages!' she exclaimed. 'Can we put it on full volume?'

Two minutes later, both Penny and Caroline were dancing, big grins on their faces, while Meat Loaf gave it his all with *Bat Out of Hell.*

59

'MORE WINE, SIR?' asked the waiter.

Without waiting for a response, he began to pour.

In his opinion, these customers were a strange bunch. Although the table had been booked for a stag party, the group included several women, one of them the stag's wife to be. And what was it with the bloke sat at the far end of the table, shooting nervous glances from behind his unfashionable glasses every time someone entered the restaurant? Strangest of all, why were they all wearing New York Yankees baseball caps? He hoped their eccentricity stretched to large tips.

'Thank you,' said Sean.

'I can't believe it's come round so quickly,' repeated Phil, for the umpteenth time. 'I haven't even thought about my speech.'

'So long as you don't mention any exes,' Eleanor warned him.

Fisher pulled his cap lower over his face. There had still been nothing in the papers concerning him, or he wouldn't have risked being here. The Inspector and his Sergeant hadn't returned to march him away, and there was no news from the castle, where life seemed to be carrying on as if nothing had happened. The calm was all very unsettling, as if he were in the eye of a storm.

Searching Caroline's house had been an unpleasant experience, one which he hoped never to repeat. Adrenalin and guilt were a toxic mix. Even so, he had become very excited when he'd discovered several polo shirts, each one with a logo stitched to the chest. He'd taken them over to a table lamp to get a closer look, but each colour had been either red or yellow. In his disappointment he had been careless, and knocked the lamp over. Quickly standing it upright again, he'd then hidden under the bed in case he'd been heard. Just as well, he thought. Thank God for Penny's quick thinking.

When they had left him alone again, he had continued his search, but found nothing more of interest. Part one of his plan had been a failure, then. Would part two fare any better? After that, he would have no alternative but to keep his promise to Jane.

'Shame you'll miss it all, Fisher,' said Sean.

'What's that?'

'My wedding? Next weekend?'

'Sorry. Thinking.'

'I know. Have you worked out all the details yet?'

He had. Himself, Jane and Phil had pored over his route endlessly, from the entrance to the tunnels in St Peter Mancroft Church, right up to the door of Harry Scarfe's office inside City Hall.

'I could do it blindfold.'

'You're crazy,' said Chris. 'You're still definitely going ahead?'

Fisher looked at Jane before nodding solemnly. 'Tomorrow night.'

'Tomorrow!'

'I reckon the sooner the better.'

Jane was suddenly subdued. 'I didn't think I'd have to say this again.'

Fisher reached for her hand. 'What's that?'

'Those tunnels are incredibly dangerous. Whatever you do, don't get lost.'

60

'I'LL HAVE TO take these off.'

Phil Henderson's Cuban heels were uncomfortable at the best of times, but on this uneven surface, they were truly painful.

'Quiet,' Fisher Bayley hissed.

They had waited until after nightfall before venturing out, making their way to St Peter Mancroft Church as quickly as they dared, doing their best not to attract the attention of any police officer who might be patrolling the streets. Fisher imagined a large poster of himself, stuck on a wanted board somewhere in the police station, every officer fully aware of the fugitive who lurked somewhere in their midst. But they had reached the church unchallenged.

Once inside, they had sat at one of the front pews, while Fisher waited for an opportunity to slip unnoticed through the trapdoor that led to the Crypt. It was then that rather than simply act as lookout, Phil had spontaneously decided he wanted to go into the tunnels with Fisher.

'You can't,' Fisher had told him. 'It doesn't matter about me. You'd lose your job if they caught you trying to break in to Scarfe's office.'

'We won't get caught. You stand a much better chance with me there. I can be lookout again.'

There was an excited, eager tone to the way Phil said this, as if he were a child contemplating some imagined adventure.

'Phil, listen to me. This is not a game. When Jane said the tunnels are dangerous, she wasn't exaggerating. I can't let you take the risk when you don't have to.'

'I know I don't have to, I want to.'

'Penny will kill you. Then she'll kill me.'

But in the end Fisher had been forced to relent, as Phil had refused to be put off. It had made using the trapdoor more problematic, but somehow they had managed to enter the Crypt unseen, where the skeletons had somewhat diminished Phil's enthusiasm, though not for long.

Now, next to the door where he and Jane had once stood together, Fisher looked down at Phil's feet in exasperation.

'Why didn't you put trainers on?'

'I didn't know I'd need them.'

'It's not too late to change your mind.'

'No way. I'm here now. Let's get on with it.'

Shaking his head, Fisher turned back to the door, which Phil claimed would lead directly into the basement archives where he worked, though it was inaccessible from the other side, having no lock. He put his ear close to the rough wooden planks, as old as the tunnel itself. As expected, he could hear nothing. Even if Phil was mistaken, he thought, and on the other side lay an office or public area of some sort, at this time of night it should be empty. The real worry was whether they would then walk straight into the arms of one of the guards who would be patrolling the building. Or were spotted by one of the building's cameras, though according to Phil, these were confined mainly to the central entrance lobby. He looked at Phil, speaking in a whisper.

'Are you ready?'

In the torchlight Phil nodded, tensing up.

Fisher had brought with him a small can of lubricant, remembering how the last time the door had been very noisy. He now used it, spraying both the bolt and the hinges. Then, as gently as possible, he began to rotate the bolt, at the same time pulling on it. It barely moved, and so he increased the pressure, at which point the bolt suddenly released and slid jerkily back into its housing with a deafening crash.

'Fuck's sake!'

Fisher listened again with his ear to the door. There was no sound in response.

'Switch your torch off,' he cautioned.

The abrupt darkness had Fisher paddling in the dark, trying to locate the bolt again, which was all that there was to pull on the door with. Finding it, he gripped tightly, drawing the door open a few inches, enough to see through to the other side. Phil, peering over his head, puffed out his cheeks with relief. The sight was a familiar one.

'We're okay. It's the stacks. We're where I thought we'd be.'

They stepped out into the dark basement of City Hall, lit only by a faint orange glow, just enough to see by. To Fisher, the huge room resembled nothing so much as a library, with row upon row of huge metal cabinets holding the countless documents Phil spent his working life with.

Their illicit entry gave Fisher the uncomfortable feeling that he'd contrived to become the very criminal he was attempting to prove he wasn't, just as he'd felt at Caroline's house. Nothing more than a common burglar. If they were caught, he would look more guilty than ever. As for Phil... Penny would never forgive him. Doing his best not to let these thoughts distract him, he carefully pulled the door to, making sure it stayed a little ajar. If anything went wrong, it was their only escape route.

'I'll lead,' insisted Phil, placing his shoes next to the door.

'You're sure there are no cameras?'

'Positive. Not the way we're going.'

'And the guards?'

'Keep your fingers crossed. As long as we don't run into them, we'll be all right.'

Fisher swallowed nervously. What they needed tonight more than anything else was a bit of luck.

The two of them reached the ground floor without

incident. They made their way carefully to one end of the building, the ambient light from the fire exit signs and office windows allowing them to see. There they climbed a staircase to the top floor, coming out onto a wide corridor, which Phil knew led to Harry Scarfe's office. The corridor was carpeted, softening the sound of their footsteps.

Most of the doors along the corridor had name plaques attached to them. Somewhere near the middle they reached the one that bore the name Councillor Scarfe. Fisher's breathing became shallow and fast, heart thumping. His mind had gone blank.

'Have you got the combination?'

Scarfe's office was protected by a numerical keypad, as were many others along the hallway. Obtaining the combination had required Phil to use guile and split-second timing, neither of which came naturally to him. Nor did lying, but he'd had no choice when convincing Tracy, Scarfe's secretary, that he urgently needed to drop into Scarfe's office, just as she was leaving by the main entrance.

'Plans for the Eye? How many more does he need? Can't it wait, Phil? I'll have to go all the way back up.'

'No need. Just give me the code and I'll leave them on his desk.'

At that point Tracy's boyfriend had hopped out of his parked car and jogged up the steps towards them.

'Are you coming, we're going to be late.'

Tracy sighed. '1 - 9 - 6 - 1. The year he was born, so he says.'

Phil grinned. 'Thanks Tracy – I won't tell anyone.'

'Make sure you don't. He gives me enough aggro as it is. All right, all right, I'm coming!'

'1 - 9 - 6 - 1,' Phil now recited. 'Told you you needed me.'

Fisher pressed the keys. There was a soft click.

'Has it worked?' Phil asked anxiously.

Fisher pushed, and the door moved. There was no sound

of an alarm.

'We're in.'

Fisher almost couldn't believe it. They were really here. All they needed now was to find something with blue silk on it. Having come this far, he dared to hope. He took a deep breath.

'Go on then,' Phil urged him. 'I'll keep lookout.'

Fisher entered the room. It was lit more brightly than the corridors, the night-time city lights coming directly in. He walked over to a tall French window, fringed outside by a narrow balcony. Beneath him lay Norwich market, nestled in its square of Victorian and Georgian buildings. Beyond that was Norwich Castle, beautifully underlit on its mound.

'Nice view,' he murmured to himself.

'Fisher! Get on with it!'

Fisher scanned the room. There seemed to be little furniture other than a TV, desk and chairs – not even a filing cabinet. His initial optimism vanished. Then he spotted a suit cover, hanging in a small alcove. Unzipping it with trembling fingers, he pulled it apart, but there was nothing inside. Suppressing his disappointment, he turned to face the room again. With nowhere else to look, he walked over to the desk. Standing behind it, he pulled at one of the drawers, which slid open silently. Harry Scarfe MP obviously didn't expect midnight visitors. He switched his torch on, careful not to let the beam shoot around the room. Inside were various papers and folders, what looked like official business.

'Anything so far?' Phil called to him.

'Not yet. Keep lookout.'

He moved to another drawer. There was something soft inside. Soft and shiny. With great care, he picked it up.

Phil leaned into the room again. 'What's that?'

'I think...' Fisher held the object up to the window. 'I think it's a pair of knickers.'

'Knickers?' Phil echoed in disbelief.

'And whose knickers would those be, sir?'

'Shit!'

Fisher froze.

Phil disappeared from the doorway. A second later came a wretched cry, quickly followed by the sound of a body falling to the ground.

Reappearing at the doorway, Phil's face was distorted with fear.

'Run!'

Fisher sprinted to the door. Curled up on the floor was a large man, wearing some sort of uniform. His peaked cap lay beside him on the floor.

'What did you do?'

'Swift kick to the balls! Let's go!'

The guard staggered back to his feet.

'You lanky bastard. Come here!'

'Run!'

Fisher and Phil hurtled towards the stairs, grabbing the banister to swing round the top step. Behind, they could hear the guard lumbering towards them, speaking into a handset.

'Jimmy, Jimmy, bottom of staircase two.' Then he yelled out, 'Stop! Stay where you are!'

When they reached the ground floor, Fisher looked up. Phil was limping down the last flight.

'You okay?'

'Fine,' panted Phil. 'Banged my toes, that's all.'

'Oi!'

'Oh shit!'

Another guard was moving towards them, much more quickly than his overweight colleague, who was now halfway down the stairs.

'He's blocking the way!' groaned Fisher. 'We've had it.'

'Follow me!'

Phil led them into the space under the stairs, Fisher scurrying blindly behind. They came to a halt.

It was a dead end.

'Fuck!'

Fisher felt sick, then realised that Phil was pulling furiously on a low door, half normal height, set back into the wall. It creaked open slightly, and then stuck.

'Quick, help me!'

Fisher joined forces, and together they pulled as hard as they could.

'Gotcha!' said a menacing voice.

The faster of the two guards stood next to the staircase, tall and broad-shouldered. There was no way past him.

'That door only goes to the basement,' he smirked. He called out to his colleague, seemingly in no hurry to apprehend them. 'It's okay, Vince, they're not going anywhere.'

The sound of heavy breathing came from the stairs.

'Good! I've got a score to settle with that lanky streak of piss.'

With a great deal of puffing and panting, the overweight guard appeared. He bent over, holding on to the metal banister.

'Give me a second... need to catch me breath.'

With a scraping sound, the door flew open, nearly causing Fisher and Phil to fall on top of one another.

'Yes!'

They bolted through. The overweight guard lunged forwards.

'They're getting away!'

'Easy, Vince. They've trapped themselves, haven't they?'

'What about the door down the other end?'

The broad-shouldered guard banged on the metal banister, causing it to vibrate.

'Bollocks. You go that way, I'll go the other.'

As he ran fast back down the corridor, towards the middle of the building, Jimmy grinned maliciously. Not much usually happened on the nightshift. Hunting down these two would be good entertainment. No point rushing it. He could try out a couple of the moves he'd practised at his martial arts class that week. Self-defence, he'd tell the police.

In the basement, Fisher and Phil scrambled through the metal canyons formed by the stacks, until they reached the dark oak door, standing ajar at the entrance to the tunnel.

The older guard's surly voice echoed across the cavernous room.

'There's no way out. Do you hear me?'

Fisher wondered where the other guard was, Jimmy. He had a nasty look about him, like he was spoiling for a fight and had found two punch bags to practice on. The oak door creaked unhappily as he thumped it open.

'They're over here!' The voice of Jimmy sounded only feet away.

Fisher stumbled after Phil into the tunnel, swinging the door closed behind him.

'Hey! HEY! That's no entry!'

The guard's body slammed into the door, nearly throwing Fisher and Phil off their feet. They recovered quickly, but Jimmy was through the gap before they could stop him.

'Gotcha!'

Without thinking, Fisher pulled the can of lubricant from his pocket and sprayed it into the guard's face.

'Aarghh!'

'Jimmy! Jimmy!'

The older guard had caught up.

Phil pushed the immobilized Jimmy into the other's path and slammed the door.

'Lock it!'

Fisher slid home the rusty bolt.

'Let's get out of here!'

They half walked, half ran, fumbling for their torches.

'Did they see your face?' Fisher asked urgently.

'What?'

'Your face, did they recognise you?'

'I don't know. I don't think so.'

If Phil had been recognised, Fisher knew their escape would be short-lived.

Behind them, an angry fist was pounding on the door.

'You're dead when we get you, do you hear me? Fucking well DEAD.'

61

THE SCREEN FROZE.

'Seen enough?'

Harry Scarfe spoke as if the image on the monitor was the direct result of Inspector Morello's incompetence. The ingratiating manner with which Scarfe had greeted Morello when they'd first met had disappeared completely. Superintendent Drake wore a similar expression of hostility, while Sergeant Robbins kept a poker face.

Morello nodded courteously, before turning to his Superintendent.

'It's Fisher Bayley, as you said, sir.'

He had quite some nerve, Morello thought, breaking into Scarfe's office, where they were all now stood. Unfortunate he'd been caught on camera. But the real question was why he'd done it. The only reason that made any sense was that he knew enough to guess Scarfe's possible involvement in Odette Novad's murder, and had been looking for proof of some sort that would clear his name.

'Frank tells me he's a suspect in your castle murder,' said Scarfe.

'With all due respect, that's privileged information,' replied Morello.

'Don't quote the rule book here,' Drake snapped. 'This is a special case. Mr Scarfe is an MP.'

'The point I'm making is, he's clearly dangerous,' said Scarfe. 'I want him caught, and the yob with him, before they can try anything like this again.'

The security camera, tucked away high in one corner of the office, had captured only the legs of Bayley's accomplice, though judging by their long thin outline, Morello felt confident he could hazard a guess as to who it was.

'I understand, Mr Scarfe. As far as the break-in is concerned, has anything been taken?'

'There's not much to take, as you can see. I use my constituency office now. Someone else will be moving in here soon.'

'Right. What about the rest of the tape? Anything from that?'

'You've seen all there is – disk space ran out.'

'Ah.'

This struck Morello as unlikely. Had Bayley actually found something then that might incriminate Scarfe? If so, why hadn't he already come forward?

'Technology.' Morello sounded sympathetic. 'Not always everything it's cracked up to be, is it?'

Scarfe said nothing, giving the Inspector a dark look. Morello moved on to motive.

'Do you know Mr Bayley?'

'Not that I'm aware of,' said Scarfe carefully.

'I see. And is there any reason you can think of why he would target you? What he might have been after?'

'How could I know that? There's nothing of value, like I said, except for the desk. Unless he was planning on making me his next victim.'

There was an awkward pause, before Morello decided there was nothing to be gained from pursuing this outburst.

'Nothing of value. Something confidential, then?'

'What are you getting at, Inspector?'

'Yes, Morello, what are you getting at?' said Superintendent Drake sharply. 'Stick to the matter in hand.'

As far as Morello was concerned, anything Scarfe might be hiding, in this office or any other, was the matter in hand.

Anything that might help him tie the MP to the murder of Odette Novad. He needed all the help he could get.

Kingsley's finances were not enough to convict with, and the opportunity to extract a confession from him had been missed. Tom Lomax's Search and Rescue unit had been pulled off to tackle another urgent case, a missing child, and Dr Briton had discovered nothing new from the ribcage. Morello had at least satisfied himself she'd not been party to any deliberate contamination of Bayley's clothing. Robbins could have been involved, as could others, but his Sergeant didn't strike him as the type – unlike Drake, who had a none too savoury reputation around the station. And Drake was much closer to Scarfe than anyone else on the investigating team, someone who Scarfe could trust. But suspicion was not enough, and Ronnie had been unable to turn up anything that could be used against him.

Which left only the blue silk thread found on the Egyptian dagger. He would liked to have searched Scarfe's home and businesses for a possible match, however unlikely, but knew that to apply for a warrant would almost certainly see Drake take him off the case, his career dead-ended.

All extremely frustrating.

He looked again around the half-empty office, as Robbins opened his notepad.

'I've talked to one of the guards, sir, a Vincent Foley. According to him, both intruders were violent. Foley was physically attacked, and his colleague, one James Shilton, had to go to hospital to have his eyes treated. They both want to press charges.'

Whatever Bayley had come here for, thought Morello, he had found only trouble.

'Did he give a description of the second man?'

'He did, but he could have been describing half the population. The only detail that stands out was his assailant being tall and thin.'

'What about security cameras in the rest of the building? Did they catch anything?'

'No sightings at all. They're limited to the main entrance and public areas.'

'Hmm. Unfortunately, they didn't use the main entrance.'

'No sir.'

The door that guarded the tunnel Bayley had escaped into (and presumably entered from) had been forced open by Robbins and two other officers, using a standard pneumatic gun. They had followed the passageway for about thirty yards, before it split in two. The left fork had ended in three small cavities, going no further. Taking the right turn, five minutes later it too had split, reaching a subterranean crossroads. Robbins hadn't been prepared to risk going any further. Whichever route Bayley had taken, and whatever his destination might have been, there was no way of knowing.

Morello faced another problem. He went over again to inspect the doorway to the office. No sign of a forced entry.

'I'll need a list of all the people who knew your access code, Mr Scarfe.'

'Easy. Myself and Tracy.'

'Tracy?'

'Tracy Watson, my PA. Or was.'

'Can we speak to her?'

'When she gets back from holiday. The diary says she's in Paris for three days.'

'If you could call me when she returns? I'll need to ask her a few questions.'

'You and me both.'

'Yes. Well.'

'I don't think there's much more you can do here, Inspector,' said Drake. It was an order, rather than an observation. 'Find out where all those tunnels go. If Bayley is hiding in there, I want him found. Clear?'

*

Morello and Robbins left City Hall and headed off immediately towards the castle. If anyone could help trace where Bayley had gone, Morello informed his Sergeant, then that person was the castle's Curator, Howard Kingsley.

En route, Morello allowed Robbins to stop by one of the market stalls, where he wolfed down a chicken pie and chips. The diet wasn't going well, and his wife was becoming suspicious. If all he ate at work was the carefully vetted packed lunch he took in every day, then how could he explain the extra six pounds that showed on the bathroom scales?

Morello stole a chip. Whether Kingsley would be able to help them or not, he didn't much care. If he had wanted Bayley, he would have arrested him that morning at the Hendersons', though not having done so looked each day like being a gamble less and less likely to pay off. The additional time it had given him to continue with his pursuit of Scarfe and Kingsley had so far yielded nothing.

At least Superintendent Drake hadn't enlisted the help of the media, he thought, which had probably also bought more time. Drake had told the press only that they had a "Person of interest" under investigation, telling Morello privately that until Bayley was caught, he didn't want his Inspector's incompetence reflecting on himself. A state of affairs that suited Morello fine.

But with or without the newspapers, Morello knew that Bayley would eventually be caught. And based on the available evidence, false or otherwise, there was every chance a jury would convict him. That would almost certainly leave Scarfe and Kingsley in the clear for good.

The odds, then, were heavily stacked in favour of the MP and the Curator. But that could change if Bayley had indeed discovered some kind of evidence hidden in Scarfe's office.

Though if that were the case, then he needed to do something about it, before it was too late.

62

'You should have left it there.'

'And rung the police,' agreed Chris.

With the wedding only two days away, Sean and Eleanor had arrived late, joining Fisher, Jane, Phil, Penny and Chris in the Hendersons' kitchen. The house was warm, despite the wintry weather outside, rattling the panes.

Fisher looked despondently at the skimpy piece of material lying in the middle of the table, mocking him for his foolishness. They were right. His initial jubilation had turned to deep despair. He couldn't cope with much more. He was exhausted, both mentally and physically. The last good night's sleep he'd had was a distant memory, and he hadn't had the appetite to eat properly for even longer. Phil too was disheartened.

'If that security bloke hadn't come when he did, we would have had time to think.'

After all the risks they'd taken, thought Fisher. All come to nothing. He picked up the thong from the table, a small puddle of soft shiny cloth. Except it wasn't cloth – it was silk.

Blue silk.

A trophy, tucked away at the back of Harry Scarfe's desk. It had to match the thread on the dagger, simply had to. And with the stuff forensics could do these days, even if the thong had been washed a hundred times, traces of DNA would still be found, microscopic, hidden in the fabric. Odette Novad's DNA. It depressed him still further to have stopped thinking of Odette as a person.

It was enough to clear his name, but for one thing. As Chris had said earlier, it was almost certain that the fabric would now hold fragments of his own DNA too – skin, sweat, whatever.

'You'd be convicting yourself,' he had warned soberly.

'Scarfe's DNA would still be on there as well though, wouldn't it?' Fisher had argued.

Phil brightened. 'That's right!'

Sean, looking much more healthy than of late, turned to Phil, almost apologetically. 'Probably is. But who's to say Fisher didn't take this thong to Scarfe's office and rub it over his chair or something, trying to incriminate him?'

'That's crazy.'

'I know that, you know that, but the police don't. Chris is right. These knickers could end up as the final nail in Fisher's coffin, not Scarfe's. He's the one in possession of them. Scarfe could deny ever having seen them.'

So close to a way out of his nightmare, accepting the truth of this had hit Fisher hard. He'd run out of options. And time. What else could he do now but give himself up, as he'd promised to, a wedding and Christmas round the corner? Attempting to break into Scarfe's business premises had from the start never been a possibility. He threw the thong away from him, sending it skidding off the table and onto the floor, no more than a cruel reminder of a fleeting relationship with a woman now dead. No one picked it up.

'At least neither of you were recognised,' said Penny, to her husband and to Fisher. She had quickly gotten over her anger at her husband's foolhardiness, glad only that he was safe.

'Just as well,' said Phil, with feeling. To divert any suspicion of his involvement, he had arrived at work that morning as usual. He'd found it a traumatic experience. 'That Jimmy was a nasty piece of work.'

'So what now?' wondered Chris out loud.

Everyone contemplated the inevitable – everyone except

Fisher.

'I'm going to the castle.'

This brought general confusion.

'Back to work?'

'Not work. To search Kingsley's office.'

Fisher knew it was a desperate thing to do, the last act of a man with nowhere else left to turn.

'Fisher, you promised.' Jane looked upset.

'I know, but look how close I've come. If Kingsley was in on it, who's to say he might not have kept something in his office too?'

'What, exactly?'

'I don't know, but it's got to be worth me looking, hasn't it?'

'Has it? And where after that?' demanded Jane angrily. 'How long are you going to keep this up for?'

'Jane –'

'You promised!'

'Do you want me to spend Christmas in prison!' Fisher was angry too now. 'And what about the wedding? Don't you want me to be there?'

'How can you say that? Why do you... you know I don't want you to...'

Jane stifled a sob. Fisher suddenly remembered there were others in the room, and he dropped his head forwards, studying the floor.

'I'm sorry. It's just... I don't want to go to prison for Christmas.'

This stark statement struck a chord, and in the truce that followed, it was agreed that if Fisher had to go to prison at all, then it could wait until after the New Year. Chris mumbled something about not being able to take time off being wanted for murder, but he was ignored. Fatigue of Fisher's dire predicament had set in, and a wedding and Christmas were a welcome distraction for them all.

In the spirit of appeasement, no one offered any further opposition to Fisher's insistence on searching Kingsley's office. In return, he flatly refused any more help, from Phil or anyone else. Jane would make sure that the door to the chamber adjoining the castle's well was unlocked, but that was all.

Later that night, lying awake in bed yet again, Fisher consoled himself with the thought that if he were caught inside the castle, he didn't care. There was a terrible predictability about what lay ahead, and he was losing the strength to fight it. He rolled over and nudged towards Jane. Behind the curtains the windows shook a little harder.

There was a storm coming.

63

From his vantage point, Fisher had a clear view down the central aisle of St Peter Mancroft Church. It was uncomfortable, but at least he was here. Sean was seated close by, Phil next to him, dressed in a morning suit. Also sitting at one of the front pews was Jane, eyes constantly flicking in his direction. Fisher wondered if they would ever be bride and groom. Was she the one? Ginny felt like a long time ago.

Watching people arrive, the colour drained suddenly from his face. He jerked his head back from the grille. Having materialised from behind a pillar, Inspector Morello and Sergeant Robbins were walking straight towards his hiding place. Before reaching him, however, they stopped, talking briefly to the Reverend. He tried to catch what was being said, but the organ player chose that moment to start warming up, the din drowning out their voices. The Inspector ended the conversation, and the two policemen treaded slowly back down the aisle, taking a seat on the groom's side at the rear of the church.

He was well hidden, he told himself, as long as he didn't put his face too close to the grille. With his breathing back under control, he adjusted his feet on the narrow ledge that supported him, to avoid getting cramp. The Crypt was freezing. He looked at his watch. Five to three. Should he take a quick walk, to keep the blood circulating?

Just then, the huge doors at the far end opened, and the organ player began in earnest. Eleanor appeared, holding her father's arm, framed in a brilliant white light. She was early.

While the organist played a favourite piece of classical music, she made her stately way past family, friends and relatives, arriving radiant at Sean's side. For a moment, neither took their gaze from the other.

The ceremony was highly emotional. Most of the congregation, Fisher imagined, were by now probably aware of Sean's condition. Though in all honesty, except for his hair, he looked almost his old self. Maybe Eleanor had given him the strength to beat the cancer trying to consume him from inside.

Fisher felt moved as the Reverend reached the final part of the service.

'Do you take this woman, to be your lawful wedded wife?'

Outside, snow was falling heavily onto the church.

'I do.'

'Do you have the ring?'

Phil stumbled forwards and kicked over a display of flowers, sending them scattering across the floor. He began to apologise profusely, a ripple of laughter travelling back through the pews, relieving the tension. The Reverend intervened.

'We can pick them up later. Do you have the ring?'

After they had solemnly made their vows, the Reverend smiled at Sean and Eleanor before continuing to his final words.

'Before these witnesses, and before God, you have given yourself unto each other, and so it is with great pleasure, that, by the power invested in me, I now pronounce you man and wife. You may kiss the bride.'

Nearly causing himself to fall over backwards, Fisher joined in the rousing cheer that followed as Mr and Mrs Cooper embraced, clinging to each other as if their lives depended on it.

64

By making his team work more overtime than was usual, Keith Sands, the site manager, had brought forward the project by nearly a month. Not that he expected a bonus.

'How long do those cables have to stay up for?'

Harry Scarfe was referring to the thick steel wires keeping the huge wheel securely in place. To his mind, they gave the impression the structure was flimsy.

'Two weeks, tops.' Sands sounded exhausted. 'Just waiting on a new gantry rail, before we pour in the last of the foundation blocks. Supplier promised us today. Once the concrete's gone off on the foundations, the cables can come down. If Eric gives us the green light. Two hundred tons of concrete takes a while to set.'

Scarfe pursed his lips, nodding. He looked up again at the enormous wheel, towering over the Forum and St Peter Mancroft Church either side of it. Not as big as the London Eye, but still impressive. In the floodlit gloom of mid afternoon, only a couple of days before New Year's Eve, it gave off an intimidating air, like a deserted spaceship.

'Has the planning engineer given us a date yet for signing off?'

'Not yet.'

'Get on to him again. I want the opening ceremony before the end of January.'

Sands grunted non-commitally. The planning department ran to a schedule known only to themselves and God.

The car horn sounded impatiently on Scarfe's Bentley,

parked just outside the gate to the compound.

'Better go. I'll see you next week,' said Scarfe, shaking hands.

The MPs visits were becoming more frequent, adding pressure to Sands' already hard-pressed team.

'Yes, Mr Scarfe.'

Sands watched as the Bentley reversed into the building site to turn around, before pulling sharply away. The woman in the passenger seat flicked her hair. Sands had only met Mrs Scarfe once or twice, but he had a good memory for faces, and of one thing he was sure – Harry Scarfe's companion bore no resemblance to her whatsoever.

65

Rising drunkenly to their feet, each person linked arms, chattering and laughing. The minute hand on the kitchen clock finally ticked to the number twelve.

'Happy New Year!' yelled everyone, Fisher Bayley loudest of all.

They all began to sing Auld Lang Syne, repeating the first verse several times, no one knowing any other words. When they had finished, Phil seemed reluctant to sit down.

'To Sean and Eleanor!' he declared, for the fifth time that evening. The news that Eleanor was pregnant had boosted even Fisher's morale.

Eleanor smiled at Sean, who was looking healthier than ever. It really did seem as if he was getting better, as he kept claiming to be.

'To us,' she said shyly, clinking a glass of orange juice with her husband's.

The party continued, music blaring.

An hour or so later, Fisher felt queasy, full of drink. Telling Jane he would be gone only a few minutes, he slipped outside for some fresh air.

On autopilot, he made his way down the back garden, through a narrow gap in the fence at the far end and onto the overgrown lane beyond, lined with wheelie bins. It was the escape route he had devised after Inspector Morello's early morning visit, though the Inspector hadn't been back since.

Turning left at the end of the lane, he began the circuit he took whenever he needed to get away – away from the planning, the what ifs, the constant worry. He only ever walked at night, the streets quiet and the windows dark, though tonight it seemed as if every other household were celebrating in style. Alone outside, he felt cut off, ghost-like, as if the cloud hanging over him had formed a barrier between himself and everyone else. Sometimes the despair was so great, a sense of isolation descended upon him even when he was with Jane.

Without her though, he would be lost, he knew that. She'd kept him sane, kept him believing that things would work out.

Might work out.

From out of nowhere, two men came running full pelt towards him, wearing hats. Police? There was nowhere to hide. He backed against a hedge, but they were on him. Then, just as fast, they ran past, a pirate and a cowboy, panting hard, paying him no attention as they hurtled round the corner and out of sight.

Fisher stood still for a moment, heart hammering, his nausea worse. If that was how two strangers in fancy dress could affect him, he thought, what would he be like walking into a police station? Part of him felt relief at the prospect, but as always, there was fear too. In truth, he was becoming dangerously accustomed to his life in the shadows – despite everything, there was a kind of peace to it. Once he gave himself up, that peace would be replaced by a prison cell and some very hostile company.

Nice choice.

The night air was cold. From a house nearby, he could make out what sounded like the country's annual homage to Slade. Calmer now, he continued his walk, thinking hard.

He still had every intention of breaking into the castle, and Howard Kingsley's office. Not tomorrow, which was Monday, New Year's Day. The castle would be closed, meaning Jane wouldn't be able to unlock the door to the well chamber for him. And Tuesday, as Jane had said, would be busy, first day back at work and all that, people working late – not so good either. But Wednesday – Wednesday, no more excuses. He would stay up all night if he had to, go through everything in Kingsley's office; desk, filing cabinets, bookcases, he'd dismantle the lot. If there were anything to be found, he would find it. He had a lucky feeling about Wednesday.

Ten minutes later, he was back at the overgrown lane. A small delta had formed where someone had urinated. Reaching the back fence of number forty-two, he climbed through the gap hidden in the corner and crossed the garden once more. From the sitting room, Slade were going off at full volume.

Jane flung her arms around him the second he was in the room. He grinned, then kissed her, long and slowly.

'Time for bed,' she whispered in his ear.

With the Pogues thumping out a tune downstairs, they made love in the Hendersons' spare bedroom, semi-naked, the duvet thrown to one side. Energy coursed through Fisher's veins. At the moment of ecstasy, his mind blanked out, and for an instant, there was only bliss.

Afterwards, lying tangled side by side, a new optimism swept over him. Wednesday the third, New Year – definitely had a lucky ring to it, he thought.

He couldn't have been more wrong.

66

Their journey had begun in Norwich at three in the morning, yet Inspector Morello and Sergeant Robbins hadn't arrived at the Novad's house until after midday. The flight had passed pleasantly enough, with a decent English breakfast on the menu – it was the connections at each end that had taken all the time. With the return trip that same evening, the day promised to be a long one.

Though it was already Wednesday, Morello still had the remnants of a hangover from New Year's Eve, causing him to squint slightly. It had been a late one. He sipped gratefully at a dark coffee, allowing time for the husband and wife sat opposite to absorb the information just given them by himself and Robbins. Also at the table were an interpreter, Una Kirk, and Sasha Janson, a Family Support Officer from the nearest town. Around them, the small wooden house shivered in the bitter wind that howled outside. The village was as remote and god-forsaken a place as any Morello had been to.

No one spoke.

Mr and Mrs Novad had taken the news that their daughter was dead with barely a reaction, Mrs Novad silently taking from a shelf a framed photograph of their daughter and laying it out in front of her. She had been a beautiful girl. Morello had explained that he and his Detective Sergeant had come in person as a mark of respect, but that details of the ongoing investigation would be relayed through the local force. The body would be returned as soon as was possible.

Morello sincerely hoped they didn't ask to see what was left of it.

It was Robbins who eventually broke the silence, shifting awkwardly in his seat.

'We're very sorry.'

The translator translated. Both Mr and Mrs Novad nodded dumbly, neither moving their eyes from the tabletop, neither showing any emotion. Each seemed paralysed, as if a dark spell had been cast over them. Odette wasn't coming home – ever.

Morello decided they should leave, and allow Sasha Janson to do her job.

Outside, an official car sat waiting for them. Robbins opened the rear door, battling with it against the freezing wind, allowing Morello to climb in before joining him. The car pulled away. Robbins had a determined look.

'I think we should pay another visit to the Hendersons, first thing tomorrow. Catch them off guard.'

Morello had seen the look in his Sergeant's eyes before, sometimes in the mirror, always after a meeting with a victim's family.

'Any particular reason?'

'Feeling I've got – like they had something to hide. Even if Bayley isn't there, I bet they know where he is.'

Morello weighed his options. 'All right. First thing.'

Robbins sat back in his seat, the car now picking up speed. 'Good. One way or another, sir, we're going to put that bastard away.'

67

While Morello and Robbins toyed with their in-flight suppers, on their way back to England, Fisher Bayley was making his way underground to the castle. The musty smell of the tunnels had become almost familiar, though the skeletons in the Crypt of St Peter Mancroft Church had made him as jumpy as when he'd first seen them. Pausing at each junction until he was sure of himself, he pictured Jane waiting for his safe arrival at the other end. Streaks of chalk began to appear along the walls, a sign he was getting close. A splashing sound made him stop, and he shone down his torch.

'Shit.'

He was in the same tunnel he had come through when he'd first escaped, and it was still flooded. The problems caused by the police divers had yet to go. With some trepidation he waded forward. If anything the water had risen, quickly reaching the top of his thighs and chilling him to the bone. Any deeper, and he would have to swim. Fortunately, the silent pool instead became shallow once more, until eventually he came out the other side, dripping wet, trousers like clingfilm. Maybe Jane could get him a towel.

He slopped soggily on, and then immediately stopped again. From somewhere up ahead he could hear the muffled sound of footsteps. There was someone else down here with him.

He switched off his torch, nearly dropping it in his haste. Whoever it was suddenly sounded very near. With a start,

Bayley saw a faint beam appear on a bend in the tunnel just ahead of him. Fighting not to panic, he turned to run, then remembered the water. Instead, in the blackness, he felt the walls for any sort of cavity or recess he might hide in. But there were none.

*

'Still here?'

Jane spun round guiltily.

'Brian! Er, yes, still here. Lots to catch up on. You?'

'Same.'

Bugger, thought Jane. It could make things difficult if Brian stayed too late.

'I'd better get on,' she said briskly.

Finch appeared not to hear her. 'How is Fisher? Any nearer to coming back?'

Bayley's long absence, due apparently to an unspecified medical condition, had become something of a talking point amongst the staff. Brian Finch had a particular interest, having become reliant on an extra pair of hands being at his disposal.

'Still quite poorly, I think.'

'Ah. That's a shame. Send him my best wishes.'

Finch strode off in the direction of the stairs, leaving Jane to continue towards the Great Hall. From there she descended into the chamber next to the well, taking out the key that would open the door to the tunnels. Except there was no need.

From where she stood, she could see that the door was already ajar.

*

Bayley's heart pounded. The torchlight was nearly on him.

Then, without warning, it came no closer, turning instead towards the wall. There was a gentle *thunk* as something was placed on the floor, followed by the unmistakeable sound of a key grating in a lock. A few seconds later, it was clear the key was not a good fit.

'For fuck's sake!'

Bayley's eyes widened in surprise. Howard Kingsley! What the hell was he doing down here? Whatever it was, he must be stressed. He never swore. Bayley edged forward, careful to remain out of sight round the tight bend, listening.

'Yes!'

The lock had obviously relented, and there was a creaking sound like a door being pushed wide. Grunting, Kingsley lifted the object he had with him, and his steps disappeared into whatever lay past the door. The darkness returned.

Feeling his way with his hands, Bayley crept round the corner. Through the open doorway, lit by a weak glow, was a short passage. It looked as if it led to one of the many storerooms scattered close to the castle. What was Kingsley putting in there? Something he obviously wanted no one else to see.

Pulse quickening, Bayley felt a vague sense of hope. Then he noticed the key. Kingsley had left it in the lock. For one wild moment, Bayley contemplated locking him in, not letting him out until he admitted the truth about Odette. But it wasn't exactly a practical idea, and keeping his boss prisoner would be unlikely to endear him to the police. Instead, he edged his way over the threshold and entered the short passage, kneeling before peering round a sharp edge.

He was looking into a large chamber, rough and featureless, like many of the storerooms. Kingsley's torch, configured as a lamp, sat on the floor, the room completely devoid of any ledges on which to rest it. In its eerie light, at the far end of the room, Bayley could see Kingsley, busy moving several large packages against the wall. Kingsley sniffed continually, wiping his nose with a handkerchief, clearly suffering from the dank air. He stood up, turning towards the spot where Bayley squatted. Bayley ducked back, but Kingsley began to walk towards him, swearing again.

'Bloody hell.'

Bayley tried desperately to hold his breath, to sink into the wall, but it was no good.

'That bloody well.'

Kingsley hadn't seen him. Something else had caught his attention. Daring to take a look, Bayley could see two more parcels, wrapped in the same plastic sheeting as the others, lying only ten feet away from where he was crouched. They sat at an angle to each other, balanced awkwardly against the wall. Kingsley picked up one of the parcels, examining it closely. Mumbling 'Better safe than sorry,' to himself, he peeled back the wrapping where it appeared loosened and carefully refolded it. He then took a roll of tape from his jacket and secured the edges.

But not before Bayley had seen what was inside.

68

Bayley's excitement mixed with fear. Was this his chance? Dare he confront Kingsley? Threaten to expose him? Seeing the Curator in a new light, Bayley couldn't help wondering if he'd underestimated his role in Odette's murder. What if he was carrying a knife?

'Fisher!'

Bayley jerked his head up. The decision had been made for him.

'How on earth... what are you doing here? Where have you been?'

Bayley stood up to face Kingsley, trying to appear confident. He walked right past him, picked up the parcel he'd just seen opened and ripped at the sheeting. Beneath the tear, the corner of a picture frame could be seen.

'Never would've had you down as a thief, Howard.'

'Thief? What are you talking about? Fisher, the police have been here. They want to talk to you.'

'A thief and a killer.'

'Killer?' A hint of fear entered Kingsley's eyes.

'That's right. Odette Novad. I've worked it all out.'

Kingsley opened his mouth to speak, but Bayley continued. He didn't want a big debate.

'Doesn't matter how I worked it out. And now I catch you stealing paintings from the castle. Ginny never was convinced with that story you gave her. What was it – some rubbish about sending these off for an arts project? Turns out she was right.'

'No, you don't understand. And it's you the police want, not me. Odette's got nothing to do with me.'

Bayley placed the painting he was holding against the wall and took a step closer to Kingsley. 'Then why aren't you scared?'

'Scared?'

'You're alone with a murderer in a place no one will ever find. What makes you think I won't kill you too?'

'I...'

'I'll tell you the answer. Because you know I didn't do it. It was Harry Scarfe, and you helped him. How much did he pay you?'

'Don't you dare –'

'No, don't *you* dare,' Bayley shouted at him. 'Think it's all right, do you, me going to prison? For something I didn't do? Do you have any idea what I've been through?'

Taken aback by Bayley's anger, Kingsley held his tongue, pulling out his handkerchief and nervously wiping his nose.

Bayley looked levelly at his former boss. Shivering in his wet trousers, he tried to regain his composure. Losing his temper was unlikely to get Kingsley on his side, and without him, he stood next to no chance against Scarfe.

It was time to take a gamble.

'I'm going to give you a choice. Tell the police who really killed Odette, and I'll forget what I've seen down here. You can sell the bloody lot, as far as I'm concerned. Otherwise, I go to Inspector Morello. You'll be sacked. And the value of this little lot, you'll be in prison right alongside me. And when Morello works out I'm not the one he wants, which he will, he'll be looking for someone else to pin the murder on. Why not a thief?'

Bayley held his breath. Would Kingsley go for it? His answer wasn't long in coming.

'I don't know who killed Odette. If it wasn't you, then I really don't. And these paintings are here to protect them.'

'Protect them? The only thing they need protecting from is you.'

'I don't have to justify myself.'

Kingsley wiped his nose again. In one corner of the cloth, his initial caught the lamplight. It was blue.

'Hey!'

Bayley had grabbed the handkerchief, staring at it as if it were made of gold.

'That's it,' he said to himself, trembling.

'Give that back!'

Bayley looked up. 'You must have used this when she was killed. Wiped off the blood with it or something.'

'What are you talking about? You've gone mad.'

Bayley grinned manically. 'There's something you don't know, Howard. Brian found a piece of silk on that dagger. Blue silk, most likely from some sort of logo he said. No one ever thought of a monogram.'

Kingsley looked alarmed. He tried to snatch the handkerchief back, but Bayley was too quick.

'I think the police will be very interested in taking a look at this. And I reckon they'll get a match.'

'You think I'd keep the same – I mean –'

'Yes! I knew it! You mean the same hanky as when Odette was killed! You complete *wanker*.'

'I had nothing to do with it! It's not the same hanky!'

'Doesn't matter if it's the same one or not – I bet you've got a set. Close enough.'

'It won't match, I'm telling you!'

'Can't afford to take that chance,' said a third voice from the shadows.

69

Far above the three men's heads, a powerful car cruised towards the city, its occupants on their way to attend an official engagement.

Caroline Scarfe gazed numbly out of the passenger window, while her husband talked into a phone as he drove, his voice hoarse. His sore throat had still not cleared up. Harry was in London for the rest of the week, and so before arriving at their engagement had insisted on stopping off at his Norwich Eye project, wanting to see what progress had been made before he went.

Caroline watched the streets go by. Her loneliness was becoming more acute. Aside from political functions like tonight, she now essentially led a single life, but without the benefits. For how much longer she could go on like this she didn't know – trapped in a loveless marriage, and trapped too by the secret she shared with her husband.

A light, steady rain was falling as they parked outside the perimeter fence that surrounded the Eye. Harry unlocked the gate that formed part of the fencing and Caroline followed him inside, the sound of people and traffic suddenly dropping, replaced by the low drone of a generator somewhere. They passed through a high screen of torn plastic sheeting, towards the base of the huge metal wheel. This close, Caroline was taken aback by its sheer size. It had a certain futuristic charm about it, arms tapering to glass pods shaped like eggs.

'Soon as the concrete is set, those cables are coming down,' said Harry enthusiastically. 'Then she'll really look the part.'

Caroline merely nodded.

'We've got the Beeb covering the opening ceremony. We're going to be on telly,' he added proudly.

The "we" seemed to refer to Harry and the wheel, rather than to Harry and his wife.

Harry's phone went off again. He answered it, turning his back to Caroline, lowering his voice to a croaky stage whisper.

'I told you, I'm busy tonight... yes... yes... I'll call when I get there...'

A woman, thought Caroline. He'd promised her no more playing around. But the odd calls had become more frequent, the attempts to hide them done with less care. As her husband stood there, alongside a neat row of cones, silhouetted against the glow of lights that pointed up towards the wheel, tears welled in her eyes.

She had never hated him more.

70

The strong flashlight was blinding. Bayley retreated with Kingsley against the back wall. The stranger's outline could dimly be seen beyond the glare of his torch, which he continued to shine deliberately straight at their faces.

'He should have let you drink that coffee.'

Bayley squinted ahead, unable to make any sense of this statement. It seemed to mean nothing to Kingsley either.

'What? Who are you? You've no right to be here.'

There were two of them, thought Bayley. Two against one. Could they overpower him?

'Doesn't matter.'

'Kemp...?' Kingsley said cautiously. 'Mr Kemp?'

The man became more threatening, moving a step closer. 'Shut up.'

Bayley could now see there was a gun in the man's right hand. What the hell was going on? Was this someone Kingsley knew? The real killer? Cold as he was, Bayley's forehead prickled hot with sweat.

Whoever he was, the man seemed to hesitate, as if unsure what to do. Then, as suddenly as he'd appeared, the man moved quickly backwards to the entrance of the chamber. There was a loud bang as the door was shut, followed by the click of the lock where Kingsley had left the key.

*

Doyle made his way back towards the castle, thinking how Scarfe had definitely got his money's worth, having him continue to trail Kingsley. And this time, Doyle hoped, Scarfe would want him to finish off the job properly. No more loose ends. If so, he would finally be on his way to Spain. Maybe a bigger boat, with Bayley dead too. And the beauty of it was, Bayley and Kingsley had each found themselves their own grave.

*

Bayley and Kingsley stood still, only their breathing breaking the complete silence. Bayley moved first, striding over to the thick wooden door in the hope it might somehow still open, but it was locked fast.

'Fuck.' He tried kicking the door, but for all the good it did he might as well have kicked the wall. 'Do you know that guy?' he asked Kingsley, coming back into the room. 'Why has he locked us in?'

Kingsley took a moment to answer. 'I think it's Mr Kemp. He came to see me about taking more of our paintings.'

Bayley looked incredulous. 'He had a gun, for Christ's sake.'

'I saw.'

'So he's not here for the art, is he?'

'He told me he was from Scarfe Technologies. That's who took the Cotman. I couldn't trust them not to take any more. That's why these paintings are here. Like I told you, I'm not a thief.'

'Was it Kemp who killed Odette? Working for Scarfe?'

Bayley got no answer, and despite repeated attempts, Kingsley remained tight-lipped.

Shivering more frequently now, Bayley went back over to the door, turning the handle again as if he might have been mistaken the first time. The door didn't budge. The thought of being caged in this underground room was already beginning to weigh on him. He decided to walk around and try to get warm. Fortunately the torch Kingsley had brought was still working, and he had his own.

As he circled the chamber, Kingsley watched him, as if suspecting a trick of some sort. There was a line, Bayley noticed, roughly two feet up, staining each of the walls.

'What's that?'

'Flood.'

Bayley thought of the paintings he'd seen earlier, balanced haphazardly against each other as if thrown there, their wrapping loose.

'Not ideal for paintings.'

'It's the only room with a lock. The flooding will stop soon, now the police are gone.'

Another half hour passed before Bayley sat down on the floor next to Kingsley. He'd been thinking.

'Kemp works for Scarfe. That's why he's locked us in. To protect his employer.'

'Protect him from what?'

Bayley held up the handkerchief. 'Evidence.' Kingsley made no attempt to take it. 'And you.'

'Me?'

'Unless you want to take all the blame.'

'There's no blame to take. Anyway, Kemp can't keep us here forever.'

'Can't he?'

Kingsley rose defiantly to his feet. He ran to the door, battering it with his fist.

'Let me out! I know you're there! Open this door!'

Bayley came up behind him. 'He's gone.'

These words seemed to deflate Kingsley.

'Harry wouldn't hurt me,' he said. 'We're family.'

This admission that Scarfe must be behind their imprisonment by Kemp lifted Bayley's spirits.

'Sure about that? He's already killed one person, hasn't he? Or got Kemp to.'

'Kemp's not...'

'Not what?'

Kingsley's eyes were downcast. 'We're family,' he repeated, sounding less convinced.

'You're in as much trouble as I am, Howard. Tell the police what you know, they'll understand.'

Kingsley looked at Bayley, but said nothing.

'Say Scarfe made you help him – threatened you with Kemp. They're bound to go easy on you.'

Like a child refusing to eat his greens, Kingsley shook his head violently, pushing past Bayley. As he did so, his feet made a splashing sound. Bayley looked down.

Water. The chamber was flooding again.

'We need to block the door with something,' said Bayley anxiously.

'There's no point – look.'

Kingsley was right. There was no water under the door itself. Instead, it was seeping up through the ground all around them. Bayley looked at the stains on the walls again. One and a half, two feet?

They could survive that.

71

THINGS COULD HAVE been so different, Caroline Scarfe liked to believe. But she knew that whether or not that was true, it was too late now. Her love for Harry had gone, replaced by a fear of what the future might hold for her.

Still with his back to his wife, Harry finished his call. Caroline tried to picture the woman at the other end; her hair, her perfume, the way she might smile, before stopping herself.

Enough torture.

Not thinking of the consequences, she ran at her husband, pushing him over the line of cones and into the wet concrete beyond. Difficult to make his speech tonight, she thought, with his suit covered in that muck.

Flailing to keep his balance, Harry lost the battle, staggering forward several feet before one leg sank up to the knee.

'What the...? You stupid bitch! What are you doing?'

He turned to face her, only partially succeeding, the other foot now also sinking beneath the surface.

'Fuck you!' Caroline screamed at him.

She ran back through the plastic sheeting, blinded by tears and rage, back through the hoarding to the car. Grappling with the door, she jumped in, started the engine and roared off, swerving to avoid a taxi coming the other way.

Back at home, she poured herself a neat gin, trembling with anger.

And dread.

When Harry finally did come through the door, his suit and his evening ruined, there was no telling how he might take it out on her. His preferred method of abuse was psychological and emotional, rather than physical, but there was always a first time.

No matter, thought Caroline.

Whatever he had in store for her, it couldn't make her life any worse.

72

'It's stopped, hasn't it?'

'I think so,' replied Bayley cautiously.

He could hear Kingsley, but couldn't see him. With both their torches out of power and lying under two feet of freezing water, they were invisible to each other.

The water had risen at first with frightening speed. If it had become necessary to swim then both men would have been doomed, but for the last hour or so the water hadn't climbed any further.

Leaning against a wall, Bayley ached with cold and tiredness – he would have given anything to sit down and rest, but there was nowhere. Craggy and crudely shaped as it was, the chamber forced him to remain upright. He'd felt his way round the walls more times than he knew, searching with increasing desperation for another exit, something he may have missed when they'd still had light. But there was no way out except for the door.

Every so often, one of the pictures, afloat in its plastic wrapping, would knock gently into him, like a cat wanting to be stroked. After the first few times he no longer jumped with alarm.

'How long will it stay like this do you think?'

'Not sure,' answered Kingsley dully.

Bayley bit his lip. They couldn't sleep standing up, and the cold was rapidly sapping his strength. When was Kemp coming back? Was he coming back? Where was Jane? Would she come looking for them?

Another bump at the back of his leg, but this time different. Something warm.

73

'If he is lost, I'm calling the police,' said Jane Meadows.

It was well after midnight. Jane sat at the Hendersons' kitchen table, highly agitated, her face streaked with tears. Fisher had never arrived at the castle. She'd ventured into the tunnel after him as far as she'd dared to, shouting his name, but had been unable to see or hear a thing, except for her own voice echoing in the dead air. No one else had been there either – Kingsley or someone must have left the door to the tunnels open by mistake.

Returning to wait back at the chamber next to the well, a while later there had been the sound of a footstep, or so she'd thought, but calling out again, she'd got no reply. Some time after ten, the security guard Barry Cleaver had heard her cries and come to investigate, forcing her to leave.

Phil and Penny were worried too. If Fisher had become disorientated, he was in very real danger. And try as they might, they could come up with no other reason as to why he hadn't kept his rendezvous with Jane.

'I think we'll have to call the police if he doesn't come back soon,' agreed Penny.

Phil nodded, getting up to put the kettle on. It was unlikely they would be getting any sleep tonight.

'Let's wait til morning,' he said, more optimistically than he felt. 'If we still haven't heard, then we'll call them.'

At that moment the phone rang. Penny jumped to pick it up.

Jane's heart leapt. 'Oh God, please let it be him.'

'Fisher?' asked Penny hopefully into the phone. 'Oh, Eleanor – yes, it's me.'

Jane slumped in her chair.

'What was that? Eleanor, are you okay? You sound upset.'

74

Fisher Bayley came to with a start. Coughing and spluttering in the icy water, he got back to his feet with difficulty. With a sickening lurch he remembered where he was, unable to see in the complete blackness of the chamber.

The need to sleep had overcome him, even his fear of what the rats might do while he was unconscious. Bayley guessed they were rats. He'd been bitten several times. Kicking out at them had seemed only to increase their determination and number, as if they sensed the presence of an animal in its death throes. Their high-pitched squeaks were like a death knell. When Kingsley had first been attacked he'd screamed non-stop. Now the only sound coming from his direction was the occasional pathetic whimper.

They were slowly being driven insane. With no way of telling how long they'd been trapped for, Bayley's body clock told him it might be morning. He was shivering uncontrollably.

'Kemp's not coming back, is he?' said Kingsley suddenly, his voice riddled with despair.

Bayley shook his head in agreement, forgetting that Kingsley was unable to see him.

'He's leaving me here to die. After all I did for him, he's leaving me here to die.'

'After all you did for Kemp?'

'Not Kemp. Harry.'

Bayley took a step in the direction of Kingsley's voice. 'What did you do for him?'

It was some time before Kingsley answered.

'I helped him, like you said. With hiding her, not killing her. I'd never do anything like that. She was already dead. It was horrible.'

Bayley waded through the water, found Kingsley and grabbed him by his soaked shirt, ripping it. His words came out distorted, dry anger catching in his throat.

'You arsehole, you total fucking –' He swung his arm and punched Kingsley hard where his face ought to have been, connecting with his cheek.

Kingsley collapsed into the water. Bayley continued to rant at him, before realising he hadn't got back up. Finding his shoulders, Bayley lifted his head out of the water and dragged him to the nearest wall, standing him up and leaning him against it. It was some time before Kingsley could speak.

'I'm sorry, I'm sorry. Please, don't hit me.'

Despite all that he'd suffered, Bayley felt a stab of guilt. It was Scarfe he wanted to hurt, not Kingsley. Though there was no doubt in his mind that Scarfe would have taken his punch and returned it with interest.

'I want to hear you say it,' said Bayley, far more calmly than he felt.

'Say what?'

'Who killed Odette. I want you to say it.'

Kingsley's voice trembled.

'Harry. It was Harry. He said it was an accident. I didn't want anything to do with it, but...' If Kingsley had expected sympathy, Bayley left him disappointed. 'You have to understand, Fisher, he gave me no choice. I... I'm sorry.'

Bayley let go of Kingsley's torn shirt and stared into the darkness. A paralysis crept over him, as he tried to take in the enormity of the confession Kingsley had just made.

It was over.It was really over. It was Harry Scarfe who had killed Odette, just as he'd thought that first time, lying in bed at the Hendersons', having escaped from the castle and from

Inspector Morello. Tears formed, building until they broke, running down his face. Wiping them away, he looked in Kingsley's direction again.

'When we get out of here, you're going to tell the Inspector what you just told me. Everything. Do you hear me?'

Kingsley gave a small sob. 'Don't you see? We're not going to get out of here. We're not...' Kingsley choked on his words, snivelling and gulping back the phlegm and spittle.

But Bayley wasn't listening to him. He'd just heard another sound, in the tunnel.

It was Jane. She'd found them.

'Jane!' he yelled out. 'Jane!'

Hope ballooned in Bayley's chest as he sloshed clumsily across the chamber. He crunched into another of the walls. Ignoring the pain, he felt his way round to the short passage that led to the door, all the time calling out Jane's name. Reaching the door he called out again, shaking the handle. But Jane wasn't there. All that could be heard was Kingsley's high-pitched and intermittent sobbing, coming from somewhere behind him.

The shock struck Bayley like a blow. He'd only imagined Jane's voice. Wanted so badly for her to be there that he'd imagined it. His mind was playing tricks on him. No one was ever going to find them. The truth about Odette would never be known. Scarfe had won. He and Kingsley were going to die in this place, and if they were lucky, they would drown before the rats overcame them.

75

THE KNOCK AT the door had never been so welcome.

'It's him!'

All three jumped up, running from the kitchen and down the hallway. Jane flung open the front door.

Standing there wasn't Fisher, but two tired looking men.

'Inspector Morello, Sergeant Robbins. Can we come in?'

Jane looked at the Inspector, horrified. It was barely six o'clock, still dark.

Bad news then – more bad news.Not dead, she thought. Please not dead.

'What's happened? Where is he?'

'Where is who, Miss?' asked Robbins brusquely, ignoring Jane's obvious distress.

Morello put his hand up. 'If we could talk inside?'

Phil and Penny exchanged a look, then nodded their assent. Both had black rings under their eyes, still red from when Eleanor had called.

With everyone seated at the kitchen table, Robbins took out his notepad, while in a tone more sensitive than his Sergeant's, Morello began.

'Am I right in thinking you work at the castle, Miss? Recognise you but can't quite place the name...'

'Jane. Jane Meadows.'

'That's right. Believe I may have spoken to you before. And who is it you're concerned about?'

Penny took Jane's hand. 'It's Fisher. He's missing.'

Robbins made a noise, but Morello continued calmly.

'He's been missing for some time, that's why we're here.'

'You don't understand,' said Jane, 'he's *really* missing. He was meant to meet me last night at the castle, but he never turned up. He's got himself lost in those tunnels. You've got to find him!' she pleaded tearfully.

'Have we now?' said Robbins angrily. 'Withholding –'

'All right, Sergeant,' Morello cut across, making Robbins angrier still. 'They'll be time enough later for that.' He looked at Jane. 'Seems Mr Bayley has a fondness for tunnels. I need to know how he got down there.'

'St Peter Mancroft Church – the Crypt. He had a map with him, but...'

'I see. And from there to the castle?'

Jane nodded, squeezing Penny's hand.

'Then it shouldn't be difficult plotting his route. Long as he hasn't wandered too far, we'll find him. We have a map too.'

'And when we do find him, he's going to wish we hadn't,' muttered Robbins under his breath. Just then his mobile rang. He took the call, and as he listened, his expression turned to one of incredulity. The call ended.

'That was Thomson on the desk, sir. Thought we'd want to know a.s.a.p. They've just had a Mrs Judith Kingsley on the phone.'

'Howard Kingsley's wife?'

'That's right. Apparently her husband never made it home last night.'

76

CAROLINE SCARFE FLINCHED. It was the third time the phone had rung in five minutes.

Having spent a sleepless night alone in the house, she had yet to face her husband. He hadn't even come home for the Bentley. She thought he must have cleaned himself up somewhere, put in an appearance maybe at the dinner function, and then gone straight to London on the train. Clutching her second gin and tonic, though it wasn't yet midday, she picked up the receiver. He couldn't be avoided forever.

'Hello?'

To her surprise, a woman's voice answered.

'Mrs Scarfe?

'Yes. Who's this?'

'Sade. Harry's PA?'

'He's not here. I think he's in London.'

'That's just the problem, he's not. Damn. He's meant to be in the House at one.'

'Sorry.'

'I've tried everywhere. You were my last hope.' Made sense to assume the last place you'd find him would be here, thought Caroline. 'Can't get him on email, and his phone's dead.'

Caroline frowned slightly. 'That's not like him.'

'No. Anyway, not your problem. Bye.'

Caroline replaced the receiver on the kitchen worktop, thinking. Harry's time spent in Parliament was sacred to him. The ceremony, the famous faces, the cameras – nothing in the world would prevent him being there.

Her scalp prickled. There was one thing that would stop him, of course. And according to his PA, the last person to see Harry seemed to be herself. The image of him struggling to break free from the concrete at the base of the Eye became fixed in her mind. Was it possible...?

Throwing the remains of her gin and tonic down the sink, she picked up her coat from the stand in the hallway and rushed out of the door.

*

Where in God's name was he? thought Doyle angrily, killing the call to Scarfe's mobile. Why didn't he answer? Doyle considered ringing his office, but held back. Scarfe had warned him never to contact him there. Which left Doyle with a problem. He couldn't leave Bayley and Kingsley left locked underground indefinitely – not without being paid for it first.

He made up his mind. Until confirmation came from Scarfe that he wanted them dead, and the money was in the bank, then Bayley and Kingsley had to be kept alive. He took another belt of whisky, scanning the bar out of habit from his corner seat. That meant they'd need water, and a bit of food. Enough to keep them going until Scarfe got in touch, the useless fucker. He'd take the supplies later, after he'd had some lunch himself.

*

'Afternoon, Mrs Scarfe.'

'Mr Sands.'

They shook hands.

'No Mr Scarfe?'

'Just me, I'm afraid. I was in the city, so I thought I'd come and take a look, see how it's coming along.'

Not quite managing to hide his relief at Harry Scarfe's absence, Keith Sands took Caroline to the site office, issuing her with a hardhat and high visibility jacket. At the same time, he gave what sounded like a well-worn diatribe on the vagaries of health and safety.

'Let's do the tour then, shall we?' he said genially, once Caroline was ready.

They went first to a small control room, where Caroline did her best to appear interested in all the Project Manager had to say. When they left the room, they walked towards the base of the Eye. Caroline felt a rising sickness, as if she were about to come face to face with a hidden monster. At last they came to the spot where she and Harry had stood the previous evening.

'That's where you'll get in and out of the pods. They don't stop moving, like the London one.'

Nodding, Caroline tried to steer Sands onto the subject she'd really come about.

'The whole thing's huge.'

'Hundred and fifteen feet,' said Sands proudly.

'Really? That's why you need the cables, I suppose.'

'No, they're only temporary. The foundations will hold her up, once the concrete's gone off. Two hundred tons we've put in. Hurricane wouldn't shift her then.'

'Two hundred tons?' repeated Caroline weakly. 'Sounds a lot.'

'It is. Sixty foot deep in parts. Like I said, nothing's going to shift her.'

At this, to his total bafflement, Caroline turned and ran, straight out of the gate. She was still wearing her hardhat and high visibility jacket.

77

It was going to be a long and painful death.

The water hadn't risen any further, but neither had it gone down.

How many days had passed, Bayley had no idea. Or maybe it was hours, he thought. It was hard to tell.

He could hardly stand. His eyes hurt from lack of sleep, and his mind felt blurred and unfocused. His whole body ached. He'd stopped shivering from the all-pervasive cold, and though his legs were too numb to be certain, he was in little doubt that the rats, getting bolder by the minute, had started to take tentative bites out of him. Almost worse was the complete and utter blackness, and the thought of the mass of rock overhead, entombing them, as if they'd been buried alive.

It was going to be a long and painful death.

Kingsley had become incoherent, falling into the water with increasing frequency, talking to himself, every so often reciting the words from an old Abba song before laughing manically, a sound as far removed from true laughter as it was possible to be. It was an added torture for Bayley, and nothing he said could make Kingsley stop.

Blacking out again himself, Bayley dropped into the water, contaminated with urine and worse. Gasping back into consciousness, he gagged on the fluid chilling his lungs. That was the fourth time. A fifth, and the water might not wake him. Then the rats would have their way.

Through his own laboured breathing, and Kingsley's

incessant babbling, Bayley heard a new sound. Something was moving towards them, through the flooded tunnel – something larger than a rat. Was that a voice? Or was he hearing things again? No, someone was outside, he was sure of it, swearing loudly. All at once, a blinding, unbearable light shone into the flooded chamber.

'Jesus!'

'Kemp?' Bayley croaked, holding his hands in front of his face. 'Kemp? Is that you?'

There was a roar, and Kingsley blundered towards the source of the light.

'Kemp?! Kemp!'

'Get off me! Get off!' There was a loud splash as Doyle pushed Kingsley away from him. 'Jesus, it stinks in here.'

Bayley tried to wade past, dragging himself through the water, making for where he thought the door must be.

'I don't think so.'

A strong arm grabbed Bayley's collar and swung him bodily around, catching his head on a wall. Bayley sank underwater. He struggled back to his knees, hot liquid running down his neck.

'You're not going anywhere unless I say you can.'

Bayley tried to stand, but his legs wouldn't work. His vision began to narrow, the torchlight fading.

Then it was gone.

Voices in his head, shouting, and as he sank quietly back beneath the water's surface, nothing.

78

Beside the bed, Inspector Morello sat upright on the only chair. The tangy odour that all hospitals seemed to have permeated everywhere, bringing back to him unpleasant memories of a childhood illness, one which had brought him close to death. The fluorescent lighting hummed steadily, illuminating the ward with a harsh glare.

At the bed opposite, a young nurse was doing her best to persuade an elderly man to swallow a small arsenal of pills. Morello formed the impression that the man was enjoying the exchange, argument being the only means by which he could compel the nurse to spend more time with him. He turned his attention back to the patient he'd come to see, propped up on several pillows, a thick bandage wrapped around his head. He was fast asleep.

Sergeant Robbins returned, carrying two plastic cups of coffee. He grimaced in a long-suffering sort of way as Morello looked up at him with mock modesty.

'How many more times do you want me to say it?' said the Sergeant, with light-hearted irritability. 'You were right, I was wrong.'

Morello grinned. 'Rest of the day should do it.'

Robbins rolled his eyes, passing Morello one of the cups, taking a glance at the patient. 'Sedatives still not worn off then?'

As if hearing him, Fisher Bayley chose that moment to stir. His eyes flickered, a vague expression on his face. Morello watched him intently.

'Mr Bayley? Can you hear me? I'm Inspector Morello. You're in hospital.'

'Hospital...?' Bayley moved his head, seeing Robbins, who gave a small smile. 'I'm out...?'

'You're safe.'

'Howard – where's Howard?'

'Don't worry, he's okay.'

'The hanky!' Bayley lifted his bedclothes and saw he was wearing a gown. 'Where is it? Where are my clothes? I need the hanky!' He tried to sit up, groaned, and collapsed back. The young nurse glanced across. 'The hanky,' he mumbled from his pillow.

'What's so important about this hanky?' asked Robbins, from the end of the bed.

'Blue silk. Same on the dagger.'

Morello sat further up in his chair. 'Who does it belong to?'

'Howard. He used it.'

Morello picked up a clear plastic bag that was leaning against the bedside table. Sealed inside were the remains of what Bayley had been wearing when he'd been admitted.

'Get these down to forensics, Sergeant. Tell them what to look for.'

Robbins took the bag and hurried from the ward. After he'd gone, Bayley closed his eyes.

'Mr Bayley? Are you okay? Can you still hear me?'

'How did you find us?' Bayley asked groggily, eyes still closed. 'I thought... I thought...'

'You've got Miss Meadows to thank for that. She had the good sense to tell us where you were. Didn't expect to find Mr Kingsley with you – or Mr Kemp.'

'Kemp wasn't with us, he was the one who locked us in.'

'So I gather from Mr Kingsley. Which explains why Kemp assaulted one of my officers and then disappeared.'

Bayley opened his eyes again, turning his head to look

directly at the Inspector. 'I'm innocent. Did Howard tell you that? I'm innocent.'

Morello allowed himself a smile. 'I know. Mr Kingsley gave a statement. Seems his near-death experience changed his view on things.'

There was a moment's silence, Bayley staring at the Inspector as he digested this, tears in his eyes. 'Thank God,' he said at last, and for the first time since he'd awoken, his features relaxed a little. 'It's over.' And with that, he fell into a deep sleep.

Morello left Bayley to look in on Kingsley again. Outside Bayley's ward, a uniformed officer stood guard. Morello gave him a nod as he passed. Within sight, further along the corridor, another officer was guarding the room where Kingsley lay. Morello had decided he was taking no chances with his star witness – his evidence against Scarfe would be crucial.

Kingsley too was asleep. Not an evil man, thought Morello, deciding there was no reason to disturb him again now. But he did have his weaknesses, as was testified to by the money Scarfe had paid him, and by the paintings found floating underground. And all too often, a man's weaknesses were where evil could find a place to hide.

79

LEAVING THE HOSPITAL, Inspector Morello drove his car back towards the station at City Hall. But as he neared the city walls, he decided on a slight detour. It was possible Caroline Scarfe might have a better idea of her missing husband's whereabouts, now she'd had a little time to get over the shock of his being wanted for murder. The search that had taken place the previous night of the Scarfes' house and grounds had unsurprisingly failed to find the missing MP.

He called Robbins.

'Was it in the bag?' Morello asked his Sergeant.

'They found it. Handkerchief with an "H" stitched on, couldn't tell the colour. Forensics are working on it now.'

'Good. Excellent. If they get a match, we can use it to make sure Kingsley doesn't change his mind about giving evidence. Any sign of Scarfe yet?'

'Still no peep. Do you think he's got wind and made a run for it?'

Morello turned into the driveway of the Scarfes' family home. 'Maybe. If Kemp was working for him, he could have given him warning. A man like Scarfe though, I'd expect him to fight, use his position. Doesn't fit.'

Robbins grunted his agreement.

Morello switched off his engine. 'Step up the search to include airports and the Channel. I want to know if he's left the country. Call me with whatever you've got, soon as you can.' He hung up and rang the doorbell.

A moment later Caroline Scarfe appeared, her face

creased from where she'd evidently been crying.

'Have you found him yet?' was the first thing she said. Her voice carried little hope.

'Not yet, Mrs Scarfe. May I come in?'

Morello sat with Caroline in the sitting room. He noticed that her right hand, holding a glass with only a piece of lemon inside it, was trembling slightly.

'I still can't believe it, Inspector.'

'It's a lot to take in.'

'Why would he do such a thing? And why won't anyone tell me who he's meant to have...'

She didn't finish her sentence.

'I'm afraid I can't discuss the details at this stage,' apologised Morello.

Mrs Scarfe nodded slowly. 'I know.'

Maybe she would make the link herself, thought Morello. Local news coverage of the "Woman Down The Well" had been pretty extensive, even without a suspect for the journalists to speculate over. Not as extensive as the coverage would be when Drake did finally call a press conference, and informed the world who their prime suspect was.

'I wanted to ask you again, now you've had a little time to think about it. Is there anywhere your husband might have gone to, other than where you would normally expect?' The rich surroundings of the house spoke to Morello of a country cottage or villa, somewhere on the Med. Probably both. 'A holiday home, perhaps?'

'I'm not sure...'

'What about abroad? Does he travel much?'

'He does a lot of business in Petrova... you think he might be there?'

'It's a possibility. Could we check to see if his passport's been taken?'

'All that sort of thing's in his study. I'll show you.'

It was a room Morello had seen in countless TV dramas.

Plenty of wood, floor to ceiling bookshelves, ornately framed oil paintings, originals he guessed, and a huge bay window looking out onto immaculate grounds.

'He usually keeps his passport in his desk,' said Caroline.

The drawers were locked. Caroline went over to the shelving by the window. She lifted a row of false book covers, revealing a white dish behind.

'He never was much of a reader,' she said, holding up a small key.

Morello unlocked the first drawer, taking it out and placing it on the desk's leather inlay. Two notebooks, a diary and a laptop. He'd take the computer for the techies to dismantle. It would be of no use to the Scene of Crime Officers, due at the house the next day, Saturday, to begin a complete sweep of every room. Robbins had argued that this was a wasted effort; they already had Kingsley's confession, and Scarfe was unlikely to have left evidence of a murder in his own home. But Morello had seen dead certs fall down before, once they'd reached the courts. With a character like Scarfe, he wanted all the ammunition he could get. No gaps through which a sharp QC could slither.

He continued with the other drawers, finding nothing of interest until he took out the last one. No passport, but instead a delicate silver chain, an ornate "O" hanging from one of the links.

'What's that doing there?' demanded Mrs Scarfe.

'Do you recognise it?'

'No I do not.'

Morello placed the necklace in an envelope from the same drawer. There was a chance Odette Novad's DNA could still be on it, if it had been hers. A smudge of sweat or flake of skin caught in the metal.

'Why are you taking it?'

'It might be an item of interest for us. If it's not, I'll make sure it's returned. Unless you have an objection?'

'No. Keep it. My name begins with a "C", Inspector, as you know.' Caroline's anger left her as quickly as it had appeared. 'I need a drink,' she announced, and went to fix herself another gin and tonic.

Morello picked up one of the notebooks, slowly flicking through it until a name caught his eye – a name he knew well. Alongside it were columns of figures and dates, and other information, in a small neat script. He re-read the page again and again, scarcely able to believe what was written there.

He'd struck gold.

80

Everyone stood around in groups, some talking, some joking even. Others remained silent. The day was cold but clear, the sky a wide blue. Bunches of early snowdrops were spread beneath the nearby woodland. The warbles and trills of birdsong coming from the direction of the trees seemed too cheerful, too hopeful almost, for a funeral. Fisher clutched Jane's hand, listening to Phil talk too much and too fast. Penny and Chris listened to him too, saying nothing.

Fisher had been out of hospital nearly a week. The day of his discharge, he had gone with Jane to the funeral parlour where Sean's body lay. The building was on a busy road north of the city, a single storey affair, squeezed between a supermarket and a fast food outlet. It seemed a sorry place in which to say last goodbyes.

Past the small reception area, he and Jane had been ushered into a white room, at the far end of which a pale wooden coffin sat, supported by a narrow table covered in cloth. Built into an alcove above the coffin was a stained glass window, backlit so that coloured shapes now appeared on his and Jane's clothing.

Hesitant, it took Fisher some moments to summon up the courage to look down at his friend. When he did, the first thing that struck him was how little there was left of the Sean he knew. Eleanor had said the end had been quick – so quick, it seemed, the cancer had in its haste almost sucked him dry. The cream silk that encased him was abundant, but the face was sunk into a misshapen mask, while the clothing looked loose, the body wasted away. For the first time in his life, Fisher felt he knew what was meant when people spoke of the soul having left the body.

'They're here,' rasped an elderly lady, her face hidden behind a black veil.

All talking immediately ceased as the hearse carrying Sean's body arrived. Eleanor stepped from one of the cars that formed the cortege, exchanging a word with her parents seated inside before walking over to Fisher and the others.

'I'm glad you're all here,' she said, her voice calm but cracked.

Together they watched as Sean's coffin was brought out. The official mourners took the weight on their shoulders. As the coffin was borne past them, Eleanor's father, Donald Rayburn, came and took his daughter into his arms. Taking small steps, the pair walked away, following Sean's coffin to where Eleanor and her unborn child would say their final farewells.

81

It was Tuesday, five am. The streets were dark and quiet. Inspector Morello hoped this was it. Since the news conference, the many dead-ends and false sightings had been extremely frustrating. One woman had even called in to claim she had been held captive by Harry Scarfe for the previous three months. Nothing, it seemed, attracted the crazies as much as the chance to appear on TV. But this latest tip-off he hadn't been able to ignore, and if Scarfe was here, his capture might also lead him to the elusive Mr Kemp.

If.

'They're all in position, sir.'

Morello nodded. He had been pleasantly surprised by the speed and efficiency of the local police force in Petrova, the hierarchy having given him carte blanche to do whatever he thought necessary. And in English, much to his shame. All the men he needed and no red tape, a refreshing change from back home, where form-filling all too often sapped vital time and energy. As a result, several small teams were now stationed outside every address in which Harry Scarfe was known to have an interest, waiting on his word.

The trap was about to close.

His search for Scarfe had taken on a new urgency since forensics had made their astonishing discovery at his Norfolk home.

At first, as expected, the Scene of Crime Officers had come up with nothing. Until that was they had examined the kitchen, using a fluorescing chemical that reacted to the presence of blood, even in microscopic quantities. The results had been spectacular. The floor, cupboards, walls, even the ceiling, all had lit up in a pattern that was unmistakeable. A mess like that usually signified that an artery had been hit, but that death hadn't been instant. Odette would have had just enough time to realise what was happening, before being lost to eternity.

Killing under his own roof, rather than at a location more anonymous and remote, suggested to Morello that it had been a spontaneous act. A crime of passion. That would fit with Kirsten Turnik's testimony that Scarfe and Odette had been having an affair, an affair that for whatever reason had gone badly wrong.

It meant he had Harry Scarfe MP up a creek so shitty that no lawyer would be able to paddle him out of it, however hard they tried. The same went for Drake. Scarfe's notebook had been helpfully detailed and difficult to explain. At first the Superintendent had tried to bluff his way out, using his seniority to ridicule the accusations put to him. When that hadn't worked, he had pleaded for the retirement option. But taking payment for planting evidence hadn't gone down well with his superiors, nor indeed those under him.

Served the bastard right, thought Morello.

'Sir?' Robbins looked at his boss expectantly.

Morello checked his watch. The team he and his Sergeant had joined, six men, fully armed, all had their eyes fixed upon him.

'Give the order,' he said.

'This is Charlie One,' barked Robbins into his handset. 'The light is green, I repeat, the light is green.'

Across Petrova, eight crack police units in full body armour leapt from hiding and raced towards their designated targets.

82

THERE WAS SOMETHING of a carnival atmosphere. Caroline Scarfe felt ridiculous, as well as nervous, particularly whenever the news cameras were pointed at her. Standing on the raised podium, she managed to pick out Penny Henderson, standing near the front of the crowd with her friends. Since Harry had gone missing they had become her friends too, and smiled and waved cheerily at her. It seemed that hundreds of people, thousands even, had braved the chilly February weather.

When Caroline had been invited to open the Norwich Eye, she had felt her husband's grip on her slip a little further. Each day for the past five weeks she had asked herself constantly, was he was really gone? The much reported police raid in Petrova had failed to unearth him. Had he drowned in the concrete foundations of the structure that stood before her now, where she had pushed him? Each day that Harry remained missing, the answer to that question seemed evermore likely to be yes.

But she had no proof, and the thought that there might yet be some lawless corner of the world harbouring him meant there was precious little peace for her – only guilt and fear. Heavy drinking hardly dented the constant worry, and for the first time she had experienced a minor panic attack, a few moments when her entire life had seemed in imminent danger of collapse. That had probably been triggered by the police, she believed, when they had requested her to vacate her home; when the kitchen had been turned into a crime scene.

She had taken a flat overlooking the river, in the centre of the city, and was comfortable enough. When Inspector Morello had called in to tell her that his forensic team had finished at number sixteen, Town Crescent, she had decided not to return. Town Crescent would never be her home again. If by Easter Harry was still missing, then would be the time to sell.

'Mrs Scarfe? Are you ready?' asked one of the officials that surrounded her.

Caroline nodded. The official smiled, as if humouring a child given a special treat.

The Mayor, a short rotund man who put Caroline in mind of Dad's Army's Captain Mainwaring, stood up to the microphone at the front of the podium. Once he had the crowds attention, he delivered a speech nearly ten minutes long, interrupted half way through by a group of protesters, chanting a slogan Caroline couldn't quite hear. When at last he introduced her, it was to great applause. Whether this was because of sympathy at the daily speculation over her husband's guilt, or relief that the Mayor had finally finished, it was difficult to tell. She decided to give a radically reduced version of the script written for her, in order that the complementary champagne could start to flow as soon as possible.

'Thank you, Lord Mayor.' Caroline fixed her eye on a point in the crowd before continuing. 'Ladies and gentlemen, it is indeed a great honour to be here, on such a special occasion. There are many people to thank for turning this project into a reality, and I'd like you all to join me now in showing our appreciation.'

She began to clap, and the crowd played gamefully along.

'This great city of ours,' she continued, setting off a loud cheer, 'has a long and illustrious past. Projects like this,' Caroline gestured towards the wheel, 'show the world that it also has a long and illustrious future.'

This brought further cheering and clapping.

'Thank you. All that remains for me to say then, is that it is with great pleasure that I declare the Norwich Eye to be... OPEN!'

She pulled down a large lever, similar to those found on the sides of old-fashioned fruit machines. Another huge cheer went up as the wheel slowly began to turn, each pod already full with dignitaries and successful bidders for tickets, grinning and waving from their shiny glass capsules.

'It works!' someone cried out, to general laughter from the crowd nearby.

To Caroline's relief the attention moved away from her. The Mayor and his entourage seemed drawn to the news cameras, like crocodiles to the sun. She stepped down from the podium and into the hospitality tent set up just behind it, spotting a waiter. He handed her a glass of champagne, which she drained in one go, taking another and wandering back outside with it.

The noise around her faded away. From where she stood, she could see, fixed to one of the wheel's two giant struts, the plaque with Harry's name on it. Until he stood trial, if he stood trial, it would remain there, the letters M and P prominent, even at this distance. The base of the Eye had been topped with red tarmac.

'Are you under there?' Caroline murmured to herself, wishing she could be certain.The man she had once loved. A part of her wept for him.

He had always talked of the Eye as being his monument to the city. If he had perished that night, she thought, when she had unthinkingly pushed him into the setting concrete, then a monument was exactly what it had become.

83

'NICE TO MEET you,' said Phil Henderson, rather formally.

It was months now since his pre-occupation with his age had at last seemed to end, coinciding with a return to his usual footwear and clothing. Rather than the hypnotherapy, Penny believed that Sean's death and Fisher's narrow escape had been responsible – a touch of perspective.

Chris grinned from ear to ear. Sarah was making quite an impression.

'And you,' replied Sarah Braintree.

Chris continued with his introductions. 'And this is Fisher and Jane.'

Sarah returned their smile, accepting a drink offered to her by Penny.

They were all stood round the small terrace that overlooked the Hendersons' garden. Easter had just come and gone, and the sun was out in earnest.

'I like what you've done with your borders,' said Sarah chattily.

'I pinch most of my ideas from Blickling Hall,' replied Penny. 'Have you been there?'

Sarah hadn't.

'You'll have to come with me and Caroline, next time we go.'

'I'd love to. Is that the same Caroline who, er...?'

'It is,' said Penny, correctly interpreting Sarah's hesitancy.

'Sorry, it's just that Chris mentioned...'

'No need to apologise. She should be here in a little while.

Anyway, changing the subject, how did you two meet?'

Sarah turned to Chris.

'Quite a funny story really, isn't it? We both joined –'

'Why don't we save that for later?' Chris interrupted her.

Sarah blushed.

'Now's good for us,' said Phil. 'What's the funny story?'

Chris took Sarah's hand. 'Go on then,' he said grumpily.

Just then Caroline appeared at the open doorway to the house, having helped herself to a glass of wine on the way.

'Hi everyone.' The forced cheerfulness didn't fit with her gaunt features and sleepless eyes. She had lost even more weight. 'Have I missed much?'

'Sarah was about to tell us how she met Chris,' said Phil promptly.

Chris glared at him.

After introducing herself to Caroline, Sarah took a deep breath. 'We met ballroom dancing – joined the group at the same time, didn't we?'

Chris grunted non-committally.

Fisher and Phil stared at Sarah in disbelief, mouths open. It was Fisher who responded first, clearly finding it difficult to picture the scene.

'Ballroom... you mean like – foxtrots, and – tangos...?'

'That's right,' said Chris defiantly.

'What's your outfit like?'

Chris regarded Phil's question with suspicion. 'What do you mean? What outfit?'

'Your spangly costume. Like they wear on the telly.'

Fisher quickly took up the theme, eyeing Chris speculatively.

'He's probably got it on now. Doesn't it chafe under those trousers?'

'I knew you two would be too immature to understand.' Chris did his best to look dismissive, made more difficult as Sarah seemed to find the exchange amusing.

Penny led Caroline away, into the garden and towards the bottom of the lawn, while Fisher and her husband continued to torment Chris as only boys knew how.

'My guess is red spangles.'

'What happens when you do the splits?'

'How is everything?' Penny asked, once they were out of earshot.

Caroline smiled weakly. 'You know.'

Penny nodded understandingly, thinking of the many nights over the last few months spent at Caroline's flat. 'Do you think the police will ever find him?'

Caroline stared into space as if she hadn't heard. When she did at last speak, she sounded drained, as if all the fight had gone out of her.

'I don't know what I think any more, Penny. If I don't get a decent night's sleep soon, I'm going to go mad.'

The combination of sleeping pills and daytime sedatives Caroline had begun to take had done little to ease her anguish. The nightmares she suffered from were as bad and as frequent as ever, and even on good days, her mood would swing from feigned optimism one moment to almost uncontrollable outbursts of temper the next.

Her antique business was also suffering, an added pressure that had become part of the downward spiral she was in. Always a moderate drinker, she now drank to excess. It was a depressing sight.

Penny decided it was time to be bold.

'Maybe it's best if they don't,' she said.

'Don't what?'

'If the police don't find him. Hiding in some hole somewhere for the rest of his life is probably the best punishment for murdering that innocent girl.'

'Who says she was innocent?' said Caroline fiercely.

They were interrupted by a commotion coming from the other end of the garden. Fisher and Phil were both standing cheek to cheek, hands joined, one arm wrapped around the others waist. They proceeded down the garden in this fashion, towards Penny and Caroline, skipping and twirling rhythmically.

'What on earth are they up to?' exclaimed Penny, though the reason for their poor imitation of a waltz was all too clear.

'Oom pah pah, oom pah pah,' sang Phil loudly.

Fisher crooned at him.

'Do you love me, Phil?'

'I do, my darling, I do.'

'Will you make me the happiest man alive?'

'I'll come and sort you two out in a minute!' shouted Chris across the garden, red in the face.

Fisher carried on. 'Maybe you can show me your spangly pants later,' he said, breathing heavily.

'Everything's spangly tonight, my love.'

Chris came running down the garden after them, Jane and Sarah in close pursuit. Fisher and Phil yelled, taking cover behind several small bushes next to Penny and Caroline.

'Boys, that's enough!' ordered Jane.

Sarah took Chris' hand, squeezing it. This seemed to have the effect of immediately calming him. Forgetting his antagonists, he kissed Sarah on the lips, prompting Fisher and Phil to make retching noises from behind the bushes. Chris broke off to grin at them good-naturedly.

'You two should come and try it one night. Keeps you fit.'

'I'd love to,' said Jane, causing Fisher to take the finger out of his mouth and goggle at her, unsure if she was being serious. 'Wouldn't we?' she said to him.

Finding this highly amusing, Phil had no time to comment before Penny sided with Jane.

'I've always wanted to learn ballroom too,' she said, giving her husband a look. 'What night is it?'

Fisher brightened.

Arrangements were made, then Penny walked with

Caroline back up the garden towards the house. Behind them, Chris fended off a volley of questions from ballroom dancing's newest recruits.

Inside the house Penny poured out two fresh glasses of wine, wondering what it was Caroline had meant before Phil and Fisher had distracted them. Not innocent? A reference to the newspapers' insistence that the dead woman and Harry had been having an affair? It wouldn't have been the first, according to Caroline. Whatever she had meant, she clearly regretted it.

'I'm sorry, Penny. I didn't mean to have a go at you just then. I just wish...'

Her words became lost in big, heavy sobs. Penny held her.

'It's okay, I'm here. It's going to be all right.'

Words she had repeated endlessly in recent months, meaningless except as a sense of comfort to both of them.

'You don't understand,' wept Caroline, over her shoulder.

'What don't I understand?'

This was as bad as Penny had ever seen her, the worst in fact.

'Is that stew ready yet, we're all starving,' called Phil cheerily, coming into the kitchen.He stopped dead in his tracks.

'Sorry darling. Er... do you want me to –'

'It's okay. Call the others, tell them it's ready.'

Throughout lunch, Caroline's brooding silence created a subdued atmosphere, no one wanting to appear insensitive. As expected, Eleanor never showed. Caroline was halfway through her seventh or eighth glass of wine when Sarah and Chris said they needed to leave. The new couple were driving to the beach at Waxham, and wanted to catch the sun. Fisher and Jane made their excuses soon after. Phil saw them to the door, returning to the kitchen again to begin clearing away the table. Penny and Caroline left him to it, going outside once more to meander slowly around the garden.

It really was a beautiful day. Caroline walked unsteadily, sniffing, a sense of hopelessness about her. Her prescription pills and the wine were a toxic mix. Feeling duty bound, Penny tried arguing with her as she had so many times of late that she was better off without Harry Scarfe. But Caroline picked holes in everything she said, until she became exasperated.

'All I'm trying to say, Caroline, is that you're a successful, intelligent, attractive woman. You can do anything with your life.'

'You never did like Harry, did you?' Caroline challenged her.

Refusing to be provoked, Penny stopped to admire a swathe of blue irises.

'I've never said that.'

'No, but you've always thought it.'

The unfairness of this caused Penny to shake with sudden anger. After everything she had done. She turned to face Caroline.

'No, I never did like him, okay? And shall I tell you why? Because he treated you like shit, that's why. You've told me yourself all the affairs you thought he'd had, and now he's killed someone. Actually killed them. He's a murderer, for God's sake! How can you defend him?'

'Stop saying that!' exploded Caroline. 'I'm not defending him, you don't understand!'

'So you keep saying. What is it I'm not supposed to understand? What?'

'Everything!' Caroline screamed at her, smashing her glass on the path.

'He's a killer!' Penny shouted back, 'he's killed an innocent girl, whatever you say!'

Caroline slapped Penny's face. The shock of it caused Penny to stagger backwards, tears coming to her eyes. A look of horror came over Caroline, and she reached out.

'I'm sorry! Please, I didn't mean –'

‘I think you’d better go,’ said Penny, as calmly as she could. She glanced at the house. Phil was at a window, tea-towel in hand. When he saw he had been spotted, he ducked out of sight.

‘Penny, please, I’m sorry, don’t make me leave, I need you. *Please.* There’s something I haven’t told you, I haven’t told anyone.’

And without warning, the words came tumbling out of her, faster and faster, as if somehow she was ridding herself of their weight. Listening, Penny grew increasingly horror-struck. Her throat was dry and constricted as she stared in stunned silence for a moment or two after Caroline had finished.

‘Are you... really sure... dead?’

Not meeting her eye, Caroline nodded dumbly.

Penny said nothing more. She couldn’t.

Her world had just changed forever.

*

Not long after, having repeatedly sworn Penny to secrecy, Caroline left. Phil went on an emergency run to the off licence nearby, leaving Penny alone on the sofa with her thoughts.

How on Earth, she wondered miserably, could she keep her promise not to tell anyone what she’d just heard? A person had been killed, murdered, and whatever her view of them, there could be no excuse for that – could there?

Even under normal circumstances, Penny all too often found the temptation to divulge confidences impossible to resist, and the more interesting the gossip, the greater the temptation. She would argue with herself that if a third person was told, then the secret held. If that person then shared it with another, and they the same, until the only secret left was how many knew it, that really wasn’t her fault.

Or so she tried to believe.

'How are you feeling?' asked Phil, putting two bottles on the coffee table beside the empty fireplace.

Penny hadn't heard her husband come back in. She looked up at him, tears in her eyes.

'There's something I need to tell you,' she said.

84

JANE SLEPT PEACEFULLY, an enviable gift she had, hands resting on the duvet that had collected around her. By her side, Fisher Bayley lay awake. He watched as a passing car caused shifting squares of light to travel along the bedroom wall. Then the shapes vanished, along with the car, leaving the room in darkness again.

He wished Phil had never said anything. How could he reconcile Caroline's confession to Penny with his belief that it was simply wrong to kill? Was it wrong whatever the provocation? What should he do? The dead couldn't seek justice themselves. Trouble was, despite the emotions stirred in him, he questioned how he could judge Caroline's moment of madness, knowing the circumstances as he did. He wanted to talk to Jane about it, regardless of his promise to Phil. To tell her the truth about why he'd woken her up the past two nights, squirming and calling out in his sleep.

Thinking of the dead reminded Fisher of Sean's funeral, which had of late left him with feelings of guilt. So many things Sean would never see, hear or do, which he would. The unfair and random nature with which Sean had been taken always made him promise to himself to make the most of whatever time he had left. Yet he knew that come the following evening, he'd probably be watching repeats on the telly and scooping up a ready-made meal. Life just wasn't made of grand ideals, at least not for him.

Jane gave a little snore, lying on her back. Fisher's thoughts changed tack, and he began to dwell on his recent ordeal, as he had every night since his discharge from hospital. The experience, looking back, seemed surreal. Searching Caroline's house, breaking into City Hall, the flooded underground chamber. The memories had become less livid, though he couldn't imagine the scars ever entirely healing.

Inspector Morello had never confided to him why he had been their chief suspect, nor whether he'd been spotted the time he had hidden in the Hendersons' bedroom cupboard. Fisher suspected he would never know the truth about that. At least in the end, he thought, everything had worked out in his favour. That was due in large part to Howard Kingsley's confession – some sort of recompense for his cowardice and greed.

Fisher returned to the present. He had a lot to be grateful for. He and Jane had grown ever closer, to the point where life before her seemed almost to have belonged to another person. To all intents and purposes, they were now living together, though nothing official had been talked about. His parents had also taken to her, which he supposed was to be expected, given their view that she was the one who had saved their son from a "watery grave", as they liked to put it.

Returning to work at the castle had felt strange and unfamiliar. He sometimes wondered whether he would ever be able to readapt, or if he wanted to – some days it all seemed so mundane and ordinary. It was only Jane that kept him feeling alive. Brian Finch was now Acting Curator, while Kingsley awaited trial in prison, having been refused bail. He'd heard a rumour that his wife Judith visited frequently, finding her husband's sudden fame as a criminal rather attractive.

Seeing Ginny Carmen again had been awkward, until it became clear that she too had met somebody else. After that, the two of them were able to settle into an amicable enough friendship, though it was clear that Jane would never forgive her for the time she'd lied to Morello and Robbins.

Another car drove past the house, its lights trailing the walls of the bedroom. It was gone two in the morning. Fisher closed his eyes. Sleep couldn't be put off forever, nor with it the vivid dreams. What was it about horror that made everyone a voyeur, like a motorist passing a fatal accident? Restless and hot, he drifted off into a shallow and troubled sleep.

It began in the Crypt, under St Peter Mancroft Church, as it had the two previous nights. In their alcoves, the skeletons were awake once more. Lining up to face Fisher, each one grabbed at him. There was no escaping their cold, hard grip. Holding him fast, they marched him through a dark tunnel, to the house where he had once broken in – the home of Caroline and Harry Scarfe.

The front door had been blown open by a squally wind, and though it was dark outside, there were no lights on. Fisher didn't want to enter. He knew what was there. But the skeletons, with their exposed teeth and hollow sockets twisted into expressions of malicious glee, dragged him through the door and towards the kitchen. He cried out, pleading, but the ridged fingers only clamped around him more tightly. Into the kitchen they pushed him, and he fell to the floor. Free from their grip, he scrabbled to get back out, but somehow his legs wouldn't work, and so he turned, as he knew he must, towards the two figures also with him on the kitchen floor.

Sat astride Harry Scarfe was Odette, naked, in a state of complete carnal abandonment. Writhing and panting she moaned, the sound becoming louder and louder until it reached a deafening pitch. Fisher looked away, putting his hands over his ears, but the floor rippled, causing him to slide to within a few feet of the pair. Suddenly there was a bang. Stood in the kitchen doorway was Caroline, dressed in black. With an instant, unthinking rage, she drew a knife from a block on the sideboard, a thick, heavy bladed carver, and with both hands drove it deep into Odette's back, the tip of the blade passing through lung and heart. Then she stepped away, shaking, leaving the handle of the carver jutting from Odette's pale and sweat-soaked skin.

Odette convulsed, spasming violently, clamping Harry inside her before collapsing sideways. Harry tried desperately to wrestle himself free, crying out in horror as Odette began to jerk uncontrollably, as if being electrocuted again and again. Her lacerated back spurted onto the tiled floor, the kitchen cupboards, the walls. She screamed, but with lungs filled with blood, streams of bright red came instead from her gaping mouth, bubbling and spattering Harry and herself in her own gore. Then her eyes flickered, her body contracted one last time, and she lay there, unmoving.

Dead.

'Fisher!'

Fisher awoke, sweat on his face, heart pumping painfully. Jane pulled him towards her, cradling him.

'Are you okay?'

He'd woken her a third night. The return of his old nightmare, he would tell her, the one where the skeletons had attacked him. Half truths were easier to remember.

'Sorry,' he mumbled. 'What time is it?'

Jane glanced at the bedside alarm. 'Half two.' She held him more closely. 'Was it that same dream?'

Fisher wiped away the sweat from his forehead. He'd been asleep less than twenty minutes. He couldn't keep going like this. He looked up, meeting Jane's eyes.

'Can you keep a secret?' he asked her.

Lightning Source UK Ltd.
Milton Keynes UK
UKOW04f1002260215

246943UK00004B/272/P

9 781908 387677